Peter Cheyney and The Murder Room

>>> This title is part of The Murder Room, our series dedicated to making available out-of-print or hard-to-find titles by classic crime writers.

Crime fiction has always held up a mirror to society. The Victorians were fascinated by sensational murder and the emerging science of detection; now we are obsessed with the forensic detail of violent death. And no other genre has so captivated and enthralled readers.

Vast troves of classic crime writing have for a long time been unavailable to all but the most dedicated frequenters of second-hand bookshops. The advent of digital publishing means that we are now able to bring you the backlists of a huge range of titles by classic and contemporary crime writers, some of which have been out of print for decades.

From the genteel amateur private eyes of the Golden Age and the femmes fatales of pulp fiction, to the morally ambiguous hard-boiled detectives of mid twentieth-century America and their descendants who walk our twenty-first century streets, The Murder Room has it all. >>>

The Murder Room
Where Criminal Minds Meet

themurderroom.com

Peter Cheyney (1896–1951)

Reginald Evelyn Peter Southouse Cheyney was born in Whitechapel in the East End of London. After serving as a lieutenant during the First World War, he worked as a police reporter and freelance investigator until he found success with his first Lemmy Caution novel. In his lifetime Cheyney was a prolific and wildly successful author, selling, in 1946 alone, over 1.5 million copies of his books. His work was also enormously popular in France, and inspired Jean-Luc Godard's character of the same name in his dystopian sci-fi film *Alphaville*. The master of British noir, in Lemmy Caution Peter Cheyney created the blueprint for the tough-talking, hard-drinking pulp fiction detective.

Lemmy Caution Novels

This Man Is Dangerous
Poison Ivy
Dames Don't Care
Can Ladies Kill?
Don't Get Me Wrong
You'd Be Surprised
Your Deal, My Lovely
Never a Dull Moment
You Can Always Duck
I'll Say She Does

Slim Callaghan Novels

The Urgent Hangman
Dangerous Curves
You Can't Keep the Change

Sorry You've Been Troubled
It Couldn't Matter Less
They Never Say When
Uneasy Terms
Dance Without Music
Calling Mr. Callaghan

The 'Dark' Series
Dark Duet
  aka *The Counterspy Murders*
Dark Hero
  aka *The Case of the Dark Hero*
Dark Interlude
  aka The Terrible Night

Your Deal, My Lovely

Peter Cheyney

An Orion book

Copyright © Peter Cheyney 1941

The right of Peter Cheyney to be identified as the author of this work
has been asserted in accordance with the Copyright, Designs and
Patents Act 1988.

This edition published by
The Orion Publishing Group Ltd
Orion House
5 Upper St Martin's Lane
London WC2H 9EA

An Hachette UK company
A CIP catalogue record for this book is available from the British Library

ISBN 978 1 4719 0150 8

www.orionbooks.co.uk

CONTENTS

CHAPTER ONE

SWEET MOMMA

I

SOME MUG by the name of Confucius—who was a guy who was supposed to know his vegetables—once issued an edict that any time he saw a sap sittin' around bein' impervious to the weather an' anything else that was goin', an' lookin' like he had been hit in the kisser with a flat-iron, the said sap was sufferin' from woman trouble.

I reckon Confucius musta been thinkin' of me.

It is as dark as hell. It is also drizzlin' with rain an' somewhere around in the skies I can hear a Heinkel dronin'. But I am not worryin' too much about any of these things because I am wonderin' about that sweet momma Carlette.

This baby has got everything you ever heard about an' then a couple of trucks-full. So far as I am concerned she is the answer to the travellin' salesman's prayer. I could tell you things about that dame's geography which would make you wonder why you are so stuck on the dame you are gettin' around with at the moment.

She is not so tall but she is certainly not short. She has got curves that you never saw in a geometry book. She has got deep an' mysterious blue eyes an' when she looks at you you can feel snakes playin' baseball in your spine. I'm tellin' you mugs with my hand on my heart that when they served out allure that baby collected for the whole family, an' I will also go so far as to say that if she had been let loose in the Garden

of Eden, Adam would have closed down for the afternoon, turned out the serpent, and started pickin'
apples like he was in the jam business.

This Carlette has also got some very nifty clothes
an' she knows how to wear 'em. Also I wish to point
out that havin' spent a lot of time walkin' up the
ship's companionway behind this dame I can tell you
that she has such a swell pair of legs that even if she
was as ugly as hell you would still know just where to
look any time you was feelin' depressed.

Me . . . I am goofy about this baby. Sittin' there
in the dark with the rain runnin' off the edge of my
fedora an' drippin' on my nose, I get around to
rememberin' her voice which is one of those voices
that sound like pourin' double cream on a satin bedspread. It is sorta soft an' low an' hoarse an' it has
got little cadences in it that register on you like you
have been smacked in the midriff by an express
truck.

I throw my wet cigarette stub away an' begin to
ruminate about one or two dames I have known in
my time. All around me are guys with darkened
torches shepherdin' the passengers off the *Florida*,
checkin' passports, examinin' luggage an' generally
rushin' around to see that nobody is bringin' in any
more trouble than is already breakin' around this
country.

Nobody seems to be worryin' about the Heinkel. I
reckon these English mugs can take anythin', an'
havin' decided that they are goin' through with this
war with Mister Hitler, they are not inclined to get
themselves too steamed up about a little matter of
bomb droppin'.

Havin' disposed of these great thoughts I get back
to thinkin' about Carlette, an' I am very interested
in the way that the old brain-box is concerned with
this baby, because I have always found that when I

2

get around to concentratin' on a dame I have always started to lay up plenty trouble for myself.

Maybe your mother told you that it was wrong to get to thinkin' about women too much. O.K. Well, take it from me the old lady was right. The only time when a guy can legitimately think about janes is when he is good an' dead. Because directly he thinks about some sweet momma he starts wishin' virtues on to her that she ain't got anyway an' when he has done this he then proceeds to tell himself that this dame is too good for him which is probably goddam right but not in the way he is thinkin'.

There is only one way to be safe with women an' that is to play a lot of 'em at once. If you get kickin' around with one honeylamb it is Mussolini's favourite ear-wig to the Royal Mint that she will take a long sideways look at you out of them cornflower-blue eyes an' in two minutes you are so gaga that you would make the village idiot look like Edison. Then, before you know what is happenin' to you, you are kiddin' yourself that you have talked her into marryin' you, instead of which the sweet little she-cuss has given one more mug the bum's rush an' got him where she wants him.

Right at this minute a big guy in a black oilskin slicker comes up to me. He says :

" Would you be Mr. Thaxby ? "

" Right first guess," I tell him. " Elmer T. Thaxby of Cold Springs, Colorado—America's foremost Nuts and Bolts salesman."

He grins.

" I'll bet, Mr. Caution," he says. " Anyhow, the nuts part is right. Have you got your identity ? "

I fish down in my inside overcoat pocket an' I bring out my Federal Bureau identity card, my Thaxby passport an' a few other documents that prove I am me. He looks over these an' says :

3

" My name's Rapps—Detective Sergeant, South-ampton Police. I've come down here to get your stuff through the Customs, Mr. Caution. I suppose you'll be wanting to get the first train up."

I ask him how the trains are goin'. He says there is one in twenty minutes—the nine-thirty, an' another one at ten-thirty. I tell him that I will take the first one. He is just goin' off when I get an idea.

" Listen, pal," I say. " There's a dame on this boat by the name of Lariat—Miss Carlette Lariat. Well, I'm sorta interested in that baby. Maybe she's goin' up on the nine-thirty too. I wonder if you could push her stuff through the Customs so's we can make that train together."

He says that would be easy. He looks at me an' says :

" You're interested in this lady ? "

" She's not workin' with me if that's what you mean," I tell him. I grin. " This is just a little personal thing.

He says he's got me. He goes off.

I sit down on a wet seat an' light another cigarette. It's sorta funny gettin' used to the darkness over here. Me—I have been in England before in the days when they had the bright lights on. Now, when you can't see a goddam thing, I reckon I like it just as much. I get up an' start walkin' along towards the Customs barrier, when somebody says :

" Hey, Mr. Thaxby ! "

I turn around an' I see it is the wireless officer off the *Florida*. This boy is a good guy an' him an' me have had plenty drinks together on the trip. He says :

" I've been rushing all around the place tryin' to get at you. I got a wireless for you half an hour before we pulled in, but I've been tied up with the old man. Here it is. Sorry about the delay."

I bust open the envelope an' read it. It is from

4

Herrick, the Chief Detective Inspector that I worked with on the Van Zelden case way back in 1936. The radio says :

" Take it you will arrive on train leaving Southampton nine thirty am sending Grant meet you at Waterloo. Will contact you in few days time good luck Mr. Thaxby.
" Herrick."

I put the radio in my pocket an' say ' Thanks a lot ' to the wireless guy. This bozo is from Cincinnati an' his name is Manders. He says :
" Well, I hope you're goin' to have a good trip, Mr. Thaxby. Mind you duck if they throw a bomb at you."
" I'll duck all right," I tell him. " How long's the *Florida* goin' to be here ? "
" I wouldn't know," he says. " I think maybe we'll stick around two-three days, but we've gotta pick up a cargo and clear. I don't think we'll be here long. Well, I'll be seein' you."
He's just turnin' away when he remembers somethin'. He says :
" Hey, Mr. Thaxby, Miss Lariat was lookin' for you."
" Was she now ? " I tell him. " Where did you see her last ? "
" She was over at the Customs," he says. " She was worried she wouldn't make that nine-thirty train."
He looks at me sort of old-fashioned. " It's a funny thing," he says, " the way a nice dame like that will fall for a guy. The more reserved they are the harder they fall."
" Oh yes ! " I tell him. " An' who was the guy that she fell for ? "
He gives me a big grin. He says :
" You don't have to start puttin' on an act ! I

5

reckon everybody knew that she was nuts about you."

I think to myself not so bad, but I put on a sorta modest look an' I say :

" Not on your life. Why, I hardly talked to the dame."

He raises his eyebrows.

" Maybe you're one of those guys that don't have to talk to a dame. It did me good to see the way her eyes followed you when you was walkin' around the deck. I reckon you're her idea of a real fella."

I give him a short punch in the ribs. I say :

" What do you wanta do—borrow some jack ? "

He laughs an' goes off in the dark. I think to myself this is nice goin', because even if I am over in this country on a job there is no reason at all why I should not have a pleasant journey up to Waterloo with this Lariat baby an' maybe fix up a little date to have dinner one time in London. After all a guy has gotta relax sometimes.

I look at my watch an' I see it is ten past nine. I ease over towards the Customs barrier. Way over in the corner I can see the Southampton copper, Rapps. I go over to him.

" It's O.K., Mr. Thaxby," he says. " Your stuff's through, so's Miss Lariat's. I got an idea she's waiting for you. Goodnight and good luck."

I tell him goodnight an' I walk through the barrier. I'm goin' pretty carefully because it is as dark as hell, an' any time you walk in the wrong direction you're liable to fall in the drink. I'm peerin' around when Manders, the wireless guy, comes up.

" O.K.," he says. " She's waitin' for you down there on the jetty. I believe your stuff's gone down to the train. Another thing," he says, " if you don't wanta waste any time, keep straight on on the right-hand side of the jetty. If you get on the other side

of the barrier it'll take you twice as long because there's
an unexploded bomb round there."

I say thanks a lot an' I walk down the jetty. Pretty
soon I can see Carlette standin' up against the wall.
I can see the tip of her nose in the light of the cigarette
she is smokin'. She has got the fur collar of her coat
turned up around her face and, believe me or believe
me not, she looks like the answer to anybody's prayer.

" Well, well," I tell her. " So it looks as if you an'
me are goin' up on the same train, which is a very
nice thing because there are one or two things I wanta
say to you."

She looks up at me an' smiles. She is one of those
dames who, when they smile, give you everything
they've got. She says sorta fresh :

" And what would Mr. Thaxby have to say to me ? "

" Well," I tell her, " I've been thinkin' one or two
things up. First of all I think you're what the doctor
ordered. I like everything about you. I like the way
you walk an' the way you put your feet on the ground.
Also you are one of those dames whose stockin' seams
are always straight up the back and both level."

" Just fancy," she says. " So you've noticed that
too."

" Why not ? " I tell her. " I was sorta interested.
But come on, we haven't any time to waste."

We start walkin' down the jetty. When we get
about fifteen yards, the moon comes up an' just for a
minute you can see one or two things, which is a nice
change. Five or six paces away is the edge of the
stone jetty. She puts her hand on my arm an' she
says, pointin' to the water :

" Isn't that wonderful ? I love to see the reflection
of moonlight on the water."

She walks over to the edge an' stands lookin' down.
I tell her :

" Well, now that you've looked at the reflection of

the moon on the water, supposin' we make this train."

" All right," she says.

She turns around an' as she does so she slips. I hear her give a little squeal an' the next thing I hear is the splash. I stand lookin' down into the water twenty feet below. When she comes up she is a good six yards from the jetty. I reckon there is a current down there. I don't waste any time. I throw off my overcoat, get rid of my shoes an' jacket an' take a dive in the drink. An' was it cold or was it !

I come up about six yards from her. I can see her tryin' to swim but she ain't got much chance with that coat on. I take a coupla nice easy strokes an' get close to her. I say :

" Take it easy. This is goin' to be all right. Just put your hand on my shoulder, willya ? "

She gives a little gulp.

" Right," she says, an' I can see she is still smilin'.

I let go a holloa that you coulda heard in Japan an' paddle around for a few seconds, after which some guy appears on the edge of the jetty an' throws me a rope. Two minutes later we're standin' up there shakin' the water off ourselves. I'm tellin' you guys that if it was cold before it is now like Iceland in the winter season.

" Look, Carlette," I tell her, " we've gotta get outa here pretty good an' quick, otherwise somebody is goin' to get lumbago. The second thing is that by the time we have got dried off we shall be lucky if we get the second train at ten-thirty. Now lets get a ripple on."

" It's O.K. by me," she says.

She slips her hand through my arm an' we make a run for it.

I reckon we're about fifteen minutes off Waterloo when I say to her :

" What about you an' me havin' a little dinner one night ? I'm goin' to be pretty busy over here, but maybe I could steal just one night off."

She says: " So you're going to be busy. I've been wondering what a man like you does."

" I can answer that one easy," I tell her. " I'm in the Nuts an' Bolts business. My uncle's factory at Cold Springs makes 'em an' I sell 'em, an' believe me the amount of nuts an' bolts they are needin' in this country at this time is nobody's business."

She says : " That's very interesting." She takes a long look at me an' she goes on : " That's funny, because I didn't think you looked like a man who sold anything."

" Except myself maybe," I crack at her. " Anyway, what about this dinner date ? "

She shakes her head.

" Nothing doing," she says. She puts her hand up an' stops me sayin' anything. " Look," she goes on, " I'm going to tell you something, and you can believe it or not, I don't want to see you again because— well, I'm rather attracted by you and I don't want to be attracted by any one at the moment. It might interfere . . ."

" With what ? " I ask her.

" I can't tell you that," she says.

" You're a funny sort of dame, Carlette," I tell her. " You tell me you don't wanta see me any more because you think you're attracted. Well, comin' over on the *Florida* you seemed to spend all the time you could keepin' away from me."

" Well," she says, " there's a reason. Nobody who's

9

got any sense likes playing with fire, you know. The
point is," she goes on, " I shall always remember this
evening. I shall always remember you getting me out
of that very cold water. I just want to leave it like
that, see ? "

" I see," I say. I look at her for a minute. Then
I go on : " It's a funny thing, you know, but I gotta
sort of idea in my head that I've met you before some
place, I don't know why. I've got a good memory
but I can't remember you. Yet how could I forget
you ? It intrigues me. I can't make it out."

She smiles. She says :

" I expect it was some other woman. I expect
there've been lots of them in your life."

I put on a sort of modest look.

" No," I tell her. " I'm not a guy who goes for
dames."

" You're telling me ! " she says.

We both laugh. I light myself a cigarette an' ask
her if she will excuse me for a minute. Then I get up
an' wander down the corridor until I find the guard's
van. This guard is a reasonable sorta guy. I give
him a pound note an' I say :

" Look, there's a lady in the restaurant car called
Miss Carlette Lariat. When we get to Waterloo she'll
go along to get her luggage from the van. You get
along too. When you get the chance give that pound
note to the porter who's takin' her luggage an' ask
him to stick around an' get the address that she gives
the taxi-driver. You got that ? "

He says he understands it all right, but ain't it a bit
irregular.

" No," I tell him, " it ain't." I give him another
three pounds. " That's for your own trouble," I say.
" Are you goin' to do it ? "

He says maybe he can see his way to doin' it.

" All right," I tell him. " When the porter gets the

address you tell him to come over an' look for me under the clock so's he can give it to me. My name's Thaxby."

He says all right, he'll do it.

I go back to Carlette, an' five or six minutes later we pull in. I said goodbye to her an' scram because I've only got a hand-bag with me, the rest of my luggage havin' been sent ahead by the Southampton copper on the nine-thirty. When I get to the barrier at the end of the platform there is a middle-sized guy with a raincoat an' a Derby hat on lookin' around him. When he sees me he comes my way. I reckon this will be Herrick's man, Grant.

" Mr. Thaxby ? " he says. He drops his voice. " Otherwise Mr. Lemmy Caution of the F.B.I. ? "

I tell him yes. He puts out his hand.

" My name's Grant," he says. " Detective Sergeant —Special Branch. Mr. Herrick sent me along to meet you. He's very sorry he has had to go up to Scotland for three or four days on a big job. He'll contact you when he comes back. In the meantime I'm at your disposal."

" That's fine," I tell him.

I ask him how he knew I was me. He puts his hand in his raincoat pocket an' brings out a picture of me, which shows you that these Scotland Yard guys are not such mugs as you would think.

I start walkin' over towards the buffet.

" Let's get a cup of coffee," I tell him, " after which we'll get around to Jermyn Street where I have fixed myself an apartment, an' I'll have a little talk to you about this case."

He says O.K. We go over to the buffet and order the coffee. When it comes I tell him I will be back in a minute, an' I scram outside, walk across an' stick around under the clock. After a minute a porter comes up to me.

11

" Are you Mr. Thaxby ? " he says.

I tell him yes. He gives me a slip of paper an' a big grin.

" That's the lady's address you wanted," he says.

I say thanks a lot an' go back to the buffet, an' when we have finished our coffee we grab a cab an' get along to Jermyn Street. On the way this Grant guy tells me all about the war over here. He is a nice sorta guy, pleasant an' easy to get along with like English coppers always are.

When we get to Jermyn Street I see the night porter, who takes me up to my apartment which I got Herrick to fix for me. I have got a bedroom, sittin'-room an' bathroom on the third floor. I tell the porter to send down to Waterloo next mornin' for my luggage an' when he has scrammed I open my suitcase an' take out a bottle of rye.

I reckon I will not waste any time on this job. I give Grant a cigarette an' a drink.

" How much has Herrick told you about this business ? " I ask him.

" Not very much," he says. " He told me you'd give me the layout ; tell me anything you want me to do."

We take a drink an' sit down. I say :

" Well, this is the story : Six months ago some guy called Whitaker, who lives in Kansas City, invents a new dive-bomber. This bomber is the berries. It's got everythin' that opens an' shuts. But Whitaker is a funny sorta guy an' he's not gettin' on with the job of gettin' the blue-prints out like he oughta."

Grant grins.

" These inventors are temperamental fellows," he says.

" You're tellin' me," I say. " O.K. Well, the Navy Department, who is very interested in this airplane, is gettin' a bit het up with Whitaker for takin' such a helluva time over the job. They wonder what's the matter with him. Then some wise guy gets an idea in his head that maybe somebody is gettin' at Whitaker —you know, fifth column stuff. So they put some Federal guy on to keep an eye on him, an' this mug finds out what the trouble was. It wasn't fifth column, it was woman—just the usual old sorta woman trouble."

Grant says : " Maybe, but the Germans could have put the woman in, couldn't they ? "

" You've got somethin' there, pal," I tell him. " Anyhow, it looks like this guy Whitaker, who has been plannin' for some time to get hitched up an' married to some girl in Kansas, has given this baby the air an' is runnin' around after some other dame. Three or four days outa every week he is chasin' around in a high-powered auto, but the funny thing is that the U.S. operative can't put his hooks on this dame. He don't know who she is, see ? So he reports back to Washington. Washington don't worry very much because on the same day they get a phone call from Whitaker from Arkansas sayin' the blue-prints are all finished an' he's comin' to Washington to hand 'em over an' that everythin' is O.K. about the air-plane, an' they can go inta production right away."

I give myself another drink an' look at him over the top of the glass.

" An' this airplane is pretty important to you guys over here," I say, " because the U.S. Government were goin' to produce plenty of 'em for the British, see ? Well, the next thing is Whitaker don't show up. He just disappears. Nobody knows where the hell he's gone an' nobody knows where the blue-prints are. So I get stuck on the job, see ? I go up to Kansas City an' I try an' get a line on this guy Whitaker. It takes me about three-four days to find out that ten days before he telephoned through to Washington that the

13

blue-prints were ready, he'd fixed himself up a passage to England."

Grant says : " What would he want to come over here for ? "

" I wouldn't know," I tell him, " but why shouldn't he come here ? It's as good a place as anywhere else, an' anyway we've got to start lookin' for this guy somewhere." I grin at him. " I've got a hunch he's over here," I say.

He says : " Well, Mr. Caution, it looks a pretty tall order to me. If you're going to start looking around Great Britain in the middle of a *blitzkrieg* for this Whitaker you ought to have an interesting time. Another thing is," he goes on, " we've got our hands pretty full. I hope we'll be able to give you as much help as we would in the ordinary course of events."

" I'll get along," I tell him. I light myself another cigarette an' give him one. " The funny thing is," I go on, " that I expected Herrick mighta had a little bit of information for me. You see, Washington had been in touch with him about me comin' over here. They gave him all the original information we had. It's not so easy for a guy to get inta this country from anywhere these days, an' I had a sort of idea that maybe Herrick might already have a line on Whitaker."

He thinks for a minute. Then he says :

" I don't know. The trouble is that Mr. Herrick was going to handle this job himself. He hoped to meet you tonight, but he got called away on a most important case. He just told me to carry on. Perhaps there's something in the folder at headquarters. When I go back there I'll have a look." He gets up. " I've got to be getting along now," he says. " Will you come down to the Yard to-morrow and let's get started on this thing ? "

" That'll suit me," I say. " I just wanta wait till

14

my clothes get here, because right now I am wearin'
someone else's suit, havin' fell in the ditch at Southampton. But I'll be down with you at eleven o'clock
to-morrow morning. Maybe Herrick left some sort of
information for me."

He says that will suit him fine.

We shake hands an' he scrams.

I get outa my clothes an' go inta the bathroom. I
give myself a warm shower an' start ruminatin' on this
Whitaker guy, an' I reckon maybe Grant is right
when he says that lookin' for Whitaker is goin' to be
like lookin' for a needle in a haystack. At the back
of my head there is an idea that the people who have
been persuading Whitaker not to cash in with the
blue-prints of that dive-bomber are not such mugs.

I give myself a rub down an' get inta my pyjamas.
Then I walk across to the sittin'-room where I have
slung down my overcoat an' feel in the breast pocket
for the leather wallet with my papers in it. Believe it
or not, the goddam wallet is gone.

I get it.

I stand there talkin' to myself an' if you mugs
coulda heard the language I used you woulda thought
you was in the Marines.

Right then the telephone rings. I hop over an' take
off the receiver. It is Grant. He says :

" Listen, Mr. Caution. After I left you I thought
I'd come back here to the Yard an' take a look through
Mr. Herrick's file just to see if he had left any notes.
Well, I'm glad I did because first of all there's a
message from him that he'll be back here tomorrow
night at about eight o'clock and would like to contact
you then ; and secondly—and I think you will agree
this is important—he has got a note of a woman's
name here—Geralda Varney. There's a query mark
against this name and a note that this woman landed
in England a week ago. I was wondering . . ."

15

" Yeah, what were you wonderin' ? " I ask him.

" I suppose there's a chance that this might be the woman that Whitaker was so keen about ? " he says.

" Why not ? " I say. " I reckon if Whitaker was keen enough on a dame to walk out on the girl he was supposed to marry, it would be good enough for him to bring her over here with him or to fix to meet her over here. Anyhow, Herrick wouldn't have a note of that name on the file unless it meant somethin'. Where is this dame ? "

" There's an address on the file—Laurel Lawn, on the other side of the Vale of Health. That's at Hampstead."

" O.K.," I tell him. " Just hold on a minute."

I stand there with the receiver in my hand doin' a little quiet thinkin'. Then I say :

" Listen, Grant, you leave this dame to me. Maybe I'll go an' have a look at her. But I won't worry you tomorrow. I'll wait till Herrick comes back. Tell him I'll get down to the Yard an' meet him there tomorrow night. That gives me time to sorta get settled in here. Is that O.K. by you ? "

He says he thinks that's the best thing. I say so long an' hang up.

I get a ripple on. I get myself back inta my clothes, put on my overcoat an' scram downstairs. Also I am beginning to feel very glad that my gun is in the shoulder holster underneath my inside jacket. I case along Jermyn Street an' turn up inta Piccadilly. The air-raid sirens are goin'. It is as dark as hell an' I have gotta feelin' that this is goin' to be a very interestin' case before we get through with it.

I walk along but I can't find what I am looking for. It is not until I get down inta Berkeley Square that I get it. As I walk down the Square a big tourin' Buick drives towards me. Inside, behind the wheel, is some dame in evenin' dress. She stops the car outside a block of mansions, gets out an' goes in. I open the door an' give a big sigh because that silly dame has left the ignition key in.

Inside five seconds I am inside that car an' rollin' up towards Piccadilly. When I get on the other side of the Park towards Knightsbridge, I pull up by the side of the road, search around in the car an' find an A.A. book in the door flap. This is my lucky night. I look at the map, start off again, put my foot down an' head for the Portsmouth road. An' all I hope is some wise guy don't try an' stop me an' ask for my identity card.

3

It is five o'clock when I pull inta Southampton. I stop the car an' ask some guy where the police station is. Then I go along there an' say I would like to see Detective Sergeant Rapps, an' that he knows me because he will remember meetin' me off the *Florida* when she docked. I say the name is Thaxby.

The station officer, who is a nice guy, says that Rapps is home in bed, but that if it's urgent he'll get him on the telephone. I say it is good an' urgent, so they get him. When he comes on the line I tell him this :

" Listen, Rapps, this is Thaxby, the Nuts an' Bolts salesman, speakin'. I had a little bit of trouble tonight and lost my papers some place. Also I wanta ask you one or two questions."

He says : " All right. Ask away."

I ask him first of all if the *Florida* is still docked. He says yes she is, that she is due to clear late tomorrow afternoon. I then say that I would like to have a few words with some guy aboard the *Florida*, an' ask him whether he could fix for me to have a dock pass to go

17

down there. He says yes he could do this once he has come an' seen that I am really me. So I say I am very sorry but that's how it's got to be.

I stick around the police station an' drink a cup of tea with these boys. Half an hour afterwards Rapps arrives an' gives me the pass. He asks me if I want any help. I tell him no I think I can handle this job on my own ; that I would like to play it that way. But that I will be glad if he will fill up the car for me.

He says O.K. I can see that he is curious, but right now I am not satisfyin' anybody's curiosity.

I smoke a cigarette while they are fillin' up the car an' then I drive down to the docks. The pass that Rapps has given me gets me past the sentry an' the dock police. It is as cold as hell. It is still drizzlin' with rain an' as I walk along to where the *Florida* is berthed I wonder just how many guys are in this thing.

Five minutes later I arrive. The gang plank is still down an' I go aboard. When I get on deck I do a little whistlin' an' some guy comes along with a lantern.

" Looky," I tell him, " this is very important. I gotta have a word with Manders, the wireless officer. Is he aboard ? "

He says yes. I then give this boyo a ten-shillin' note an' tell him to get along an' roust Manders out an' tell him somebody wants to see him urgent. He goes off.

When he has gone I walk around an' smoke. Most of the time I am thinkin' about Carlette. After ten minutes I hear somebody comin' my way. It's the deck watchman an' Manders. As they come level with the gang plank I get hold of Manders by the arm. I say :

" Hello, Manders. Don't say you've forgotten me.

18

My name's Thaxby. I wanta have a little talk with you."

He opens his mouth to say something, but I dig the muzzle of the gun that I have got in my overcoat pocket inta his ribs.

He says : " O.K. Let's talk."

I say : " I'm not talkin' here, Manders. Let's take a walk around the dock."

He goes down the gang plank an' I go after him. We walk fifty or sixty yards away from the *Florida* around behind the Customs sheds. Then he stops. He turns around.

" So what ? " he says.

" It was a sweet set-up, Manders, wasn't it ? " I say, " that you fixed up with your little pal Carlette ? "

He says : " I think you're crazy. I don't know what you mean."

" Like hell you don't," I tell him. " I'm wise to you. You fixed up for that dame to fall over the edge of the pier when we came off the boat, because you knew I would go in after her, because it was dark an' there was nobody else there. I *had* to go in after her. You also knew I wouldn't be such a mug as to go in with a heavy overcoat like I am wearin' an' you were also aware of the fact that I keep my papers in a leather wallet in the breast pocket of that overcoat. So while I am swimmin' around in the drink rescuing that hell-cat you or one of your pals pinched my papers—my identity card, passport and everything. Well, what have you gotta say ? "

He looks at me. His eyes are glitterin' like a snake's.

" Listen, Mr. Thaxby . . ." he says. Then he shoots out his foot and gets me below the knee. I go down but before I hit the ground he kicks me in the face. It feels as if half my jaw is gone. I don't say a word. I drop the gun outa my hand an' lie doggo like I was poleaxed. I can hear him breathin'. He waits half

19

a minute. I reckon he is waitin' to see if I move.
When I don't he kicks the gun outa his way an' bends
down over me. I can feel his breath on my face.

I let go a sorta moan. It seems to satisfy him.
Under his breath I hear him say, " Schweinhund ! "
which tells me all I wanta know. He grabs hold of
me by the collar of my coat an' starts draggin' me
along. It does not take me very long to work out
what this baby is goin' to do with me. I reckon he
is goin' to push me over in the drink, all of which
will prove to you guys that this bozo is not a nice
bozo.

He is not finding the job too easy, because I have
let the whole of my weight go limp, an' after a bit
he gives himself a rest. He leaves me for a minute
an' when he comes back he puts a coupla bricks in
my overcoat pocket just to make certain I do not
come up an' haunt him. After which he gets goin'
an' starts draggin' me some more. In a coupla minutes
we come to the pier edge. He has another rest an'
then stoops down to get hold of me again.

This is my big moment.

I slip my left arm around his neck an' get hold of
his left wrist with my right hand. He is wrigglin' an'
kickin' like an eel, but I get him where I want him.
His face is pressed inta the thick nap of my overcoat.

" Listen, bastard," I tell him, " I don't like you one
little bit an' even if I am a ' schweinhund ' you will
realise that I am a very strong sorta ' schweinhund.'
I am also goin' to tell you somethin' else. You ain't
goin' to see Berlin any more."

I heave myself over on my right side an' throw him
over my shoulder. As he hits the ground I let him go.
I get up on one knee an' as he tries to get up I crack
him under the jaw. His head goes back an' hits the
pier with a bump. I drag him over an' prop him up

against one of the pier stanchions. Then I start smackin'
him across the kisser. After a coupla minutes he
decides to come to.

"Look," I tell him, "you tell me something."

He says : " I'm not goin' to tell you anything."

"Oh yes, you are," I say. "You're goin' to tell
me this—or else I'm goin' to hold a cigarette-lighter
under your nostrils until you decide to talk. It is
about that dame Carlette. I reckon this dame is the
one that Whitaker skedaddled with, ain't she ? She's
the one who was after those blue-prints ; workin' in
with your bunch ? "

He says : " Why not an' what then ? "

" That's all I wanta know," I tell him.

He leans his head back against the stanchion. He
gives a little groan an' at the same time lashes out at
my face with his feet. This time I'm lucky. He misses.
I bust him one on the snout that woulda put an
elephant to sleep. I get up. It is all very nice an'
quiet around me—as dark as hell an' still drizzlin'. I
bend down an' get a fireman's lift on the boy. Then
I take the bricks outa my pockets an' stick 'em in his.
I carry him to the edge of the pier an' let him go in
with a nice easy plop, after which I light myself a
cigarette, go around an' search for my gun, find it,
put it in my pocket an' walk off the dock.

All of which will show you mugs that there is one
wireless officer that Mr. Hitler won't use any more.

4

It is ten o'clock an' a nice day when I get back to
London. I leave the car in Berkeley Square near
where I found it. Then I walk back to my apartment
in Jermyn Street, take a hot shower, four fingers of
rye an' go to bed. Believe me, I am feelin' good an'

21

tired. I have got a bruise on my jaw that looks like a map of the world.

Just before I go to sleep I do a spot of quiet thinkin'. It looks to me as if I might do quite a bit of business today, with a bit of luck, off my own bat, an' I think I'll play one or two little ideas I have got in my head before I go to see Herrick.

I ring down to the janitor an' tell him to give me a call at four o'clock. Then I go to sleep an' believe it or not I never even dream about anythin'.

I get up at four an' wander around my apartment thinkin' things out. I have some breakfast an' get inta a suit of my own clothes. Then I get hold of the piece of paper that the porter gave me last night at Waterloo with Carlette's address on it. This baby is livin' at a place called Sheldon Mansions in St. John's Wood.

I go downstairs, get myself a cab an' get out to the Sheldon Mansions. I have a word with the porter there who tells me that Miss Lariat has gotta place on the first floor. I go up an' ring the doorbell. While I am waitin' I get a little bit of a thrill. I am wonderin' whether I am really goin' to see this dame, whether I have got the right address. However, I don't have to wonder very long, because right then the door opens an' there is Carlette. I have already told you mugs about this baby, but I am tellin' you that if you had seen her standin' there with a little smile playin' about her mouth, dressed in a black lace negligée, maybe you woulda got as big a kick outa lookin' at her as I did.

" How's it goin', Carlette ? " I say.

She opens the door wide.

" Well, here's a surprise," she says. " Mr. Thaxby ! . . . And how did you find out where I was living ? "

I give her a big grin. I go into the hallway after her, hang my hat up on a peg an' take my overcoat off.

" I am a clever mug sometimes," I say. " I did a
little bribin' on that train last night. The porter who
put you inta that taxi slipped me the address you
gave the driver."

" Ah ha ! " she says. " You would think of a little
thing like that. Come in."

We go inta a sittin'-room. There is a big fire burnin'
and the curtains are drawn. She says :

" Would you like a drink ? "

Then she goes over to the sideboard an' mixes me
one.

I stand in front of the fireplace watchin' her. When
she comes back with the drink she says :

" What is this, Mr. Thaxby ? " She smiles up at
me. " I've got an idea you've got designs on me,"
she says.

" You're tellin' me," I say. I start grinnin'. " Ain't
you the goddam little bitch ? " I tell her. " I reckon
you've got enough nerve for forty-seven other janes.
But maybe this is where you meet your Waterloo—
an' I don't mean the station either."

Her expression changes. Her eyes get sorta hard.
She says :

" I don't think I understand what you're talking
about."

" Oh no ? " I tell her. " Well, you sit down there
an' I'll tell you. You an' me are goin' to have a little
heart to heart talk, Carlette. At least I'm goin' to do
some talkin' an' then you're goin' to start. You
wouldn't know who I was, would you ? "

She goes over to the settee an' sits down. Now I
have found that life is divided into two sorts of dames
—the dame who shows a large slice of leg when she
decides to sit on a settee, an' the dame who doesn't.
Me—I am inclined to go for the ones who don't,
which is the class that she don't belong to. She says :

" Mr. Thaxby, I think you're a little bit crazy. I

also think you're presuming on a shipboard acquaintance to make yourself unpleasant."

I put my hand up.

" You wait a minute, baby," I tell her. " I haven't started gettin' unpleasant yet. Maybe you're one of these ignorant dames. Maybe they haven't even got around to tellin' you the facts of life. So I'll jog your memory a little bit.

" My name is Caution—Lemuel H. Caution. I'm an agent of the Federal Bureau of Investigation, an' you know goddam well before I came over here I went up to Kansas City to find out what had happened to a guy called Whitaker—a mug who'd invented a new dive-bomber, but who'd been a little bit tardy about cashin' in the blue-prints. When I get up there I find this guy has scrammed an' in the process he has also walked out on the dame he was supposed to marry. The reason he's walked out is because he's stuck on some other dame who is playin' along with a mob who're tryin' to get their hooks on those blue-prints. Well, we got an idea that this Whitaker has come over here to England, so I come over too. Maybe it's a coincidence that you were on the same boat. Also I reckon that you know that you got what it takes an' that stand-offish attitude of yours on the trip was the very thing that would make me interested."

She leans back in the corner of the settee an' she puts her hands behind her head. She says :

" How interesting. I think you must have been going to the movies."

" Like hell," I tell her. I go on : " When we're half an hour out of Southampton I give the wireless officer, that guy Manders—I don't suppose you'd know *him* either—a radio to send to Herrick of Scotland Yard, tellin' him when I'm arrivin'. Well, Manders never sends that radio. He probably sends another one sayin' I am goin' to be three or four days

24

late or something like that just to keep 'em quiet at this end. So this fixes Herrick, who is not expectin' to see Caution for one or two days anyway. Manders gives me a fake reply supposed to come from Herrick, tellin' me that he is sendin' a guy called Grant to meet my train at Waterloo. The next thing is that somebody has got to get hold of my papers—my passport, my Federal Bureau of Investigation Identity Card an' the other stuff I got relating to this case—so Manders an' you fix up a nice little job.

" When the *Florida* docks he comes over to me an' tells me a big story about you havin' fallen for me in a big way, suggests that we go up to London together. He also fixes with you that you do that big act about fallin' in the drink, knowin' that I'll come in after you, thereby givin' him a chance to grab my papers out of my overcoat.

" All right. Directly the mug has done this, he rings up another of your boy friends. This guy meets me at Waterloo Station, tells me that he's Grant from Scotland Yard, but the mug don't ask me for my Identity Card, which he oughta have done, because he knows durned well I haven't got it. He brings a picture of me outa his pocket an' says that's how he knows I am me. This is where the boyo makes his first mistake. Also he does not say anything about my not havin' come up on the train that left Southampton at nine-thirty, which was the train mentioned in the phoney radio that was supposed to come from Herrick an' he does not say anything about this because he knows goddam well that I was goin' to miss that train.

This mug then comes around to my apartment with me an' tells me that Herrick is away for a coupla days an' will not be back until tonight. He suggests that I see him then. Well, here's a nice set-up. My papers have been pinched. I am not goin' to try an'

see Herrick because I've been told he's not there, an'
Herrick is not worryin' about me because he has had
a fake radio sayin' I'm not arrivin' for a coupla days.

" O.K. This mug Grant then pulls another fast
one. Just when I am goin' to bed he rings me up an'
tells me he is speakin' from Scotland Yard. He says
he has been through the file an' found the name of
some dame livin' out at Hampstead ; that he reckons
that this is the dame that got Whitaker to come over
here, which is a lot more punk because *you* are that
dame."

I give her a big grin.

" Anyway," I tell her, " this Grant guy thinks I've
fallen for this stuff, so he is not worryin' about me for
a little while. He is also certain that I will not contact
Herrick anyway until tonight, which is about the
only thing he is right about, an' how do you like that,
baby ? "

She gets up. She goes over to the sideboard an' gets
herself a cigarette. She lights it, blows a puff of
smoke an' looks at me. She is still smilin'.

" I don't like it a bit," she says. " I think it's
hooey. You say you're Caution of the F.B.I." She
shrugs her shoulders. " Well, you can't prove it.
Where's your F.B.I. Identity Card ? Supposing I ring
the bell and ask the porter to have you thrown out
on your ear ? What are you going to do then ? Another
thing," she goes on, " maybe I can prove to you that
you're wrong."

" Oh yeah ! " I tell her. " You go ahead with it,
but it'll have to be pretty good, an' anyway I wouldn't
believe you. I'm wise to you, Carlette."

She goes over to a desk in the corner, an' gets hold
of a document case. She unlocks it. She pulls out a
lotta papers from inside.

" Come over here, Mr. Know-All," she says, " and
have a look at this."

I ease over to the desk an' look at the papers. The top one is a newspaper cuttin'. As I put my hands on the desk to read this cuttin', I see her hand shoot out an' grab a paper-weight on the end of the desk. I swing around. I put up my left hand an' I just give her a nice little quiet smack under the jaw. She drops the paper-weight, she gives a sort of sigh an' I catch her as she falls. I carry her over an' lay her down on the settee.

I take a look around. I open the drawers in the desk, look through the papers. There is nothing there. The stuff looks as if it mighta been left by the previous tenant. I walk across an' open the door that leads out of the sittin'-room. The place is dark because the curtains are drawn, but it smells very good. There is a suggestion of perfume in the air like somebody had been usin' some nice bath salts or somethin'. Me—I have gotta nose for scent an' I certainly go for this scent because it is very good.

I step inta the room an' fumble around for the light switch, but I don't worry about this business for very long, because right at this minute somebody catches me a helluva smack over the dome. I do a flop on the floor. Everything goes nice an' dark an' believe me, I am not worryin' about anything any more.

An' I do not even dream.

CHAPTER TWO

I

SOME SENSE begins to trickle back inta my head. In other words I begin to get the idea that I am still alive even if I have just had a head-on collision with a dive-bomber. Every time I try to move my head it is like somebody is hittin' me with a coke hammer.

I relax an' after a few minutes my brain-box begins to tick over an' I realise that I have been taken for a sweet ride by this Carlette baby with the willin' assistance of the guy who was hidin' in her bedroom. Which just shows you that the dome of a " G " man is just as liable to get a mean bust as any other sonofabitch.

Havin' dealt with these deep thoughts I open one eye just a piece an' take a look around. I am lyin' in the sittin'-room with my head just inside the bedroom door where I have been dragged by somebody—maybe the guy who socked me. From where I am lyin' I can see Carlette parked on the settee. She is lyin' back smokin' a cigarette an' on the table by the side of her well within reach of her pretty little fingers is a .38 automatic.

I get wise to this baby. Something way back of my brain clicks an' tells me that this Carlette Lariat is just nobody else but a dame called Carlette Francini, one of the toughest and hottest mommas that ever rolled a mug for his dough.

This baby has done a bit of everything an' got away with most of it. Dope peddlin', a spot of kidnappin'

28

and any other sorta skulduggery that came her way.

I give a sigh an' begin to think of what I would like to do to this hell-cat if I got the chance, but after a minute I lay off this because these vindictive thoughts are not likely to get me any place.

So I start bein' constructive. I lay there, waitin' for my head to stop buzzin', tryin' to think of what has happened to me on other times that I have got myself sandbagged or slipped a Micky Finn in some dame's apartment, but believe it or not, I haveta come to the conclusion that the circumstances are not quite the same, an' that if I am goin' to get myself outa this jam I have got to be very clever an' very quick, because I do not reckon that these bozos are goin' to hand me a bunch of roses to speed me on my way. They will do somethin' else with me an' I do not think it will be so nice.

I ease myself up against the side of the door an' let go a big sigh. I open my eyes just in time to see Carlette grab the automatic an' point it in my direction. I give her a wan sorta smile.

" Look, Carlette," I tell her. " Maybe you think that this is all very clever an' sweet, but believe me, you brown snake, by the time I am through with you what I am goin' to do to you would make the early Christian martyrs look like the annual festival of the Two Forks Help-The-Troops Association. If you think you can get away with this sorta hooey you must be even more nutty than your ma knew about."

She gets up, pulls her stockin's up an' takes the cigarette outa her mouth. Then she walks over to where I am half lyin' against the wall an' stands there lookin' down at me like I was somethin' washed up by a tidal wave.

When she starts speakin' her voice an' everything is quite different. She is not the honeybabe I knew on

29

the *Florida*. No, sir. She sounds tough an' nasty. She says :

"Whatever my ma knew she had enough sense to have a child with some brains, fly-cop."

She looks sorta far away for a minute an' then she goes on :

"Ma always wanted me to be the sorta girl that men look up to, but the trouble with me was that I wanted to be the sorta baby they look round at, an' that's the way it is. Anyhow," she says, "I reckon I got enough of what it takes to handle a big mug like you, because if your lady friend could see you now, lookin' like you was tryin' to remember where you stuck your chewin' gum last night, she would take one look an' a run-out powder, you big false alarm."

"Hooey," I tell her. "You are just another of these cheap gun molls with big ideas an' no brains. You make me sick. You are one of these babies who are so goddam dumb that any time you put your step-ins on wrong way round you think you gotta walk backwards all day. You got a swell pan an' you think you can skate through life on that instead of which by the time you are through you will have worn the seat of your pants out tryin' to slide round corners. Carlette," I continue, "to me you are just a big tub of lard with an ingrowin' temper an' no horse sense."

"You ain't tellin' me," she says. "Look, smart guy, this is one time when I do not want any wise-cracks from you. I don't like you . . . see ? I never did like you, you wisecrackin' Federal bastard, an' if you don't get that ugly trap of yours sewn up I'm gonna give you such a helluva deal that havin' your head sawn off would be pleasant compared with it. You got that ? "

"I got it," I tell her. "An' I also remember you now—you cheap four-flushin' jane. If you was not

the baby who was tried with the Panzetti an'
McGonnigle mob way back in '36 for murder an'
kidnappin' then I am the Flyin' Dutchman. Although
how I could ever forget a pan like yours is beyond
me an' you have permission to quote me at full
length."

"You don't say !" she says sorta acid. "Well . . .
you're right. But I beat that rap an' if you think I'm
takin' any back talk from you you can think some
more. An' here's somethin' to be goin' on with."

She takes a short step back an' then she kicks me in
the face. An' when I say kick I mean just that. My
head goes back with a smack against the doorpost
an' my nose begins to feel as if it belongs to some guy
in the next street. A coupla of my teeth are evincin'
a strong desire to part company with their colleagues
an' my cheek is cut to hell where the sharp toe of her
georgette shoe has caught it.

"An' how do you like that, pal ?" she says.

She stands there smilin'. Believe it or not that
woman is a sweet sorta dame. I reckon that when
she was a kid her big amusement was pullin' cats'
tails out.

"I don't like it at all," I tell her. "But don't you
worry about me, Carlette. You just give yourself a
nice happy time, because one of these fine days I am
goin' to get around to you an' then I will celebrate
plenty."

"Maybe, sourpuss, an' maybe not," she says.
"Anything you can do to me is O.K. by me." She
starts laughin'. "Hear me laugh," she says. "Mister
Lemmy Caution, the big ' G ' man, fallin' for me like
a ton of coke. Did you go for my act on the *Florida*
or did you—you big lug ! If you coulda heard me an'
the boy friend laughin' our heads off at you you
woulda wanted to jump in the sea an' bite a shark."

"Nice goin', you tramp," I tell her. "So Manders,

31

the wireless guy on the *Florida*, was your boy friend, hey? I suppose he was another of the Panzetti mob that was workin' with you on this racket. Well, believe it or not, kiddo, that boy friend knows more about bitin' fish than I ever shall, because right where he is at the present moment there are plenty fish."

" What the hell do you mean by that? " she says. She looks concerned. I reckon maybe she was stuck on Manders.

" Oh, nothin'," I tell her. " But whatever you an' your lousy mob are aimin' to do with me, the fact remains that I pushed the Manders guy over the edge of the pier at Southampton with a brick in each pocket an' I reckon he's still sinkin'. That makes it sorta even . . . hey, sister? "

She flushes as red as a tomato. She says :

" If I thought you was tellin' the truth, you lousy copper, I'd cut your throat now . . . but I don't believe you. . . . You're bluffin'."

" Punk," I say. " Manders is as dead as last week's hamburger an' right now that boyo is providin' a nice meal for the local fish. That makes you practically a widow so far as love is concerned, an' I hope the next time you get married it will be to a rattlesnake, an' believe me I'd be sorry for the rattler. Another thing," I go on, " is that you are takin' some big chances, Carlette. You're feelin' pretty good right now. Anything I can do would make you smile, says you, but ain't you forgettin' that there are some other guys workin' with me on this business. What about these English coppers? You can't get away with this stuff over here, baby. They'll have you before you know it."

" Nuts," she says. " First of all Herrick don't know you've arrived. So far as he's concerned you're just gonna disappear into thin air. So nobody is goin' to worry about the big ' G ' man Lemmy Caution for quite a while."

"Maybe an' maybe not," I crack back at her,
"but at the same time if I hadn't come around here
lookin' for you, thinkin' that you was Carlette Lariat
instead of that cheap mobster's pet Carlette Francini,
the position would not be like this. I was unlucky,"
I go on, "I just didn't know that your other boy
friend was hidin' in the bedroom."

She laughs.

"You're dead right, copper," she says. "He was
here when I opened the door for you, an' I reckon he
heard your voice an' got under cover. I'm glad he
did."

"I suppose he's gone to get himself a drink to
celebrate," I say.

"You'd like to know, mug," she says. "But don't
worry, he'll be back, an' when he arrives we got a
nice little idea we're gonna work on you. You're
goin' out of this place in a big laundry basket an'
nobody is ever gonna hear of you again."

I do not say anything to this because believe it or
not these guys would think nothin' of doin' a little
thing like that. I lean my head back against the
doorpost an' give a sorta sigh as if I wasn't feelin' so
good. Then, I give a groan an' let my head fall back
on the floor with a bump, just as if I'd passed out.

I lie there with my eyes closed, but I have got my
left eyelid open just a little bit an' I am watchin' her.
She stands there lookin' at me for a minute an' then
she does what I hoped she was goin' to do. She walks
over to the sideboard an' she comes back with a big
glass water jug. She is still totin' the gun in her right
hand an' she comes an' stands over me an' starts
dribblin' the water outa the jug over my face.

"Come on, you big sissy," she says. "If you haveta
faint just because of what I handed out to you, I
wonder what you're gonna do when Willie comes
back an' gets to work on you."

33

I open my eyes sorta slow. Then I give a moan an'
do a big act that I am tryin' to sit up an' that I can't
quite make it. I waggle my head about like I was a
concussion case an' let go another groan.

She calls me by a very rude name an' she steps in
a bit closer an' tilts the jug so that the rest of the
water slops right over my face. I sit up quick an' take
a sudden kick at the jug. It comes off. I knock the
jug right outa her hand an' it catches her a nasty
smack just underneath the waist-line. She gives a
helluva gasp, tries to get the gun up but she can't
make it. She squeezes the trigger an' puts a bullet in
the floor between my legs, drops the gun an' then she
goes right out. I reckon I have knocked every bit of
wind outa this dame that she ever had—an' then
some.

I do not waste any time. I get up, grab the rod,
go out to the hallway and put the bolt on the apartment door because I do not wanta be surprised by
the guy Willie if he comes back.

When I get back to the sittin'-room, Carlette is still
rollin' about, makin' funny noises. I pick her up an'
stick her on the couch. Then I go inta the bedroom
an' take the cord of a dressing-gown that I find in
there an' tie her up so she looks like a trussed chicken.

I then get some water outa the bathroom an' give
her a drink. By this time she has got her breath back
an' is lookin' at me like a meetin' of the Associated
Brothers of Satan tryin' to decide which is the slowest
method of boilin' some guy alive.

" It just shows you, sweetheart," I tell her, " that
everything works out for the best an' that nobody
should ever give up hope."

She puts up a sickly sort of grin. She says :

" O.K., Caution. Maybe you think you're doin'
fine. But you ain't gotta hope. I got plenty of friends
over here who will take care of you."

" All right, honey," I tell her. " You have a good hate but it ain't goin' to get you anywhere. Just excuse me while I make arrangements for the disposal of the carcass."

I go out an' take a look around the flat. On the far side of the kitchen is a big coal cupboard, an' while it ain't exactly full there is enough coal an' coke inside to make things interestin' for Carlette. I go back to the sittin'-room, pick her up an' take her into the kitchen. I dump her in the coal-cellar.

" I reckon you can shout your head off here, baby," I tell her, " an' nobody ain't goin' to hear you. If you get hungry just cut yourself a nice piece of coal."

I will not tell you what that dame said to me because even if you understood it you wouldn't believe that words like that could come out of a mouth that is as pretty as Carlette's, all of which will go to prove to you guys that because a woman has got a very nice pan an' a sweet set of curves it does not mean that she cannot be very nasty at times.

I shut the cupboard door just at the time she is tellin' me what she hopes will happen to my great grandchildren, lock it an' put the key in my pocket.

I then go back to the sittin'-room, grab myself four fingers of rye whisky out of the bottle an' proceed to do a little quiet thinkin'.

First of all I reckon that the guy who was hidin' in the bedroom was some guy that I do not know at the moment. What I mean is I reckon he was not the phoney Grant guy because if he hadda been, Carlette, when she had me on the end of that gun of hers, couldn't have resisted tellin' me all about it. If I am right in this idea, then the Grant guy does not know that I have been to see Carlette, because he does not know that I got her address, an' because he will believe that I will stick around today like I said an' go an' see Herrick at the Yard some time tonight.

35

But the Grant guy will have an idea of something that I *will* do. He will have this idea because he put it into my head. An' the reason he did this was because this was because this bozo has got a little scheme of his own. An' I think I know what it is.

I give myself another quick drink just to keep the cold out an' go into the bathroom. When I take a look at myself in the mirror I nearly throw a fit because my pan looks like territory that Mister Hitler has been occupyin'. My nose an' cheek are cut an' I have got an eye that looks like I have been havin' a rough house with Joe Louis.

I get to work on myself with a wet towel, after which I grab my hat an' coat, close the apartment door behind me an' ease downstairs.

On the ground floor I find the porter. I reckon this guy looks pretty intelligent because he takes a look at my pan but don't even blink an eyelid.

I take out my bill-fold an' rustle out a five-pound note. I say :

" There has been a little trouble at Miss Lariat's place. I'm her brother an' I had a spot of trouble with the guy who was up there. Maybe you remember him goin' up."

He says yes he does.

" Well, that guy is bad medicine," I go on. " He's been chasin' around after my sister, an' she don't like it. When I told him to scram he hit me with a china vase. You can see what he did to my pan."

He says yes he can see that too.

" O.K.," I tell him. " Well, if that guy comes around here again—an' I expect he will—you might tell him that Miss Lariat has gone, an' that she don't want to see him. Don't let him get away with anything around here."

He says he supposes that Miss Lariat will confirm what I'm tellin' him.

" Sure, she will," I say. " But she don't want to be disturbed till late tonight. She's lyin' down. She's sorta upset about things."

I slip him the five-pound note an' he says he understands everything perfectly an' that if Mr. Kritsch comes round he will see that he does not get up to the apartment.

" That's fine," I say. " An' when the guy goes maybe he'll take a cab some place. If you want to earn another five you might use your ears an' listen to the address he gives the driver."

He says he'll do anything he can, an' that the drivers on the cab-rank there are all sorta friends of his so he reckons that if Kritsch takes a cab he can find out the address.

I say thanks a lot an' scram.

I ease around the corner an' I get myself a cab an' drive back to Jermyn Street. I take a look at my watch an' see that it is just seven o'clock.

Maybe this ain't goin' to be such a bad day after all.

2

It is seven-thirty when I get down to Scotland Yard. There is an air-raid goin' on but nobody seems to be takin' a lot of notice. While I am goin' down there in the cab I can see places that have been blown flat by the Hitler boys ; but there is still a helluva lot of London standin' up on its feet an' I reckon these German bastards will haveta pull their socks up if they think they're gonna win the war that way.

Herrick gives me the big hand. He takes a look at my pan an' I can see he is wonderin' just how I managed to get myself lookin' like I have been run over by a steam-roller. I tell him that I fell off a bus in the black-out an' I hope he believes it. We check

37

up together an' it is as plain as a dead codfish on the drawin'-room carpet that these thugs have pulled a fast one on us. Herrick ain't been away anywhere at all. He's been stickin' around waitin' for me to show up.

But it shows that these guys know their stuff. It shows us that they know that the Whitaker mug is in this country an' that they knew I was comin' over on the *Florida*. Carlette was stuck in to take care of me, an' the wireless operator was one of these Gestapo/ U.A.-1 boys that they got planted all around the world just waitin' to be a menace to one an' all when required.

I ask Herrick if he has got any idea as to who the Grant guy was, an' we go through the pictures in the rogues' gallery at the Yard but I can't find him there. In any event I do not reckon that this guy is English. I got an idea that he is a bird who speaks English goddam well but will probably turn out to be some sorta wop when we find him.

I don't say anything to Herrick about Carlette an' the show-down I have had with that baby. I do not say a word about this because I got one or two ideas that I will let you in on. But I give him the works about Manders. I tell him how I went back to Southampton an' had a rough-house with that palooka, an' how, when we was strugglin', he fell over the pier edge an' never come up again. Herrick looks at me sorta old-fashioned when I pull this one on him but he says that this is O.K. by him an' that it will probably save a lotta trouble in the long run.

He then takes me along an' we have a word with the Assistant Commissioner, who is a nice guy an' makes you feel like these top-coppers always do when you are in England, an' that is that they have been wastin' all their lives until they met you. The Assistant Commissioner, whose name is Strevens, says that he has already been in touch with Federal Headquarters in Washington about the Whitaker guy, and that at the moment they are concerned with two angles on this case. First of all they wanta know why Whitaker decided to come over to England, an' secondly havin' decided to do so how it was that he got inta the country without them knowin'. He asks me if I have got any ideas on these questions.

I tell him that I have got plenty ideas. I tell him that it is my considered opinion that this guy Whitaker got plenty frightened of something in a hurry an' decided that America was not a very safe place for him to be in. I reckon that Whitaker was right there, because as you guys probably know there are a helluva lot of German guys operatin' in the United States tryin' to throw a spanner in the works. These guys know that if England is goin' to cane Hitler—an' I personally don't reckon there is much ' if ' about the job—then she is dependent a helluva lot on American production both in armaments an' especially planes. The Germans reckon that they can win a big battle if they can stop production at the source. I tell Strevens that everything in this job stinks of the foreign department of the Gestapo, U.A.-1 they call it, an' that the way I see the job is this :

Here is this guy Whitaker. He is a fella that nobody knows a hell of a lot about except that he has been in the airplane business for a long time. He invents this new dive-bomber an' the Federal Government are out to buy it off him. So it ain't money that is worryin' him because he musta known goddam well that the U.S. Government woulda paid him more for selling the patent rights in his invention to them than the Germans could for not doin' it.

Point number two is that this guy is engaged to some dame in Kansas. He is goin' to marry this baby. When I was kickin' around in Kansas I tried to contact this momma but couldn't. She had scrammed off

39

some place an' nobody knew where she was. O.K. Well, for some reason or other the Whitaker guy hitches up with some other dame. This second dame is a tough baby put in by U.A.-1 to get next to Whitaker an' get the plans of the dive-bomber off him.

Maybe Whitaker gets wise to this an' decides to scram because he thinks these mugs will get him if he don't. So he comes over to England an' there you are.

Now you mugs will know that I am holdin' out on Strevens an' Herrick an' maybe you will wonder why, but if you will stick around for a minute I will wise you up to what is in my mind.

Strevens says that maybe I am right an' that if Whitaker has got himself into this country the way I suggest he has not got a dog's chance of stayin' under cover because everybody knows that there has been a big national check-up in Britain an' that everybody has to tote around an identity card, that you can't get any food unless you are registered for rations an' that even if Whitaker is stayin' at some hotel they have still got to know all about him an' that even if he is American an' a friendly neutral the police will wanta know all about him.

So he says that he reckons that Whitaker has slipped into the country usin' another name an' with a passport that he has got from somewhere or other, but that this is not worryin' them a great deal because they know the approximate date when he musta come over here an' that Herrick is havin' a check-up of entries into the country from the United States ; that it is merely a matter of checkin' up an' that they reckon that they will have their hooks on the boyo before a week is out.

He says that if I stick around with Herrick an' co-operate with him there is no doubt that Herrick

40

will pull the boy in an' I can then take over an' find out what the trouble is.

Herrick then says that it is not quite like that. He tells the Assistant Commissioner about Manders, the wireless operator on the *Florida*, an' how this guy sent him a phoney radio an' handed me a phoney one purportin' to come from Herrick. Herrick says that the idea in this was to stop me gettin' up to London on time an' that it looks as if somebody or other hopes to do some business with Whitaker before I can get at him.

Strevens then says if that is so it is all the more reason why we should get a move on an' find this inventor before the rats get at him, an' that he would like to be advised as to what is happenin' from time to time.

I then go back to Herrick's room with him. We talk for a bit an' he says that he will get the Special Branch an' the Home Security people to get busy with this job pronto an' that he reckons he will have some news for me within a day or so.

I tell him that this will suit me very well an' that I will get back to my apartment an' do some unpackin' an' drink a little whisky an' generally hang around until I hear from him.

After which I ease off, grab myself a cab an' go back to Jermyn Street.

When I get there I open myself a bottle of rye an' do a little quiet ruminatin'. Maybe you guys are wonderin' why I have not opened up an' told Herrick an' the Assistant Commissioner the works about this business. O.K. Well, here's the reason.

I reckon that if I had told Herrick about Carlette he woulda pulled her in pronto an' that is one thing I do not want. The second thing is if I had told him anythin' about the address the phoney Grant guy had given me—the Laurel Lawn dump out at Hampstead

41

—he woulda got busy there too. It is a stone certainty
that he would not have let me do what I am plannin'
to do because he woulda reckoned the game might
not have been worth the candle.

Because way back in my own mind I have got some
private ideas on this business. I reckon that the
German mob—the U.A.-1 boys—got wise to the fact
that Whitaker had invented a new dive-bomber an'
that they put Panzetti's old mob in to try an' get the
blue-prints. I reckon they paid 'em plenty for doin'
it. This is how Carlette gets inta the game. Carlette
is put in to get next to Whitaker an' for some reason
her idea is to get him outa the country an' into
England.

Well . . . they wouldn't try an' pull this off unless
they had got something—an' somebody—ready-eyed
over here—somebody who was goin' to look after
Whitaker when he got here. So after they have got
the boyo to start over here, Carlette sticks around an'
waits for me to come over, because they are already
wise to the fact that I have been put on the job by
the Federal Government.

An' they have got a sweet set-up for me. Carlette
comes over on the same boat as me, an' Manders—
who is probably one of the U.A.-1 boys—is fixed on
the boat as wireless operator. Their idea is to get me
outa the way before I even see Herrick after *they have
got hold of my identification papers*—an' I reckon I know
why they wanted them. So Manders an' Carlette pull
a fast one on me an' get the papers an' then the next
thing is to get me very nicely rubbed out before
Herrick even knows what is happenin', because, by
the time he does find out, they reckon they will have
the job very nicely trimmed off an' finished.

So there you are.

3

It is a quarter to nine when I finish off with these deep thoughts an' I am hopin' that I have not left the job I am thinkin' of doin' too late. I grab the telephone an' dial ' Enquiry.' This takes me a helluva time owin' to the fact that there is an air-raid on an' the A.A. guns are shootin' like hell an' devils, an' when they ain't some goddam Jerry is droppin' an occasional bomb around the neighbourhood just to show that there ain't any favouritism an' that he regards me as a military objective.

When I get ' Enquiry ' I tell 'em that I am very sorry to worry 'em at a time like this but I am a stranger around here an' that I am very desirous of getting the telephone number of a dump called Laurel Lawn, out at the Vale of Health, Hampstead. I say that I do not know the name of the subscriber, havin' lost it, but that it is important I should get the number.

After a bit they tell me that they cannot give me the number because the service at that address has been discontinued, which gives me a laugh because that is how I thought it was goin' to be.

I ring downstairs an' order some sandwiches an' coffee. After which I get ready for action. I open up my big trunk an' take out a little .25 automatic pistol that I tote around with me. This pistol goes in a wire clip that I fix inside the right sleeve of my coat. By pressin' my arm against anything I open the clip an' the gun slips down into my hand.

I then put on my overcoat an' stick my Luger pistol in the right-hand pocket, after which I ease downstairs an' walk along into Regent Street, where I pick

43

ι'ɒ a cab. I tell the driver to take me out to the Vale
of Health at Hampstead.

Sitting back in the cab I relax an' do a big grin
when I think of what Herrick would say if he knew
the fast one I am pullin' on him. Me, I have always
found that when you get an idea you gotta play it the
way it comes to you an' that whatever happens you
got to do it quick.

I remember one time when I was up in Cincinnati
on a forgery case. One night I was sittin' around
some honeybabe's flat tellin' her the story of my life.
After which she tells me that her husband is a little
runt of a guy who is so mean that he won't even spend
a week-end, that he don't understand her an' that her
soul is just strugglin' for romance, an' that directly she
clapped eyes on me somethin' inside her went pop an'
that she knew somethin' excitin' was goin' to happen.
She then goes on to tell me that the only reason why
she ain't divorced the little gazebo that she is tied up
to is that she is a sensitive dame an' cannot bear
publicity.

She then gives a big sigh an' throws her arms
around my neck an' says, " Lemmy . . . I cannot live
without you. I am all yours."

Just at this moment my eye sorta wanders around
the apartment an' in the corner I see a pile of press-
cuttin' books, so I gently disengage myself from the
stranglehold that this dame has got on me an' say I
will be back in a minute.

I then scram outside an' ask the lift guy whether
the dame is married an' if so who she is married to.
Havin' slipped him a five-spot he proceeds to divulge
to me that she is the hottest momma around those
parts, that she has been married seventeen times an'
that the guy who is her life partner at the moment
is a prize-fighter who is lookin' for a chance to walk
out on her. The said prize-fighter havin' told one an'

all that he would rather be tied up to a coupla hard-boiled rattlesnakes than the blue-eyed armful who has just been puttin' the fluence on me.

I then stand around the corner in the corridor where I can see the door of the dame's apartment, an' two minutes afterwards some guy who is about seven feet high an' looks like a gorilla with toothache rushes up to the apartment an' starts hollerin, " What are you doin' with my wife ! " After which I ease quietly down the stairs, buy myself a double rye an' ruminate that it was a swell piece of deduction on my part to ask why a dame who don't like publicity should keep a coupla press-cuttin' books. All of which will maybe prove something to you guys if you think about it long enough.

It is a quarter-past nine when I get out to the Vale of Health. I pay off the cab an' do a little walkin'. It has started to rain an' it is also as dark as hell. After askin' a coupla guys the way I find this Laurel Lawn. It is a big sorta house set back off the main road, standin' in a fair size bit of ground with a wall around it. There are some iron gates, one of which is open, an' a car drive leadin' up to the front.

I do not go through the gates, which is maybe what somebody would expect me to do. Instead I ease around to the back of the house an' do a big climbin' act. I get up over the wall and drop down on the other side inta some damp shrubbery place. I take a look around but I cannot see or hear anything at all. The house is as quiet as the local morgue.

I look around tryin' to find some way in. After a bit I find a sorta pantry window about six feet off the ground. I smack the catch off this with the butt of my Luger an' push myself through. When I am inside I re-fix the black-out curtain over the window an' snap on my cigarette-lighter.

I am in a sorta butler's pantry. There are a lotta

45

empty jars an' bottles around but it don't look to me as if anybody has been livin' in this dump.

I push open the door an' walk through the kitchen that is on the other side. I then gumshoe along a long passage that I reckon leads to the front of the house. There are rooms leadin' off this passage but they are all empty. One or two of 'em have got furniture inside but the stuff is all covered with drapes an' there is a helluva lot of dust about the place.

In the hallway facin' the front door there is a stairway leadin' upstairs an' I ease up this. I am goin' very gently an' not makin' any noise at all. Halfway up the stairs there is a turn an' when I get around it I can see a spot of light comin' from under a door along the first-floor corridor.

I stand still an' listen but I cannot hear a thing. I ease up the stairs an' along the corridor. When I get to the door I bend down an' take a look through the keyhole. Opposite me I can see a fire burnin' in the grate an' a chair pulled up by it. I listen for five minutes but nothin' happens so I take hold of the doorhandle an' start easin' it gently around. I get the door open an' take a peek inta the room.

It is a fair-size room like the others. Most of the furniture is covered but there are a coupla chairs pulled up by the fire an' a table standin' by.

I walk over to the table. Just when I get there I smell cigarette smoke. Somebody has been smokin' Turkish cigarettes. I undo my overcoat an' put my hand in my pocket for my cigarette case. I am just pullin' it out when somebody says :

" Put your hands on the table and keep them there. If you move I shall kill you."

Boy . . . oh boy . . . ! Has this dame got a voice or has she. It is a low sorta soft voice with a vibration that makes your ears tingle. An' when she speaks she clips her words off like they come out of a machine-

gun. Standin' there I start wonderin' whether it is
possible for a dame who has got a voice as swell as this
to have anything else worth while besides.

I start grinnin'. I am still facin' the table. I say :
" I suppose I can fish out this cigarette, lady. I
haven't smoked for quite a while."

She says : " Stay where you are. You can drop
your case on the table and help yourself from there."

I says thanks a lot. I drop the case on the table,
open it an' take out a cigarette. While I am doin' this
she comes round an' stands in front of me.

Did I tell you that dame had a voice ? Well, I'm
tellin' you right now that she had everything else that
matched it. When I look up at this baby I get knocked
for a row of pins.

Me—I have seen some dames in my time. But I
am tellin' you that any swell dame I ever saw before
looks like a deformity compared with this honey.

She is wearin' a Persian lamb three-quarter coat.
The coat is open an' underneath she has got on a black
flannel frock with sapphire blue collar an' cuffs. I
don't wonder that the dress she is wearin' sorta hugs
her figure because with the shape she has got she could
wear an old sack an' look like Casanova's best bet.

Underneath a sapphire blue turban with a platinum
pin stuck in the front I can see some swell waves of
red hair an' when I say red I mean the real stuff—the
colour that Titian put his trade-mark on. Her com-
plexion is like the cream on the top of the milk an'
her eyes are sorta soft, blue an' languid. She has got
black eyebrows an' long curly eyelashes that look as
wicked as hell.

I give a gasp. I reckon that this baby has just gotta
have *something* wrong with her. So I take a look at
her ankles. Believe me they was right too. One quick
look at those ankles woulda made grandpa get up an'
dance. An' the black sheer silk stockin's an' little

47

Oxfords that she is wearin' finish off a picture that woulda made your favourite film star look like the dame who comes in to do the manglin'. Oh boy . . . oh boy . . . oh boy !

On her left hand she has got a green kid gauntlet drivin' glove an' in the right she is holdin' a .32 snub automatic with the muzzle pointin' somewhere in the region of my guts. But I am so goofy about this lamb-pie that I do not even worry.

I say to her : " Lady, I shall be very pleased if you will slip me a light because I need tobacco. I gotta have something to quieten my nerves down. Any time I look at a dame who is double-loaded with beauty like you are I go all funny. You are my favourite sight."

Her expression does not change. She looks very serious. She puts her left hand inta her coat pocket an' brings out a lighter an' a little gold cigarette case. She opens the case on the table with one hand, takes out a cigarette an' lights it, an' pushes the lighter across the table to me.

" You can light your cigarette," she says. " But keep your hands over the table. If you don't I'm going to shoot. You understand ? "

" I'm ahead of you, lady," I tell her.

I pick up the lighter an' light my cigarette. I draw a long breath of tobacco smoke right down inta my lungs an' I take a quick look at the lighter as I put it back on the table. On it, let into the gold in little seed pearls, I see the initials G. V.

So there you are.

She is still standin' there lookin' at me as if I was something you find under a rock.

I give her a big grin.

" Lady," I tell her. " If you will just relax for a minute and not worry too much about lettin' your trigger-finger fumble with that gun, I will probably

48

set your mind at rest about a whole lotta things. First of all you have got me all wrong. My name is Lemuel H. Caution of the Federal Bureau of Investigation, Department of Justice of the United States of America. An' you are Geralda Varney an' you are the red-head who was engaged to marry that big mug Elmer Whitaker, the boyo who . . ."

She interrupts me in a very cold voice. I am tellin' you that when she speaks it is like skatin' time in Alaska. She says :

" I don't think I should worry to tell me any lies if I were you. The thing that you have to do at this moment is to concentrate on saving your own worthless life. I tell you—and I mean it—that unless I get the complete truth from you before I leave this room tonight, I am going to kill you like a dog."

" Look, Miss Varney," I tell her. " If I am gonna get myself killed I am not very particular as to whether I get ironed out like a dog or any other sorta animal. But I got the idea in my head that you are takin' yourself a little bit too seriously. Why don't you relax ? "

She says : " I suppose by this time you are becoming a little tired of pretending to be Mr. Caution."

I give a big sigh. You guys will realise that this is a very difficult situation for me.

I say : " O.K., lady, so I am not the real Lemmy Caution. So I suppose if you know that then you musta met the real fella. Maybe you will tell me when an' where you saw this palooka because believe it or not I am that guy."

She laughs.

She says : " I met the real Lemmy Caution this afternoon. He *was* the real Caution. He was able to produce to me his identity papers, his Federal Bureau Card and all other papers necessary to show me that he was the man he purported to be. He was also good enough to tell me of the attempt that had been made to steal his papers and that *you* would probably be coming to this house tonight."

" I see," I tell her. " This bein' so maybe you will tell me who *I* am, because right now, I am not quite sure."

" I do not know who you are," she says. " But I do know that this afternoon you called on your accomplice Carlette Francini. I have also been told that you were coming here tonight for the purpose of meeting another member of either your gang or the German Intelligence Service, who are paying you."

Now I know I am right. I also get it that I gotta do something good an' quick about this business or else there is gonna be some sweet trouble knocking around.

I sit myself down in the big chair, keeping both my hands on the table. I have definitely got the idea in my head that this baby means business an' that she don't like me. She will squeeze that gun just as soon as look at me, an' this thought does not appeal to me a little bit.

Me . . . I have been kickin' around with dames for long enough to know that when a red-head like this one has made up her mind that she does not like you an' that you are somebody else an' not you, an' that you are a big bad member of some gang that she is not very fond of, she is just as likely to let you have it an' worry afterwards as she is to powder her nose.

Because any of you mugs who gets the idea in his head that a dame cannot iron you out as quick as a member of the male sex is only qualifyin' for the local nut-house. All the best babies I have known could kill you as easy as any thug. Dames are like that—the softer they look the tougher they come.

Me . . . I remember a dame I met up with one time in Gettysburg when I was up there on a kidnap job.

50

This baby was so sweet that every time you looked at her you wanted to rush out, sing a coupla psalms an' look around for the chance of bein' a better man. I have known bozos meet up with this dame an' go home an' beat up their legal wives just outa sheer boyish fun an' exuberance.

An' do I fall for her or do I ? I will not keep you in suspense. I do. But I also take a quick peek at this doll an' I tell myself that there is a whole lotta trouble wrapped up in this bundle of woman an' that if I wish to preserve my sanity an' also keep myself all in one piece I will be a wise guy if I do a big exit.

But I hesitate an' at the last minute I think I will just go around an' see her once again just for old time's sake. When I get around there she throws me a long lingerin' look, puts her arm around my neck an' hands me out a kiss that woulda taken the linin' off a battleship. Then she says in a demure sorta voice :

" Lemmy, I am for you an' you are my proper mate. The fact that I already have a coupla husbands is not goin' to come between you an' me. Why should true love worry about a little thing like that. Go get your grip an' let us leave for some sweet spot far from the city where we can get next to Nature an' realise the sanctity of true love."

I say that this is O.K. by me but that I am on business an' that I got a lotta work to do an' that maybe I will come back an' see her some time next year if I am around them parts. She looks at me sorta sweet. Then she gives me a soft little smile. She says :

" I understand, my heart. You do not have to tell me any more. But there is just one thing before you go. I want you to take with you a little memento of me."

She goes over to a drawer that is filled with bunches

of lavender an' flowers, an' I think that she is maybe goin' to give me a posy to wear next my shirt so's every time it tickles I will remember her. But don't you believe it. When she turns around she has lugged out a .45 army automatic an' she starts an artillery bombardment on me that woulda made me look like a nutmeg grater if I hadn'ta got around the door quicker than you can think.

All of which will prove to you palookas that because a dame looks sweet an' speaks sweet it does not mean that she cannot cut your throat from ear to ear at any given moment with one hand an' pluck rose-petals with the other.

So when I look at this dame Geralda I realise that it is stickin' out a foot that if I wanta get out of this *an' get her out of it*—because I can see what is on the carpet—I have got to be clever an' I also see that it is no good at all for me to try an' tell the truth because that will get me nowhere at all. I reckon I will try something else.

" O.K., lady," I tell her. " It looks to me as if the game is up an' that you are wise to the works, so I reckon the best thing I can do is to come clean an' wise you up to what is happenin'. But you gotta make a deal with me. You gotta give me a break if I play ball with you."

She looks at me as if I was a piece of stale drippin'.

" I will make no promises," she says. " But if I am satisfied with the information that I get from you then I may allow you to leave here alive. I will promise nothing beyond that."

I nod my head.

" I get it," I say. " You are gonna pump me dry an' then you are goin' off to meet this guy who says he is Caution an' tell him the works an' he is goin' to get after me an' fix me. An' I have heard about that guy. He would just as soon iron me out as look at me. So I might as well keep my trap sewn up now an' let you bump me off an' how do you like that? "

She looks a little bit disappointed. She waits for a minute an' then she says :

" It is perfectly true that I shall probably inform Mr. Caution of any conversation I have with you. But that does not mean that you will not have a chance. I do not think that either Mr. Caution or myself are worried with small fry like you. It's the people who are paying you that we want."

This is a sweet one. So I am small fry as well as not bein' me. I ask you!

I say : " O.K. Well, what do you wanta know? "

She drops the gun an' lets the barrel rest on the edge of the table. All the time I am lookin' at her mouth. I reckon that I have never seen a mouth like she has got. When she shows her teeth it is like lookin' at strawberries an' cream.

" I have only one question to ask you," she says. " And you will answer it immediately. You will answer it or I shall kill you. Where is Elmer Whitaker? "

I get up. I look at her as if somebody had hit me across the face with a flat-iron. I make a pair of big eyes an' I let my jaw sag. I do an act that woulda put Clark Gable in the Amateurs' Hour class.

I say sorta hoarse : " D'you realise what you are askin' me . . . ? "

I flop down in the chair an' clasp my hands in front of me like I have seen guys do on the stage when the situation is hopeless."

She says : " Are you going to answer me or not? "

" Look, lady," I tell her. " You are makin' things very tough for me. You have asked me where Whitaker is an' I have either gotta tell you or you are goin' to give it to me . . . an' I don't wanta die."

I get up an' I look at her sorta pathetic.

" D'you realise," I say, " that whatever I do I am signin' my own death warrant. If I tell you where Whitaker is Panzetti an' the German guys will know it musta been me. You know what those guys will do to me . . . they won't even shoot me. They'll take such a long time puttin' me out that I'll die about six hundred times before I hand in my dinner pail. Do you get that ? "

" What do I care ? " she says. " What have they done to Elmer. How do I know what they have done to him ? "

I flop down in the chair again. I say :

" O.K., lady. I'm goin' to spill the beans. I'll tell you the whole truth. But for the love of mike if you gotta drink around here let me have it. I'm feelin' all in because I know this is the beginnin' of the end for me."

She says : " Stay where you are and put your hands on the table."

Then she starts backin' away from me, still holdin' the gun on me. She goes to a little table on the other side of the room where I can see a handbag lyin'. She opens it with one hand—still watchin' me—an' brings out a flask. She comes back an' puts it on the table.

" There's your drink," she says. " Take it and get busy. I haven't a lot of time to waste."

I think that she don't know that neither of us have got any time to waste. I put out my hand an' pick up the flask. I unscrew the top of it an' go through the motion of puttin' the flask up to my mouth. When it is nearly there I give it a flick an' send a stream of raw liquor right in her eyes.

I drop flat as she gives a little scream. Then she drops the gun. She has got her hands over her eyes an' she is howlin' like a kid.

I jump around the table an' get the gun. Then I

get hold of her an' grab both her wrists behind her back. She is sobbin' with pain.

"Look, you little mug," I tell her. "You stop howlin' an' talk sense to me otherwise I reckon that you'll have something good to howl about. How'd you get here? Have you got a car?"

She hesitates. She is still moanin'.

"Get goin', baby, an' talk," I tell her. "Otherwise I'll pour some more of that raw liquor in your eyes. Where's your car parked?"

She takes her hands away from her face. She says in a low voice:

"One day I'll kill you for this."

I give her a good smack across the behind.

"I ain't interested in what you're gonna do one day," I tell her. "Where's the car?"

She says the car is in the garage around the side of the house.

"O.K.," I tell her. "Well, we're goin' there *pronto*. An' we ain't goin' down the front staircase either. An' if you as much as open that pretty little trap of yours I'm goin' to smack the pants right off you. Now get goin'!"

I push her through the doorway an' down the stairs. I take her along the back corridor, through into the kitchen an' into the pantry. I tell her to get through the little window.

She says she won't do it.

"Oh yes, you will, baby," I tell her, "an' if your reason for refusin' is that you think you won't get them pretty hips of yours through, don't worry. I'll push you through all right. The other thing is even if I do see your legs it won't be the first time I've seen a dame's calves. So get busy."

I grab her with one hand an' push her up towards the window. She gets her head out an' I give her one good heave. She goes through—fur coat an' all.

55

Directly she is through I stick my head out after her.

"Just stay where you are an' wait for your uncle, the big gangster," I tell her. "Otherwise I'm goin' to blow daylight into you."

I wiggle myself through the window an' drop down beside her. A bit of moon has come up an' I can see her eyes blazin'.

"O.K., sweetheart," I tell her. "Just relax an' save your bad temper. Where's the garage?"

I follow her around the side of the house an' there is a brick garage standin' a good thirty yards away from the house. I push her over to it. She opens the door. Inside I can see a big car.

I open the car door an' take out the key. Then I tell her to get inside. She hesitates for a moment but I give her a good push an' she cannons into the seat.

"You goddamned thug," she says. "One day I'll tear you in pieces for this."

"You'd be surprised, sweetheart," I tell her.

I lean over her an' give her an honest to goodness kiss right on them swell lips of hers. She smacks me across the face.

"That's O.K., baby," I tell her. "It was worth it. You taste just like the doctor ordered. Now you stick around here an' croon until I come back for you."

I lock the car doors an' scram. I find a key to the garage doors hangin' up on a nail an' I close an' lock them too.

Then I ease back to the house. I wriggle myself through the pantry window back into the house. I scram up the stairs into the room we was in, an' leave the door half-way open so that just a spot of light shows down the stairs.

Then I go downstairs into the dark hallway. I sit myself down in the middle of the passage that runs from the front to the back close against the wall, with the Luger in my hand, waitin'.

4

I reckon that by now it is about eleven o'clock, an' just at this time a church clock strikes an' tells me that I am right.

I settle back against the wall an' wish I could smoke a cigarette. When I have been wishin' this for about another five minutes I hear a noise outside the front door. A coupla seconds after this somebody puts a key in the front lock an' opens the door very quietly. A guy comes inta the hall an' shuts the door behind him.

But while he was shuttin' it I get a look at him against the background of the open doorway. There is just enough moon for me to see who this boyo is. Sure as a gun it is the phoney Grant guy—the guy who met me at Waterloo Station.

I squeeze back against the wall an' even stop myself breathin'. The mug is carryin' a little suitcase in his hand an' I can hear him put it down, very gently, on the floor of the hallway. Then he starts gumshoein' up the stairs.

Half-way up he stops, an' I reckon he has seen the light from the door on the first floor that I have left half-open. He stands there for a minute an' then he starts comin' down the stairs again,

I get scared. I wonder if this guy is goin' to scram. I think that maybe havin' heard no sound comin' from the room upstairs he reckons that there ain't any one there.

I hear him get down to the hallway an' pick up the little suitcase an' I expect that the next thing he is goin' to do is to open the front door an' do a big exit act. I get ready to get up an' go after him. But he don't do this. He starts creepin' along the passageway towards me. I squeeze myself up against the wall as he goes past an' believe it or not I can hear him breathin'.

When he is well past me I get up on to my feet an' listen. He goes inta the kitchen an' I see him put a little flashlamp on. He sticks the suitcase down on the floor, opens it, fiddles about inside it for a minute an' then switches off the torch. He starts comin' back my way. I press myself up against the wall as he goes past but he is so goddam close I coulda spat right in his eye an' not missed him.

He goes into the hallway and starts openin' the front door, very quietly. He is takin' a lot of care that he don't make any noise at all. Just when he has got the door-handle turned an' is swingin' it open I go for him. I take half a dozen good leaps an' I bust him right on top of the dome with the butt-end of the Luger. He gives a big sigh an' flops.

I shut the front door an' feel in the pocket of his overcoat for the little torch. When I find it I switch it on an' take a look at him. It is the Grant guy all right.

I chuck him over my shoulder an' start to carry him up the stairs. The boy is plenty heavy an' I am very glad when I get him up to the first-floor room. I put him down in one of the big chairs by the fire an' light myself a cigarette an' I am tellin' you bozos that I am now feelin' rather pleased about things.

On the floor is Geralda's whisky flask lyin' where it fell. I pick this up an' I am very glad to see that it is still half-full. I take a little swig at it myself just to kill the influenza germs, an' then I stick the flask in his mouth an' tilt the whisky that is left down his throat. After this an' a little face slappin' the boyo begins to return to earth.

He puts his hands up to his head an' then he opens his eyes. He begins to try an' look around him but he don't sorta like the light. He closes his eyes again an' gives a groan.

I frisk him. He has got a Mauser automatic pistol in his right-hand hip an' a passport in the breast pocket of his overcoat. The passport says that he is Giacomo Fratti, that he is an American citizen an' that his home address is in Oklahoma. There is a New York Consulate check stamp on the passport dated five weeks before. There is nothing else on the guy except a funny little sorta metal key that he has got in his trousers pocket an' some loose change an' twelve pounds English money.

So I was right when I thought this guy was a wop. I give him an easy smack across the kisser.

" All right, Fratti," I tell him. " You come up for air because you an' me are gonna do a little quiet talkin' an' before we part you are goin' to tell me just as much of your life story as I don't haveta smack out of you. So get goin' before I start work on you."

He blinks at me two or three times an' then he says :

" Listen, Caution, you can't get away with this stuff around here. This is England, this ain't America."

" Look, pal," I tell him, " I am not particularly interested in your knowledge of geography. Right now I know this is England an' I am also aware that there is an air-raid on, an' I am also aware that if I was to stick my rod in your mouth an' blow the top of your head right off I would still be O.K. with the guys over here when I tell 'em my little piece about you. So don't let anythin' like that worry you, because I know plenty."

He says : " Yeah . . . well, if you know so much, you don't want me to do any talkin'."

I give a big sigh.

" It is always the trouble with you thugs," I tell

59

him, "that you haveta get fresh, which is something I do not like."

I put out my hand an' I get hold of him by the collar. I yank him up on to his feet an' I bust him one on the kisser that is such a mean sock that I hurt my knuckles.

He decides to do a backfall over the back of the chair. When he hits the floor he stays there. He is bleedin' like a stuck pig an' makin' a moanin' noise that sounds just like the tide comin' in.

I go around to him an' I pick him up. There is a four-leg chair standin' against the wall. I plant him down on this an' then I pick up the chair an' him an' step back about three paces. I then throw the chair an' him against the wall . . . hard.

The chair busts an' his head hits the wall like it was a cannon-ball. He subsides on the floor. After a minute he puts his hands over his face an' starts weepin'.

"Tough guy, hey?" I tell him. "I thought you was one of these palookas who are not doin' any talkin'. Maybe you would like to change your mind an' start in, an' any time you decide to play ball you will kindly indicate in the usual manner."

I then put him up against the wall an' start smackin' him hard across the beezer. He does not like this one little bit. He pulls back his leg an' aims a kick at my guts that woulda put me right inta the burial parlour class if it had contacted.

I then get to work on this mug. I proceed to give him everything that I ever learned durin' my toughest moments. I invent new things for the boy. By the time I have finished with him he looks like somebody had thrown him inta the gearbox of a battleship that was steamin' backwards.

In five minutes' time he decides that he wishes to talk to me.

I stick him in the big arm-chair an' believe me
every time I look at this guy it almost hurts *me*. Two
of his teeth are missin', both his eyes are a nice art
shade of purple, one side of his jaw is not matchin'
up very well with the other an' his nose is sorta
pointin' at an angle of thirty degrees from true north.

"Look, Fratti," I tell him. "As you will have
gathered by now I am not a friend of yours. In fact
I will go so far as to say that I do not like you one
little bit. I will also state that if you do not now ante
up the truth an' the whole truth I am gonna fix you
so that the only thing that you will be any use for is
a pattern for wallpaper."

He runs his tongue over his lips that are about twice
their size. He says he's talkin'.

"O.K.," I say. "Well, first of all I wish to know
the name an' whereabouts of the guy who was given
my identity papers after Manders an' Carlette Francini
pulled that act on me."

He says he don't know. He swears he don't know.
He says that the job's been played so goddam clever
that nobody in this racket knows what anybody else
is doin'.

"O.K.," I tell him. "I will accept that just for
the moment. But you did know that this guy who is
callin' himself Caution was goin' to see Geralda Varney
today, didn't you?"

He says yes he did.

"An' you knew that he was goin' to tell her to
come here tonight so that she could help trap the guy
that he told her was the phoney Caution—*me*. An'
you probably also knew that she said she'd do this
because he told her you'd be around an' that all she'd
have to do would be to pulla gun on me an' hold me
here until you—or somebody else got here to take
care of me. Right?"

He says that this is right.

61

" Who're you workin' for ? " I ask him.

He shrugs his shoulders.

" This isn't going to do me any good," he says. " You know what Panzetti will do to me if I squeal."

" That's nothin' to what I'll do to you if you don't," I crack back at him. " So you're workin' for Panzetti. An' who's he workin' for ? "

He looks down at his wrist-watch which by some miracle has not got itself broken in the recent schimozzle an' I can see some little beads of sweat come out on his forehead. I wonder why.

" Look, Caution," he says, " if you'll give me a break an' let me get out of here so's I can get out of England before Panzetti gets his hooks on me I'll tell you all I know. But I've got to get out quick."

" You tell me what you know," I say, " an' we'll consider what's gonna happen to you after you've talked."

He looks at his watch again an' then he says, the words sorta tumblin' out of his mouth :

" For Christ's sake. We gotta get out of here. We've gotta get out quick ! "

" Yeah," I say. " An' why ? "

He says : " I brought a suitcase with me when I came here. There's a time bomb inside." He starts sweatin' like hell. " It was Panzetti's idea," he goes on. " Panzetti's working for some bunch of Germans. They've paid him plenty to get hold of the dive-bomber plans that Whitaker was working on. When Whitaker came over here Panzetti got scared about something—I don't know what. They aimed to pinch your papers an' put some guy in to pretend to be you to meet up with this Varney dame an' get her along here to-night. I was tipped off to meet you as Grant, the guy from Scotland Yard, an' to try an' stop you contactin' Herrick until late tonight. That's why I told you he was away. Then I telephoned you an' said that I'd found this address an' the name Geralda Varney on the folder in his office because Panzetti reckoned you'd come out here tonight to meet up with this dame and find out who an' what she was after."

He starts rubbin' his hands together. He is scared sick.

" I was to hang about outside an' wait for you to arrive. We knew the dame would come because she wanted to find out where Whitaker was. When you were both in here I was to plant the suitcase with the time-bomb in it downstairs an' get out. There's enough T.N.T. in that machine to blow this house to hell. But nobody would have thought anything of it. There's always an air-raid on and this house is empty. They'd have thought that either some German plane had dropped a bomb or else a delayed action bomb had exploded. It was a sweet set-up. Well . . . it hasn't come off and that bomb is timed to go off in fifteen minutes . . . so now you know."

" Nice work," I tell him. " You're a swell bunch of mugs, ain't you ? So you reckoned to get rid of the Varney dame an' me in one go. A sweet idea."

I take a quick look at him. I reckon this thug is so knocked about that there ain't any fight left in him.

" O.K.," I tell him. " Well, you're goin' to get out of here when you've done a piece of work for me. An' I'll tell you what you're goin' to do. I'm goin' outside to get Miss Varney. An' when I bring her back you're goin' to tell her the whole works or else I'm goin' to leave you to go up with that bomb. Well ? "

He says O.K.

I go over to the window an' I grab one of the curtain cords. I tie his hands down to his ankles good enough to hold him until I get back. Then I light

63

myself a cigarette an' ease over to the door. When I get there I turn around an' ask :

" How long is it before that goddam bomb is due ? "

He screws his head down to look at his watch. He says :

" It's goin' in thirteen minutes. For God's sake be quick."

" You've got lots of time," I tell him. " It's goin' to take me two minutes to get that dame here an' two minutes for you to tell her the works. That leaves nine minutes for us to get outa here. So just relax."

I scram down the stairs like hell an' devils. I ease through the passage outa the pantry window an' over to the garage. I unlock the door an' go across to the car.

" Come on, Geralda," I say. " I have got a sweet little surprise for you."

There is just silence. I switch on Fratti's torch that I have got in my pocket an' take a look at the car. That tells me all I wanta know. The window by the driver's seat is broken an' Geralda has scrammed.

I take a look around the garage. In the back wall, opposite the door is a window an' that is bust too. So now you know. That honeybabe has taken a run-out powder just at the time I wanted her around to get a load of truth into her system. All of which will prove to you that a good-lookin' dame is seldom in the place that she is wanted in at the moment she is wanted, which is somethin' else that this Confucius guy thought of first.

I light myself a cigarette an' shrug my shoulders. Life is just like that. Every time you get something nicely planned out some dame busts up the works.

I start to walk across the garage to the door. It looks to me as if the best thing I can do is to collect this Fratti guy before the balloon bursts, take him back to Scotland Yard, tell Herrick the works an' start fresh from there.

I put my hand on the door an' something lifts me up an' throws me across the garage like I was a piece of paper. There is a roar that makes my ear-drums tingle an' half the roof of the garage decides to part company with the walls. There is dust an' rubbish flyin' about the place like a volcano had burst.

I get up an' get outside. I look towards the house. Half of it is not there. There is just a big gapin' hole.

I feel in my pocket for my cigarettes an' light one.

I reckon that Fratti musta miscalculated about that bomb.

I get over the back wall because I can hear some people comin' in by the front gates. I reckon these are police and air-raid guys with whom I do not wish to have any conversation right now. I drop down on the other side an' start walkin' in a circle that will bring me back to Hampstead. After about half an hour I get into the main street an' pick up a cab that is crawlin' along. The "All Clear" is just goin' an' I tell the driver to take me along to Sheldon Mansions in St. John's Wood, because I think it is time that somebody let little Carlette get outa that coal-cellar where I left her.

While we are goin' there I do some heavy thinkin'. First of all, although this bomb business was not so good for that mug Fratti it is maybe goin' to be good for me. I got an idea about this.

I relax back in the corner of the cab an' smoke a cigarette an' start thinkin' about guys like the late Fratti. These punks are the world's biggest mugs. They're tough an' they're sometimes smart. All they want is easy money providin' they don't haveta work for it. But in the long run they work a goddam sight harder than any legitimate guy, get themselves pushed around plenty and then get blasted to hell just because

65

some guy who makes their time-bombs makes a little mistake in the timin'.

I start thinkin' about Panzetti—the guy who was behind Fratti—an' I promise myself that if ever I get my hooks on this bozo I will put my trade-mark all over him.

Panzetti is a wop. The guy is an Italian-American, who usta specialise in the kidnap business an' run a few vice houses on the side. I reckon he was just the right bozo for the German U.A.-1 boys to get hold of for a job like this. First of all he is so screwy that he ain't even afraid of bein' ironed out, an' secondly he is about the toughest proposition that Mr. J. Edgar Hoover an' the Federal Bureau have ever got themselves up against. Panzetti is pure poison.

But the fact remains that he will hear about the bomb at Laurel Lawn. He will do a big grin an' think that he has got rid of Geralda Varney an' Lemmy Caution in one fell swoop. He reckons that this will leave the field nice an' clear for the fake Caution guy —whoever he is—an' enable 'em to get this mug Whitaker just where they want him.

An' if what Fratti said was true that he didn't know anything very much about the job except his own part in it, then it is a good chance that the blowin' up of Laurel Lawn was the only job that he had to do after pretendin' to be Grant of Scotland Yard an' fixin' it so I went there. That bein' so maybe he has already been paid off an' nobody is goin' to worry about the fact that he don't turn up any more. The more I think of this the more I like the idea that I have got germinatin' at the back of my head.

I throw my cigarette away an' light a fresh one. After another quarter of an hour we start gettin' near to Sheldon Mansions. Just before we get there an air-raid warnin' goes. I pay off the cab an' go into

66

the dump. There are two-three people walkin' about the hallway in their dressin'-gowns smokin' an' meanderin' around on their way to the shelter.

I ask the night guy if he knows where the day-porter is an' he says yes that the guy I want is down-stairs. I slip this boyo a half-crown an' ask him to go down an' get the day-porter up to the hall because I wanta speak to him.

A few minutes afterwards this guy comes up. He is the guy that I slipped the fiver earlier in the day an' he remembers me all right.

" What happened about Mr. Kritsch ? " I ask him. He grins at me.

" Mr. Kritsch came back about half an hour after you'd gone," he says. " I told him what you said and he said it was a lot of rubbish. He said Miss Lariat hadn't got a brother. He said he was going upstairs to see what had happened to her.

" About a quarter of an hour afterwards," he goes on, " he came down with Miss Lariat. Both of 'em looked worried about something. Mr. Kritsch asked me to get 'em a cab and they went off. He said they wouldn't be back. I went over to the rank later and got the address from the driver like you said. He drove them a long way—out to Maidenhead—to a place called The Melander Club. He dropped 'em there."

I tell him thanks a lot an' give him the other fiver I promised him. He looks pretty pleased about this. He says :

" Of course you aren't *really* Miss Lariat's brother, are you, sir ? "

I tell him no, that any time I had to be Miss Lariat's brother I would go find myself a nice lake an' jump in it.

Then I scram, leavin' him standin' there with his mouth open.

I walk a little way. The rain has started again an'
it is as dark as hell. Away above I can hear some
German planes dronin' about. I start thinkin' what
I would like to do to these guys an' then I get the
great thought that maybe cleanin' up the job I am
on will do more than anything else.

After a bit I get a cab an' drive back to Jermyn
Street.

I give myself a long shot of rye, a warm shower
an' ring down to the night guy that I would like to
be called at eleven next mornin'.

I think that maybe then I will have a heart to heart
talk with Herrick.

After which I take another shot of rye an' get
myself inta bed. I am goddam tired but the joke is
I don't get off to sleep.

No, sir. I just lay there lookin' at the ceilin' an'
thinkin' about that dame Geralda Varney. I would
lke to know just where that dame is.

Because believe it or not that baby has got something that the other ones have not. I am tellin' you
that the south view of this dame from the east when
she is walkin' north would make a blind man take to
hard liquor.

Because you gotta realise that I am very partial to
dames an' I am all the more partial to this one because
she has not only got what it takes but she has also
got plenty of guts an' I went for the way she stuck
me up in that Laurel Lawn dump.

I reckon this Geralda is pretty sore. She is pretty
sore because she must know that it was Carlette
Francini who got the Whitaker mug to come over
here an' she musta guessed that Carlette didn't do it
by hypnotism either. So she will not like Carlette.

She is some more sore because she thinks that I am
a phoney frontin' as Lemmy Caution for the purpose
of gettin' at the Whitaker mug once again. An' she

will not be too pleased with the fact that I got the best of her over the argument.

In fact I will go so far as to say that it looks to me that any time she sees me again she is likely to be tough.

This gives me a grin because I have always found the tougher they sound the nicer they are. You get me?

But between you an' me an' the old doorpost I am worried about that dame.

CHAPTER THREE

YOUR DEAL, MY LOVELY

I

NEXT MORNIN' the mug from downstairs calls me like I told him, but I don't get up. I just stick around in bed lookin' at the ceilin' tellin' myself fairy tales.

The first fairy tale I tell myself is that I reckon that this Geralda Varney is O.K. right now ; that after she bust out of that garage at Hampstead the dame has gone home an' gone to bed, an' is probably sleepin' some place like the babes in the wood.

All the same I reckon that I am only kiddin' myself. If little Geralda is not in a bad spot then I am an Indian Princess with the ague. Because it is as plain to me as a negress on a white bedspread that after she got outa that place the little mug has gone scrammin' off to find the phoney guy who is callin' himself Caution, an' she is gonna tell him the whole works an' how she nearly got me an' how I slipped it over on her an' how somethin' has gotta be done about me. After which Willie Kritsch—because I reckon he is the bozo who is totin' my identification papers around —is goin' to come to the conclusion that things are not goin' to be so good while I am loose. He will also deduct—an' he won't even haveta use a ready reckoner to do it—that after a bit Geralda is goin' to get plenty tired of playin' this game on her own. He will conclude that the little sweet will go shootin' her pretty mouth off to some copper an' so the next thing he will think of is that Geralda must be put on ice until such time as they have dealt with me.

They might bump this dame. An' that is the logical thing for them to do because in a minute she is goin' to start askin' questions, an' when a dame starts askin' questions you might just as well give her the works an' finish her off permanently so as to keep her ruby lips from splutterin' the wrong stuff at the right moment.

I heave myself out of bed an' take a warm shower. Outside there is a winter sun shinin' an' lookin' outa my window down inta Jermyn Street I can see well-dressed dames walkin' around just as if life was just a matter of window shoppin' an' there was not any blitz on at all.

I pick out a swell suit that I have got an' a silk shirt an' ring for breakfast. I finish eatin' an' give myself one little shot of bourbon just to put the polish on the furniture.

I then grab off the telephone an' call Herrick. When he comes on the line I say my piece.

" Look, Herrick," I tell him. " I reckon I been holdin' out on you. There are one or two angles on this Whitaker case that you don't know about. . . ."

" Such as . . ." he says, an' I can visualise him grinnin'.

" Such as a dame called Carlette Francini who is a mobster's frail who was put in on the *Florida* to get next to me an' work in with Manders, the wireless guy ; an' such as a boy friend of hers called Willie Kritsch who is so blood-stained that he would make Hengist an' Horsa look like a sissy dance-hall duo ; an' such as the boyo who was callin' himself Grant of Scotland Yard but who is nobody else but Giacomo Fratti, another torpedo who got himself blown up last night in a house at Hampstead because a time-bomb that he was totin' around didn't keep its date on time. See ? "

He says he sees. He also says that he is not at all surprised that I have been at my old tricks again an'

71

holdin' out on him, an' that he hopes from now on I am goin' to be a good guy an' work in. Because he says that this is not America an' the law has got an entirely different angle around here an' that if I start usin' my technique on the lines for which I have gotta reputation in U.S.A. I am liable to start another *blitzkrieg* besides the one Adolf is workin' on at the moment.

I then say that I reckon he is right an' that I think we oughta have lunch together an' that we can discuss the whole works an' formulate some plan of campaign that is not likely to give anybody in authority too much of a pain in the eyeballs ; but that in the meantime I will be glad if he will send me around a Police Pass or somethin' so that I can prove I am me, because at the moment I have nothin' in writin' to distinguish between Lemmy Caution of the Federal Bureau of Investigation an' Mae West's stand-in.

He says O.K. he will send a Police Pass round for me right away an' that he will collect me in Jermyn Street at one-thirty.

I give myself a cigarette an' start gettin' the intellect box to work. By an' large I reckon that this job is goin' to be tougher than shootin' craps an' that the sooner somebody does a little heavy thinkin' about it the better. However, I cannot see any light at the moment, so after walkin' around the sittin'-room for twenty minutes I get into my overcoat an' go downstairs.

When I get to the entrance hall there is a guy from Herrick askin' for me. The guy has got a Police Pass with my picture attached an' a note from Herrick. The note says :

"*I will be with you at one-thirty. I had a word with the Assistant Commissioner and told him that you'd been holding out on us. He said that having regard to the*

72

*way you handled the Van Zelden case back in '37 your
system didn't seem so bad, but that in this business we've
got to be careful. We will discuss the whole thing when
I see you.—Yours,*

" *C. J. Herrick.*"

I tear the note up an' put the Police Pass in the
secret pocket I have built inta my waistcoat. So I
reckon I am now set up with two very nice identities.
First of all I have got Police papers as Lemmy Caution
of the F.B.I. an' secondly I have got Fratti's passport,
identity card an' permit. So I am very nicely fixed
for the idea that I have got sizzlin' at the back of my
dome.

The sun is shinin' plenty. I am feelin' so good that
I would not change places with a guy who was bein'
burned to death over a slow fire, but I am still a bit
het up about that baby Geralda.

I have told you guys before that I have taken a run
around with a dame or two in my life ; but I am also
tellin' you that I have never seen so much sweet what-
have-you-got done up in one package as this Geralda.
I do not wish to rhapsodise to you mugs because maybe
you are married an' have other serious troubles, but
I am tellin' you that this doll has got so much to look
at—an' everything in the right places too—that it
makes you gasp like an' old warhorse who has just
remembered a date he had forty-two years ago. You
got me ?

Walkin' up Regent Street I get to ruminatin' about
dames. What is it that makes one dame so different to
another. There are plenty dames who are lookers,
who have got this an' that an' who know how to
swing it prettily, but at the same time they sorta miss.
Because the whole thing with a dame is personality
an' the way she puts herself over.

I remember one time I was hit for a home run by

73

some honeybelle I saw up in Miami. She was sittin'
in a hotel lounge an' I'm tellin' you that if Henry
The Eighth coulda taken one look at the dame's
curves he woulda given orders for the Royal Bed-
chamber to be repapered in scarlet an' paid off the
public executioner. After which he woulda taken
some quick steps to alter the whole history of England
an' Good Queen Bess woulda been born a blonde.

I look at this dame an' I think that here is something that you read about in books. So I put on a
winnin' smile an' I ease over to her an' open up a
little *conversazione* on lines that woulda made The
World's Greatest Lovers look like a book of cookery
hints.

She throws me a sweet smile but when she opens
her mouth an' starts speakin' it was just like listenin'
to a 1920 model in low gear after the big end was
seized up. I'm tellin' you that dame had a voice so
terrible that it woulda made an automatic nutmeg
grater sound like somebody playin' the flute. An' when
she walked she packed a waddle that was so acute that
she practically needed a compass to steer by.

All of which will show you guys that you very
seldom get all the goods in one package an' that
customers are advised to open up the case an' inspect
the merchandise before they get home otherwise no
exchanges can be made.

But this Geralda has got the whole set-up. She
is the complete picture. Any time you get tired of
thinkin' about her face you can put in a little overtime
on ponderin' on her shape or the way she walks, an'
when you get tired of that—if you *could* get tired of
that—you can always get around to rememberin' the
way she speaks an' how you just have to watch her
lips when the words come out.

I am tellin' you one an' all if I was stranded on a
South Sea Island with this baby I would not even

worry to tune up my ukelele. I would just stick around an' make a play for that jane that woulda made Casanova look like an old hayseed.

Because you bozos know just as well as I can tell you that the whole trouble in this little old world is due to dames. The guy who said that the dame always pays was talkin' out of his right ear. Dames always pay but they take goddam good care they get the doin's off some mug before the account comes in. Every dame is armed for the battle. The ugly ones have got sense an' the sweet mommas have got the stuff that makes you lose any brains *you* originally had.

An' any guys who do not believe me can take a look at the universe today, after which they can go out an' give themselves a cold bath. If Hitler would lay off tryin' to be the big world-conqueror an' would sling a mean look at some warm momma with the right sorta beauty Field Marshal Goering would be travellin' in cash registers, Ribbentrop would be back sellin' cut whisky to mugs, an' the S.S. boys would be gettin' themselves a job outside the local cinema an' thinkin' themselves goddam lucky if they could get two plates of black sausage on Sunday.

By this time I am half-way up Regent Street an' I get a sudden hunch that I would like a whisky sour before I start thinkin' of gettin' back to meet up with Herrick. I remember a little Club stuck away up on a second floor near Cork Street that I usta use when I was over here on the Poison Ivy Case, so I turn down Conduit Street an' start walkin' that way.

When I am half-way down the street I get an idea that somebody has put a tail on me. I stop an' look in a shop window. Over my shoulder I can see, about twenty yards away between me an' Regent Street a big car has pulled up an' a dame is gettin'

75

out. She is dressed in black with a fox fur an' a cute hat.

I light a cigarette an' go on my way. When I am turnin' into Cork Street I take another peek over my shoulder an' the jane is still in sight.

I find the place I am lookin' for an' go up the stairs. There is nobody inside except the doll who is tendin' the bar. I order a large whisky sour, lean up against the bar an' draw the smoke down inta my lungs. I reckon that life could be a lot worse.

I sink the drink an' order another one. I am just gettin' around to thinkin' that life is gettin' brighter every minute when the door opens an' the dame in the black suit comes in.

This dame is a cutie all right. She is wearin' a black suit cut by some guy that knew his curves, a white silk shirt with a frill in the front, a fox fur that cost some dough an' white kid gauntlet gloves. There is a little bit of veil hangin' down from her tailored hat that makes her look good an' mysterious.

I ask the jane behind the bar for another whisky sour. While I am drinkin' it I am lookin' over the edge of the glass at the dame in black.

She stands around in the doorway for a minute an' then she comes right in an' parks herself on a high stool right next to me. She has a very nice thing in legs an' I reckon her silk stockin's cost money. Also her shoes are expensive.

This dame is the sort of dame that looks very good on a high stool. She orders a double Scotch with a chaser, takes a little gold cigarette case out of a nifty patent leather handbag with gold clasps, an' relaxes.

I flick my lighter an' hold it for her cigarette. She screws around a little on the stool an' looks at me. She smiles. She has nice teeth.

I sigh to myself. Because it looks as if I am meeting with some very nice lines in janes these days.

76

She says : " Thanks a lot, Mister Caution." She then screws around again, lifts her glass an' sinks the whole issue before you could whistle.

" Lady," I tell her, " I am very interested in the way you drink Scotch. Also I am curious about how you know who I am, an' what are you drinkin' this time ? "

She says thanks a lot and that she will take another slug of Scotch. I order this an' one for myself. I light a fresh cigarette an' wait for the ball to open.

She blows a smoke-ring. When she does this she purses up her mouth an' her mouth is not so hard to look at.

She says : " Mister Caution, as you probably know life can be very difficult around London for a girl like me. There are moments when I feel that I want a whole lot of advice from the sorta guy that you look as if you are."

" Lady," I tell her. " You don't know how right you are. At the same time I would be very interested in how you know that I am me an' also havin' regard to the fact that you have been chasin' me around for the last ten minutes I reckon you was snoopin' about outside my dump in Jermyn Street this mornin' waitin' for me to blow. Correct ? "

" Correct," she says. She crosses her legs—an' she is not a bit mean in the process either. She goes on : " Of course you wouldn't know anything about me, would you ? " She gives me a big smile.

" I'm not so sure," I tell her. " I've got a very good memory, but it only works when it wants to. How about a little drink ? "

She says yes, she thinks that is a good idea. We have more Scotches. She stubs out her cigarette. Maybe, I think, we will now get down to a little business.

She opens the case an' takes another cigarette out.

77

When the case is open I can see, right at one end, four or five slim brown cigarettes. I grin to myself. They look to me like *marihuana*. So it looks as if the dame is a reefer fan. An' they always talk . . . well . . . sometimes.

She draws the smoke down into her lungs. Then she says :

" The name is Kells . . . Montana Kells. Maybe you heard it . . . Lemmy. . . . Hey ? "

I laugh.

" You're tellin' me, babe," I tell her. " I been tryin' to place you ever since you came in at the door. You usta get around with Fenzer in the days when Chicago was as open as last week's sardine can. I also got an idea they pulled you in when they slammed Fenzer in the pen, an' that would be about four years ago."

" Yeah," she says. " The bastards sent me up for a year. Of course it was a frame."

I nod.

" It always is," I tell her. " Nobody ever got sent up who really deserved it. It's always them lousy coppers. How d'you like it over here ? "

" It's all right—up to now," she says. " I'm beginnin' to dislike it just a little bit ; but maybe things will get better."

" You bet," I tell her. " They always do. That is if they don't get worse. But maybe you been vaccinated against things gettin' worse."

She finishes the Scotch in front of her. Then she wiggles around an' looks at me. She has got nice sorta eyes. They are soft an' brown an' pleadin'.

" I don't see why I should sit around here an' let you buy Scotch all the time," she says. " I got a little dump near here—a service apartment. Why not come along an' let me fix you a drink an' some lunch."

I look at my watch. It is nearly one-thirty. I grin because I am gettin' the idea that once again I am goin' to stand up Herrick.

"That sounds swell, Montana," I tell her. "But what exactly is the big idea? You ain't tellin' me that you have fallen for my personality with a big bump are you? Maybe you remember that it was me who pulled your boy friend in—I mean Fenzer."

She starts pullin' on her gloves.

"I know," she says. "An' I didn't ever give a hoot in hell. Fenzer was a meal ticket, that was all. An' you know how it is, Lemmy, once you get stuck with a mob you've got to stay put otherwise somebody starts writing their initials on you, up a back alley, with a hand gun."

She gets up.

"Fenzer was a tough case," she goes on. "He was very hard-boiled an' loaded with sin . . . plenty of it, but there are some guys who are even worse than Fenzer—by a helluva ride."

I raise my eyebrows.

"Such as . . . ?" I ask sorta innocent.

"Such as a guy like . . . well, a guy like Panzetti, for instance," she says. "Panzetti is what I call a bad guy. He's bad because he likes it that way. If somebody was to pay him to be different he wouldn't even take the dough. He's nuts an' he's poison. That guy is as deadly as a snake an' twice as slick."

She stands there smilin' at me. She says :

"Are you comin', Lemmy?" Her voice is like treacle. Way back behind that piece of veil she is wearin' I can see her eyes big an' soft an' round.

"Yeah . . ." I tell her. "I'd be glad to come . . . now."

"Something made you change your mind, didn't it?" says Montana. "I wonder what that could have been?"

79

"I wouldn't know," I say. "Maybe it was hearin' the name Panzetti. There are some guys I like talkin' about an' some guys I don't, but Panzetti is a guy that I am always willin' to talk about or listen about . . . see?"

"I see," she says. "Let's go."

I pay for the drinks an' we go. Outside, the car is waitin'. It is a big Lancia. The guy at the wheel has got the sort of face that makes you think that so far as he is concerned everything smells.

We get inside an' Montana tells him to go home. I relax in the corner an' ponder.

Montana don't say anything. But she takes a long sideways look at me.

I reckon that dame could snap a mean garter if she felt that way.

2

About three o'clock I take a look at my wrist an' see what the time is. I reckon that Herrick will be pretty sick of waitin' for me. It just shows you that a detective's life is full of mystery, don't it? I hope that Herrick will take it that way.

Montana has certainly got a very nice set-up around here. Her apartment is big an' well-furnished. There is a big curtained door that is a bit open, an' through it I can see a big bed with a purple silk bedspread. Maybe she has that to remind her of the purple mob that she usta get around with in the old days.

An' the lunch was very good. There was some soup an' a little Scotch, an' a Lobster Newburg with some more Scotch, an' a chicken with fixin's an' a helluva lot of Scotch an' coffee, after which we have drunk a little Scotch. Me . . . I am so full of Scotch that all

80

I need is some bagpipes an' I'd think my name was MacGregor.

Montana is lyin' over on the big settee showin' a very nice piece of leg sorta accidentally. I have told you mugs that there are several sorts of dames—as regards showin' legs I mean. There is the dame who likes her legs an' shows 'em, an' there is the dame who likes 'em an' shows 'em by accident. This second dame is the artistic dame. I am comin' to the conclusion that Montana is an artistic dame. But just how artistic I am not quite sure.

I draw a gulp of smoke down inta my lungs an' send it tricklin' out of one nostril. Me—I have always had an idea that Special Agents of the F.B.I. do not get enough light an' shade in their lives an' I am feelin' very good with myself because I think that inta my drab career there is goin' to come a splash of colour an' I got a big idea that splash is goin' to be Montana.

She says sorta dreamy : " Are you O.K., Lemmy . . . or would you like some Scotch ? "

She don't wait for me to answer. She gets up an' pours a big slug into my glass an' splashes in some soda water. She comes over to me with the glass. She says :

" Life is damn funny, ain't it ? The last time I remember seein' you—before I hung around your place in Jermyn Street this morning, I mean—was in Philadelphia the day they tried Fenzer. You were sitting in the well of the Court an' you were wearing a grey suit with a pale blue silk shirt an' a navy tie. I liked you then. Even although I knew that I was gonna win something over you—an' I won a year in the pen—I still sorta liked you. Is that goddam funny or is it ? "

She puts the glass down. Then she bends over me an' the next thing I know is that she has got her arms around my neck an' is drapin' herself across my lap.

Her mouth is pressed up close to mine an' she starts puttin' some work in on a kiss that woulda made Cleopatra look like an amateur.

She says sorta hoarse : " Lemmy, I'm crazy about you. You got something that drives me goofy."

" That's my personality, honey," I tell her. " I get it from my great-grandfather. He was the fourteenth love-child of a fourteenth love-child an' any time he usta look at a dame she usta curl up her toes, spit, uncross her fingers an' surrender. My great-grandmother usta say that neckin' with that guy was like bein' strangled to death—it was O.K. after you'd finished strugglin'."

She sits back an' takes a long look at me. She says : " Don't I mean nothin' to you at all ? "

I pick her up an' I dump her back on the settee.

" Look, Montana," I tell her. " Maybe you will think that I am sufferin' from a compound fracture of the intelligence. But I am more interested in booty than beauty. I am a guy who is inclined to be very careful of dames who are lookers like you are because my old Ma always usta tell me that when a guy falls inta a woman's arms he also falls inta her clutches. Also," I continue, " I would not like to lead you up the garden or do anything that would make you feel inclined to go mean on me. So let us get down to hard cases."

She goes over to the sideboard an' pours herself out another shot of Scotch. By now this baby is lookin' a bit wild-eyed.

" An' what the hell do you mean by that ? " she says.

" Listen, honey," I tell her. " Maybe I am only a Federal Agent, but I have not yet got ferns growin' outa my ears, an' I am not entirely built of lead above the neck. First of all you hang around my apartment in Jermyn Street this mornin' an' do a big tailin' act.

82

Well . . . why? How did you know I was livin' in Jermyn Street? The second thing is this lunch an' liquor an' love stuff are all the big build-up for something. The third thing is that Giacomo Fratti, the guy with a bomb complex, tried to blow the pants off me last night with some funny bomb he was totin' around and did not make the grade owin' to the bomb goin' sour on him an' decidin' to explode at the wrong moment.

" So what is the result? Fratti don't show up to report that I am no more. Not only that, but the Geralda Varney dame has gone shoutin' her head off to Willie Kritsch—who she believes is me—that I stuck her in a garage last night an' got away with it. So somebody don't like it an' I am makin' a guess who that somebody is. You got me, sweetheart? "

She nods her head.

" Go on, you big lug," she says. " I could listen to you for hours if somebody would give me a sleepin' draught."

" O.K.," I tell her. " So what is the next act? I'll tell *you*. The next act is that a sweet an' nicely gingered-up cutey by the name of Montana Kells is put in to contact me an' try an' pull somethin' else on me. An' I am now stickin' around waitin' to see what you are goin' to pull."

She sinks the Scotch in one gulp. Then she sits down on the settee an' leans forward lookin' at me like she was afraid I was goin' to disappear at any minute."

" Look, Lemmy," she says. " Don't let anybody kid you that people don't think you've got brains. Everybody knows your record an' everybody knows you've pulled more chestnuts outa the fire for Uncle Sam than any other goddam Federal copper. Because you got what it takes an' you are always one jump

83

ahead of the market. But here is one time where you ain't as far ahead as you think."

She leans forward some more. This dame is gettin' so intense that she is forgettin' to show her legs, so you must realise that the situation is serious so far as she is concerned.

" You think I'm workin' for the Panzetti mob," she whispers. " Well, you're goddam right. I *was* but I ain't now. This is where I get the chance to take a run-out powder an' I'm takin' it. I been playin' for weeks to get it an' now it's come my way I'm gonna take it.

" You know Panzetti. That guy is so goddam cruel that he would make any ordinary killer look like a Sunday school treat. If Panzetti thought I was goin' in to play with you he'd put the finger on me as soon as look at his watch. He is like that. An' he packs a lotta dough in his pants an' even over here where the law is so straight that you can't buy a copper there is still a war on an' you can get away with plenty."

I light myself a fresh cigarette.

" Go on, sweetheart," I say. " You are beginnin' to arouse my interest."

" First of all," she says, " Fratti was supposed to come through this mornin' an' report that you an' that Varney dame had been blasted to hell. He don't. He don't because you've slipped it over both the Varney dame, who was the lure to get you around to that house, an' Fratti who was supposed to finish the pair of you.

" O.K. Well, then that goddam Varney bitch goes runnin' back to Willie Kritsch who she thinks is Lemmy Caution just because he's got your papers, an' tells him the works. Kritsch gets through to Panzetti an' tells him that Geralda is on the loose again an' that he does not know what has happened to you an' Fratti.

" So Panzetti is still stickin' around waitin' for Fratti to show up an' you can bet your life he is just bubblin' over with good humour, because he wanted to play this thing without a lot of noise. He wanted to play it without pullin' the law over here in on the job. He was all set to be finished an' done with it before anybody knew what was happenin'."

" So what's the answer ? " I ask her.

" He's put me in to do a deal," she says. " He's put me in to do a deal with you. He called me an' told me to hang around an' contact you somehow when you left your apartment. He said I was to try an' fix things with you. But I ain't goin' to. I'm takin' a run-out powder on Panzetti like I told you."

She comes across an' drops on her knees in front of me. She says :

" Lemmy, I'm tellin' you the truth. I been tryin' to get away from the Panzetti bunch for two years. I couldn't make it over there but I got a chance here. I'm playin' ball with you. I'll spill every goddam thing I know an' all you got to do is to look after me, give me a break and don't let that goddam thug get his hooks on me. Well . . . *is that a deal* ? "

She gets up. She stands lookin' down at me. I can see she is tremblin'.

I light myself a cigarette.

" O.K., Montana," I tell her. " It's a deal."

She goes over an' gets the bottle an' we have a little Scotch on that. After which she starts walkin' around the apartment cryin' like somebody was payin' her to do it. I just sit back an' relax. I have seen dames cry before an' anyway I am not quite certain what she is cryin' about. It might be emotion, it might be relief an' it might be Scotch. Personally speakin' I think it is Scotch.

After a bit she grabs herself a cigarette an' subsides

85

on the couch. She takes a long drag at the cigarette and then she says :

" This job's goin' to be a honey. That's the way Panzetti saw it. I don't know how he got on to it in the first place, but I got an idea that some of the German people who are running the Hitler bund in the States got at him an' showed him some real money. Well . . . Panzetti is a guy who can always do with jack even if he is already double-loaded with it. So he listens.

" Then he gets after Whitaker. This Whitaker is a mug. Clever at his job but solid above the ears where a dame is concerned. He is engaged to be married to this dame Geralda Varney. Panzetti gets a slant on her an' finds out that she is a cool customer an' that she is tryin' to stall Whitaker from runnin' around with too many dames. So he puts in Carlette. Well, I reckon you know Carlette. That broad has got herself medals for puttin' the fluence on hard-boiled guys an' for her Whitaker is just a push-over. She gets next to Whitaker, shows him a good time an' some liquor, teaches him seven hundred and fifty-two different ways of neckin', an' before the sap knows whether he is comin' or goin' she has got him where she wants him.

" Right then the U.S. Government start takin' an interest in this bomber he's invented. An' he tells Carlette that he is goin' to sell it to the Navy Department. She says oh yeah an' takes him out that night to the Grapevine Inn where Panzetti has got a coupla gorillas waitin' for him. After dinner Carlette goes to powder her nose an' the boys get to work on Whitaker. They push him around a bit an' he don't like it. He scares easy an' when they scram an' Carlette comes back he is lookin' like a coupla strawberry jellies that have got themselves windblown. The guy is frightened sick.

86

" So she tells him that he's gotta be careful, that maybe some gangster has heard about the bomber an' is tryin' to muscle in. Next day he gets an anonymous note sayin' that unless he is prepared to hand over the plans of the bomber somebody is going to cut his nose off with a hacksaw. This just about finishes him off. He tells Carlette an' she says the thing for them to do is to scram an' come over here, where they will be safe because there ain't any gangsters in this country. So he comes. The idea bein' that he shall go first an' Carlette will follow him over.

" The next thing is Panzetti fixes to come over here. He has got a set-up all arranged—a business that he's been runnin' for some time. But first he tells Carlette to stick around for a bit an' see what happens. She finds out that you are gum-shoein' about Kansas City tryin' to find Whitaker an' when you come over she comes on the same boat. The wireless guy Manders is a wop who is workin' for the German Secret Service an' he an' Carlette reckon they can take care of you.

" They get your papers off you an' Manders calls through an' tips Panzetti off directly he's got 'em. He has given you a phoney radio supposed to have come from Scotland Yard an' sent another phoney one to them so they ain't expectin' you. Panzetti then puts in Fratti who has been workin' for him over here for some time, an' Fratti meets you at the railway depot an' says he's Grant from Scotland Yard. All he's got to do is to stall you from goin' to Police Headquarters here an' give you some dope about the dame called Geralda Varney who is livin' out at Hampstead. Just about the same time Willie Kritsch—pretendin' to be you—is tellin' the Varney dame that if she wants to help find Whitaker she'd better go out to the Hampstead dump an' meet one of the mobsters who is holdin' him—that is *you*."

" The idea is to get both you mugs out there an'

then Fratti is comin' along to blow hell outa everybody. They know that there will be an air-raid on at that time an' it will be just another house bombed, that's all. That settles you an' her. You're both outa the way. Nobody knows anything about either of you an' Panzetti can get on with the job of makin' Whitaker finish off them plans that he was workin' on but that aren't quite completed. So there you are."

I nod my head.

" Fine, Montana," I tell her. " That sounds like the works to me. Tell me something. Did Fratti know Willie Kritsch an' Carlette Francini. Had he met up with 'em before ? "

She shakes her head.

" Nobody knows anybody in this game except the people who have to work together—an' *me*. I know the whole works. I reckon Panzetti has gotta trust somebody an' he thinks I'm O.K." She laughs like she thinks it is funny.

" Just another little question," I say. " If Fratti ain't shown up or called through Panzetti couldn't know he was dead. So for all Panzetti knows he might be alive now. That bein' so how does Panzetti know that I'm livin' in Jermyn Street ? "

" That's easy," she says. " Didn't you take Fratti back to your place after he'd met you when you thought he was Grant. Directly he left you he called through to Panzetti, before he called you with that phoney stuff about bein' at the Yard an' seein' Herrick's folder. I was there when he came through."

" Right," I say. " So the set-up is this. The Varney dame goes rushin' back to Kritsch an' Carlette an' tells 'em that I slipped one over on her but she got away. Where did she go back to to tell 'em this ? "

She says : " Carlette an' Kritsch have got a place

in St. John's Wood—an apartment in a dump called Sheldon Mansions."

" That sounds O.K. to me," I tell her. " Well, Montana, it looks to me like you have turned over about twenty-four new leaves and are beginnin' to tell the truth at last, which must be a nice change. All right . . . well, what was the deal that Carlo Panzetti wanted to do with me. An' why the hell should that cheap lug have the goddam nerve to think I'd do a deal with a two-timin' cold-blooded lump of hot-seat fodder like him."

She shrugs her shoulders. She gets up an' goes over to the sideboard an' pours herself out a big shot of whisky. She drinks it down neat, like it was water. This baby must have a stomach like a battleship boiler. She flops back on the settee. She says :

" Panzetti reckons you gotta do a deal."

I open my eyes.

" So I *gotta* do a deal, have I ? Well . . . ain't that just too bad. An' tell me why, honeybunch ? "

She grins.

" Carlo has got brains. You gotta admit that," she says. " You know him. He'd double-cross his own mother an' roast his grandma over a slow fire an' get a big laugh out of it."

She leans forward. Her eyes are poppin'.

" What the hell do you think Panzetti laid to get Whitaker over here for ? " she says. " He coulda pinched them plans off him in America if he'd wanted to. That or bumped him first an' then took 'em. Well . . . use your brains, Lemmy. Panzetti is aimin' to double-cross the guys who have paid him to get the plans . . . the German bunch."

I give a whistle.

" This sounds like somethin'," I tell her. " O.K. Go ahead. What's the deal ? "

She grabs herself another cigarette an' lights it.

89

" For Christ's sake," she says. " You gotta look
after me, Lemmy. *You gotta.* . . . If Panzetti knew
what I was spillin' to you he'd fill a bath with paraffin,
put me in it an' light it. He'd kill me so goddam slow
I'd be prayin' for somebody to cut my throat for a
nice change."

I grin at her.

" Don't worry, cutie," I tell her. " I'm gonna look
after you all right. I'm goin' to make you my special
business. Go ahead. What is the big deal that Panzetti
wants to do with me. If he's talkin' any sort of sense
I might even listen."

" Here's the set-up," she says. " Panzetti got
Whitaker over here so as to get away from the Heinies.
He knows that if he'd crossed 'em up in America
they'da got him. They're plenty strong out there. If
you don't believe me read the Dies Committee reports.
But you know all about that. O.K. Well, over here
Panzetti can do what he likes. The Germans can't
get at him an' he's got their dough. Not only has he
got their dough but he's also got Whitaker an' the
bomber plans. An' if that ain't enough he's got
Geralda too. An' if that ain't something to deal with
then I've got cork legs."

" You haven't, honey," I tell her. " I know. I
been lookin' at 'em practically ever since I met up
with you to-day. An' I think them rose-coloured
suspenders are just too cute. But don't let me interrupt. You've told me what Carlo Panzetti has got.
Now you tell me what the deal is."

" I'm goin' to tell you," she says. " I'm not
only goin' to tell you but I'm also goin' to wise you
up as to how you can outsmart that guy. Here it
is."

She comes over an' flops down beside me.

" You gotta lay off Carlo," she says. " You gotta
let him an' Kritsch an' Carlette an' the whole shootin'

match ride. An' you gotta fix that with the English police."

"Like hell," I tell her. " Can't you see the English police listenin' to that sorta stuff. This is England, baby."

" So what," she says. " Panzetti reckons they gotta listen. Does Britain want the Whitaker dive-bomber or don't she ? Panzetti says that you gotta lay off him. He's had two hundred thousand dollars from the Jerries in America. He's goin' to stick to that dough. You got to guarantee to lay off him an' his mob an' so have the English police. Panzetti knows that you can fix that if you want to. Well . . . when that's agreed he's prepared to be generous. He's goin' to let Whitaker loose an' he's goin' to let the Varney dame go. He ain't even goin' to take a smack at her first. He'll let them two go like a little gentleman an' then . . ."

" An' what then ? " I ask her.

" He is prepared to sell the plans of the Whitaker bomber to the British an' American governments," she says. " An' he says he ain't askin' much. He's askin' just two hundred an' fifty thousand dollars."

I think for a minute. I light myself a cigarette an' inhale. I am beginnin' to think that this guy Carlo Panzetti has really got some brains. After all what the hell is a quarter of a million dollars in a war that's costin' about ten million a day ?

I say : " An' supposin' I don't like the deal. What's the answer to that one ? "

She shrugs her shoulders. She puts a lot inta that shrug. Then she says :

" Panzetti told me to tell you that if you didn't put the O.K. on his proposal then you could kiss Varney an' Whitaker good-bye. He said he'd slit Whitaker's throat himself an' take pleasure in it, an' he also told me to tell you that he'd got somethin'

else on ice for the Varney dame before she got the
works. He said he reckoned you'd understand."

I nod my head.

" I reckon he'd made it pretty hot for that dame,"
I tell her. " I reckon she'd be goddam glad to die
after Panzetti got through with her. An' after that he
hands the blue-prints over to the Germans. Nice
work ! "

I get up.

" So this is the big deal, is it ? " I say. " An' you
wanta walk out on Panzetti, an' you're goin' to help
me to fix that bastard. O.K., baby, an' I'm tellin'
you I reckon you're right. That Carlo Panzetti is no
guy for a dame to get around with—not if she wants
to keep in one piece for long."

I walk over to the sideboard an' give myself a little
drink. I am thinkin' hard. After a minute she says :

" I told you I'd wise you up as to how you can get
topsides with that yegg, didn't I ? O.K. Well, now
I'm gonna prove it."

I sit down.

" That's the sorta talk I like to hear, Montana," I
tell her. " Go right ahead, baby. My ears are
flappin'."

She says : " Panzetti was sure that you'd do the
deal. He was so goddam sure that he's fixed to have
the Varney dame an' Whitaker moved to a place
where you could get at 'em. He wasn't goin' to tell
you where they were until I'd contacted him an' told
him that the deal was on. Then you was goin' to be
told where you could get 'em. After that Panzetti was
goin' to get in touch with you again an' let you know
where the money for the plans—the two hundred and
fifty grand—was to be paid over. When that was paid
he was goin' to hand over the blue-prints an' not until.
But he was goin' to spring Whitaker an' Varney as a
guarantee of good faith."

"That don't sound so good to me, Montana," I say. "If he was gonna spring Whitaker what was to prevent that mug from drawing a fresh set of plans for us? He invented the bomber, didn't he?"

She looks at me sorta old-fashioned.

"Don't be silly," she says. "You oughta know Carlo better than that. Whitaker won't draw any plans for months. It'll take half a year to get him walkin' straight."

"Meanin' what?" I ask her.

"Meanin' that Carlo has been at his usual tricks," she says. "He's been injectin' Whitaker with dope ever since that mug finished doin' the blue-prints. The guy is half loopy. He won't even be able to draw a straight line until he's had plenty medical treatment. Panzetti is nobody's fool. I reckon if he don't get some quick action he'll start in on the Varney dame. I should think he might invent something really good an' sweet for her. He don't like pretty women. He's sorta perverse . . . but maybe they told you."

I get up.

"O.K., Montana," I tell her. "So you wanta walk out on Panzetti an' you want me to look after you. All right. Well, now you can cash in an' tell me how we upset this clever bastard. An' it looks as if we gotta be quick."

"You're right," she says. "An' the first thing you gotta do is to get your hooks on Whitaker an' the Varney bit. You can do that all right. I know where they are."

"Now you're talkin', honey," I tell her. "Talk fast an' plenty. Where are they?"

"Whitaker is at some dump near a place called Newbury," she says. "A little dump near Highclere in Berkshire. There's a house there in the big park— a place called Casino Lodge. Panzetti rented it

93

months ago. Whitaker's there an' they're gonna send the Varney dame there some time this evenin'. You can go get 'em. It's a pushover."

" How far is this place ? " I ask her.

" Sixty-five miles," she says, " or thereabouts."

I look at my watch. It is four o'clock.

" Look, Montana," I tell her. " I'm gonna take a chance on you. I believe you're tellin' me the truth. I'm goin' down to this dump right now."

" Yeah," she says. " An' what about me ? You're gonna leave me flat where that rat can get at me. What do you think Carlo is gonna do to me ? He knows I'm here. He knows . . ."

" Look, honey," I tell her. " Why don't you go some place where you'll be safe ? Why don't you go back to the States ? Believe me, Panzetti won't ever get outa this country. I'm gonna make it my business to see that he don't."

" That'll suit me," she says. " But I want to get away quick. I'm not stickin' around here one minute longer than I got to."

" O.K.," I tell her.

I go over to the writin' desk in the corner of the room an' I grab a piece of paper an' I write a note to Herrick. I say :

" *Dear Herrick,—I'm sorry I stood you up again today, but things are crackin' an' I had to get on with it. The bearer of this note is Miss Montana Kells who has rendered me a big service. She is on our side. She wants to get back to the States good and quick, which I think would be a good thing. Please give her every assistance.*"

I sign the note an' address it to Herrick. I show it to her an' put it in an envelope.

" Get your things packed," I tell her. " An' then take this note down to Scotland Yard. See Herrick,

94

he'll look after you. What time will you be goin' down there ? "

She says she reckons she'll get down there tomorrow early. She says Panzetti won't know what's hit him until then, an' so she'll be safe if she sees Herrick then.

" That's all right," I tell her. " Now I wanta car. What about that lug who was drivin' that big Lancia you got ? "

" He's O.K., Lemmy," she says. " He knows how I'm playin' this. I'll call him around at the garage an' tell him to hand the car over to you. Then he can scram. He's got friends on this side."

She goes over to the telephone an' she calls a number. She tells the chauffeur guy to hand the Lancia over to me. She tells him that everything is O.K. an' he needn't worry an' that he is to pack his grip an' get out.

Then she comes over to me an' puts out her hand.

" Good luck to you, Lemmy," she says. " I'll see you back on Broadway an' don't forget you've gotta see me through. If you don't get Panzetti he's goin' to get me."

" Don't worry, kid," I tell her.

" Tony is waitin' for you around at the garage," she says. " He'll hand over the car to you. You might give him this."

She goes over to the desk, opens a drawer an' takes out five hundred dollars in bills.

" Tell him that's the pay-off," she says. " An' tell him to scram an' get under cover quick."

" O.K., baby," I say. " An' you get your things packed, get down an' see Herrick an' get outa here. This ain't goin' to be a healthy country for you."

She puts her face up to mine an' she gives me a kiss. I'm tellin' you guys that she put some work in on that kiss. Then she stands off.

" I was always a mug for you, Lemmy," she says.

95

"But I'll be seein' you. One of these days I wanta have a long private talk with you."

"Me too . . ." I tell her. I give her a playful smack an' I walk to the door. When I get there I turn around an' take a look at her. She is lookin' at me with big, soft brown eyes like a gazelle.

I reckon she is a very sweet dame.

Outside in the street I light a cigarette. Then I start walkin' around to the garage, which is in a mews around the back of the block. I find the place an' ring the bell.

It is the usual sort of mews garage, with the car-room underneath an' a little flat over it. After a coupla minutes the chauffeur guy comes down. He grins at me.

"O.K., Mr. Caution," he says. "I had a word with Miss Kells. The car is all ready for you."

"Look, pal," I tell him. "Have you got a telephone here?"

He says yes. He leads the way up the stairs into a little sittin'-room. The telephone is in the corner.

I put my hand in my coat.

"Miss Kells gave me five hundred bucks to give you pal," I tell him. "An' she said you was to get under cover an' scram. See . . . ?"

He says he sees all right.

"But," I go on, "I ain't goin' to give you the dough. I've got something else for you instead. Somethin' just as good."

I bring my hand out of my shoulder holster with the Luger in it. I hit him once across the jaw with the barrel. He hits the floor with a bump.

I frisk him. I take his keys an' a little .32 he is carryin' in his hip. I go down to the garage, unlock it an' get a length of rope. I go back an' start ropin' this guy together. I tie him in so many knots that I reckon it will take four years to get him loose. But I leave his hands tied on a length of rope that will let him move 'em a little way.

While I am workin' on him he starts comin' round, so I smack his head back on the floor an' put him to sleep again.

I drag him inta the kitchen an' leave him under the table. I shut all the windows. I stick a bottle of milk I find there within reach of his hand.

" O.K., pal," I tell him. " You can stick around here until I come back for you. An' I hope it won't be long. You can shout your head off here but nobody'll hear you. I hope I get around to you before the milk gives out."

He has got his eyes open. He calls me a very rude name.

I lock the kitchen door. I go inta the sittin'-room an' telephone through to Herrick at Scotland Yard. I am lucky. He is there. When he comes on the line I say :

" Listen, Herrick, I ain't got a lot of time to talk to you right now because I am very busy. But I wanta tell you something. I reckon some time today or tomorrow a dame by the name of Montana Kells is gonna try an' contact you. She's got a note from me tellin' you to help her. She wants to go to America quick. You got that ? "

He says he's got it.

" O.K.," I tell him. " If that dame shows up you pinch her an' throw her in the can. She's poison. She's in with the mob who have got Whitaker."

He says he'll hold her until I show up.

" Thanks, Herrick," I tell him. " An' there's just one other little thing you might do. Just get a telephone message over the diplomatic wire to F.B.I. Headquarters in Washington. Ask 'em to give you a report on the last known whereabouts of Carlo Panzetti. Tell 'em it's for me. You got that ? "

He says he's got it.

I say : " An' don't think I'm holdin' out on you because I'm not. But things have been movin' around here an' I gotta do something quick. Maybe I'll be seein' you tomorrow."

He says he hopes so an' that any time I have got ten minutes to spare I might like to let him know somethin' about what I am doin'. He says it's an old Spanish custom.

I told you he was a nice guy.

CHAPTER FOUR

THE FALL GUY

I

I GET ON to the Great West Road when the dusk is fallin'. The car is a honey an' I am steppin' on the gas, because I do not wanta be stuck around drivin' in the country in a black-out. Outside Maidenhead I go inta a huddle with an Automobile Association guy who is able to put me on the right road. This guy knows where Casino Lodge is, an' lets me know how I can make it, which is a lucky thing for me, because so far as I can make out the place is stuck right in the middle of some woods around Burghclere.

It is as cold as the meat safe. But the light is holdin' up an' I can still see to roll the bus along. The day is one of them grey sorta days that they get over here in England, the sorta day that makes you sentimental an' start thinkin' about fires an' a bottle of rye an' a dame in a fur-collared loungin' robe with the right ideas.

Life is like that, ain't it? No sooner do you get set on doin' one thing than you wanta do something else. When you are on a case you think it would be swell to be neckin' some blonde baby who is as round as a cannon-ball an' twice as dangerous. An' just when you are in the middle of a big scene with some honeypot with nice ways your old mind goes kickin' back to some case you was once on an' you start thinkin' how good it mighta been if you'd done something different to what you did.

99

One time I was assigned to a big kidnap case. Some millionaire's son—a kid of seven named Jakie Periera—was snatched an' held for two million dollars. I stuck around on that job for six weeks concentratin' like hell but I couldn't think up a goddam thing. Then, one night, at a dump near Miami, I ran inta some sweet package that has got so much of everything in the right place that it positively hurts you to look at her except through smoked glasses, who slings me one of them ' Take-a-long-look-baby-I'm-hard-to-make ' glances. After which I ease over an' introduce myself to her with that old-world courtesy that either gets you to first base in record time or wins you a smack on the beezer that can be heard out in Siam.

This dame goes for me. She not only goes for me but she also goes *plenty*. After discussin' the weather an' other topical events we get along to some club an' dance until the small hours, after which she asks me am I artistic, an' when I tell her that I am so goddam artistic that I woulda made Benvenuto Cellini look like a margarine salesman, she says O.K. then I should go back with her to her apartment because she wishes to show me an etchin' she has got. I then tell her that this is one hundred per cent with me an' we get around to a swell apartment with white rugs an' ivory wallpaper. She goes out of the room an' believe it or not when she comes back she has actually got an etchin' in her hand, an' when I get over the shock I take a look at it an' see that it is the picture of a kid in rags sittin' in front of a garage with a broken sign up, somewhere out in the sticks.

I throw the etchin' on the chair an' proceed to embrace this baby like I was out to win the bear-huggin' championship of Europe, an' while she is nestlin' in my arms I take a look over her shoulder at the etchin' an' I see that the face of the kid in the picture is the face of the Periera kid. I then ask her where she got the etchin' an' she tells me a friend of hers done it. I ask for his address an' she tells me, after which I make a break for the door, scram without even takin' my hat an' in two hours I have got the kid an' the kidnap gang pinched.

All of which will show you guys that love will find a way, but I have often wondered what it woulda been like to know that dame for an hour or so longer. Because the next time I see her on the street she looks at me with one of them indignant ' What-has-she-got-that-I-can't-use-better ' looks an' I can't even tell her that I am just another martyr to duty.

The Lancia rolls along. I find some dump at Reading that sells Lucky Strikes, an' when I have got through the town I open the pack with one hand, light myself one an' start thinkin' about Montana.

I reckon that Montana is the berries all right. This dame is so goddam clever that one day she's gonna cut herself shavin'. An' she thinks I am the fall guy. She thinks that I was gonna fall for that line she handed out to me about her being frightened of Panzetti an' wantin' to get out an' be a good little girl.

The trouble with frails like Montana is that they are not content to play a thing along nice an' easy. They have to stick embroidery on anythin'. If she hadda had any sense she woulda realised that I was gonna catch her out if she started goin' into details. But she has to do it. She has to do it because she thinks she is gettin' away with it an' also because she is so full of Scotch that she ain't watchin' her step properly. All of which should show you guys that a clever dame don't talk too much an' also sticks to soft drinks any time when she is playin' around with a tough proposition.

It is good an' dark when I run through Newbury.

I get outa the other side of the town, drive for four miles an' then look for the side road. After a bit I find it. It is a good road runnin' through a thick woodland. I roll along nice an' slow lookin' for the white double gates that the A.A. guy told me about, the gates that lead to the path that skirts a lake an' passes by the Casino Lodge.

After a bit I come to the gates. I pull up, get out an' open 'em up. I drive the car through an' park it alongside the track under some trees. I stand there for a minute considerin' things.

This place is as dark as hell an' smells plenty damp. Stretchin' in front of me, on both sides of the wide pathway, are trees an' thickets. The rain has started to drizzle down an' away down the road that I have come by I can see a little mist comin' up.

Standin' there I start wonderin' just why the hell any guy with brains should elect to get himself a job like I got. But I reckon that's the way it goes. Every guy who joins the Federal Service always sees himself walkin' about in swell-cut tuxedos, lampin' lovely dames all the time, winnin' himself medals an' generally havin' one helluva time, instead of which all he gets is wet feet, a cold in the head, an' finishes up by winnin' a first-class tellin' off from the Director for not playin' the job different.

So what. . . . I stand there listenin' but all I can hear is some goddam owl hootin', the rain drippin' an' my brogue-cut oxfords that set me back twenty-five dollars at Strands on Fifth Avenue squelchin' in about four inches of real old-fashioned English mud. Me, I am goddam awful fond of the country—on the Christmas cards—but when it is like it is right now you can have it an' you know just what you can do with it.

I pull out the pack of Lucky Strikes an' light one. I hold the lighter so that the flame shows. Then I

102

stick the weed in my mouth an' start walkin' down the path through the woods. I am whistlin' to myself a nifty little tune that Ben Bernie usta play called " Everything You Got Lady," which is just another of them tunes that makes you think of the girl friend an' a little quiet neckin' in the twilight. Maybe I forgot to tell you palookas that I am a very poetic sorta cuss an' when I am not hurryin' around after some bunch of thugs I am the sorta guy who would read a lotta poetry an' speak like a radio announcer if ever I got the time to get around to it an' practise.

After I have walked a hundred yards or so I throw the cigarette away an' turn off left across the woods an' start doublin' back, through the thickets, in a big circle, towards where I left the car. After a while I come back to the gates. I stand behind a big clump of rhododendron leaves watchin' the smart alec who is runnin' the rule over my car. I cannot see very well from where I am so I ease over quietly until I am only a few feet off the pathway. The guy has got his head stuck in the car an' is usin' a little hand-torch. He is on the other side from me.

After a bit he comes around an' opens the door on my side. He looks around for a bit an' when he pulls his head out I see it is Freddy (Two-Time) Zokka that usta get around with the McInnigle mob when they was doin' loft work in '35.

I give a cough. He jumps away from the car like somebody has stuck a knife in his rear-piece an' goes for his breast pocket. When he pulls his hand out he is holdin' a snub-nose belly gun an' has recovered his nerve sufficiently to take a look at me.

" Hello, Two-Time," I say sorta pleasant. " How-d'ya like the heap ? She's a nice car, ain't she ? Maybe if you stick around long enough with Mister Panzetti you'll have enough jack to buy yourself a scooter—that is if they don't fry your seat off you

103

first. They tell me they got an electric chair that would just about fit that fat behind of yours."

He says : " Yeah. . . . Well now, if it ain't Mister Lemmy Caution, the big ' G ' man. Why don't you take it easy, pal, otherwise this iron might go off an' make a hole in your belly just underneath your navel. An' they tell me it hurts plenty."

" They musta told you," I crack at him. " Because *you* wouldn't know. The only time you ever shot anybody, punk, was in the back while they was asleep. Why don't you put that rod away an' try an' be intelligent ? "

" Oh yeah," he says. He has got a sneer on his face that makes him look like his mother was thinkin' of a Chinaman just before he was born. " Why don't you shut your big mouth, Caution ? You don't amount to anything the way you are fixed right now an' all I gotta do is to crease you an' chuck you in the lily pond an' nobody wouldn't ever miss you."

" Just fancy that now, sourguts," I tell him. " I know somebody who would miss me plenty an' so do you."

I get myself a fresh cigarette out an' light it.

" Look, you cheap bastard," I tell him, " I'm gonna tell you what I'm goin' to do to you an' you're goin' to like it. The last thing you're gonna do is to squeeze that trigger because you know as well as I do that Mister Panzetti—that lousy tub of snakes' brains— didn't aim to get me down here to get myself rubbed out by a low-down son of a tramp like you are. You are also well aware of the fact that if you was to iron me out your boss would be so goddam annoyed with you that he would probably cut your throat, which would save the executioner a lot of trouble an' some electricity some time."

I go over to him an' I put my hand out. He backs

away an' hits himself against the wing of the Lancia. I get my hand on the barrel of the gun an' push it away an' I bring my other fist over an' clock him right on top of his ugly nose.

He lets go the gun an' droops over the car bonnet. While he is still off balance I let him have another one in the windbag. I hit him low down in the belly an' he gives an odd sort of yelp an' subsides with his face in two inches of mud.

I throw the gun into the thicket. Then I get hold of him an' stick him up on the car step. After a few minutes he starts gettin' the colour back into his face.

I say : " Listen, handsome. I know all about it. You was sent down here to wait for me to come in, an' then you was gonna go over the car. Maybe you was goin' to let the tyres down or take out the rotor cap so's I wouldn't be able to get away too quick afterwards. But don't you try an' kid me that I ain't safe down here. I reckon if any of you cheap mobsters was to try an' iron me out Panzetti would be so annoyed that he'd throw you to the lions."

He don't say anythin'. I yank him up onto his feet.

" Look, bughouse," I tell him, " you start walkin' down the road an' you keep on walkin'. When you get to Newbury maybe they got a train you can get to London. When you get there you go around an' see Montana Kells—if she's still in that dump of hers —an' tell her that I am not such a mug as she thinks I am. Another thing," I go on, " if I was you, Two-Time, I would take a whole lot of trouble to keep outa my way in the future because if I get my hooks on you again I am goin' to do somethin' to you that would make Chinese torture look like the Neighbour-hood Friendly Hour on a national hook-up. So get goin', you big gorilla, an' don't stop."

105

I give him a good push in the pan just to show there is no ill-feelin'. He don't say anything. He just goes outa the gate an' starts walkin' down the road holdin' his guts.

I start walkin' down the pathway again. Presently, after I have walked for a good ten minutes, the path narrows. On each side of me are big rhododendron bushes an' trees an' ferns an' what have you got. I reckon there is so much shrubbery around here that if you got lost you could stick around permanently an' live on wild rabbits.

I walk on. After a bit I come to a little clearin'. On the left side of the path is the edge of a lake. It is a big lake an' the mist is hangin' over the top of the water. The sound of the rain drizzlin' down, the plop of the water against the bank where the wind is pushin' it an' the general atmosphere are all about as cheerful as somebody's last night on earth.

I keep on walkin'. I walk around the path that leads round the edge of the lake, whistlin' quietly to myself an' wonderin' just what the next act in the set-up is goin' to be.

After a bit the path widens. Just in front of me there is a big clearin' an' on the other side is a lodge. It is an old-time place an' the white pillars by the doorway show up plenty. I give a big sigh. It looks as if I have arrived.

I go up the two-three steps that lead up to the portico an' pull down the bell-handle. There is a pause an' then somewhere, about fourteen miles away, I can hear the bell ringin'. It is one of them cracked bells that you can hear any time you have a nightmare. I stick around, but nothin' happens. Nobody comes.

I throw my cigarette stub away an' light a fresh one. Then I try the knobs on the double doors. They open. I go inside, switch on my torch, close the doors behind me an' take a look around.

I am in an old-fashioned hallway. The furniture is good even if it is dusty. On the wall on my right is a big oil-paintin' an' underneath is written : ' *George Soames Ellinghurst, First Lord Calvoran.*' I take a look at the picture an' come to the conclusion that George was a swell guy even if he does look as if he was born with a stiff neck.

I walk across the hall. On the left, on the other side of the hall, is a wide sorta circular stairway with big oak balustrades.

I start walkin' up an' believe it or not every time I put my foot down I can hear an echo. I get to thinkin' that this must be the haunted house that you see on the movies.

I get to the first landin'. I stand there listenin'. The place is as quiet as the local graveyard, except now an' again there is an odd creakin'.

I let go a bawl that you coulda heard in Russia.

" Whitaker . . ." I yell. " Are you around here ? "

From somewhere above me comes a sorta moanin' noise. It is a low desperate sorta groan. The sorta noise Aunt Priscilla makes when somebody tells her that her marriage lines are phoney an' that she has been livin' in sin for the last forty-seven years.

I go up to the next landin'. The light of the torch shows me a long corridor runnin' from side to side of the Lodge. All along it are hangin' pictures of more members of the Calvoran family' There are so many of these guys that I reckon that George, the guy whose mug is hangin' in the hallway, musta been very fond of his wife. I take a look at 'em as I walk along an' believe me they all look like the guy downstairs, so there is no truth in the rumours that these English Countesses in the old days usta get around with odd guys—either that or else the artist who done the pictures was a tactful sorta cuss.

I let go another yell, an' after a minute there comes an answerin' groan. Only it is a bit louder this time. It seems to me to come from the end of the corridor. I ease along there. There is a door on my right an' I open it an' flash the torch in.

In the middle of the room, which is as old-time as the rest of this dump, is a big antique six-legged table. There is a guy stretched out on this table. He is spread-eagled. His arms are tied to the top legs an' his legs to the bottom ones. I switch my torch on his face. Somebody has stuck a gag in his mouth, but he has managed to get half of it out. His face is thin an' white an' his eyes are as tired as hell. This guy does not look at all happy.

I take a look around the room. On a little table by the shuttered window are some bottles of Scotch, a syphon an' some clean glasses. There is not anybody else around so far as I can see.

I go over to the door, shut it and turn the key in the lock. I find the light switch an' turn on the light. Then I go over to the table an' get out my penknife. I start cuttin' the guy loose.

I say : " Well, Mister Whitaker, I been lookin' for you. I'm glad to find you all in one piece."

He tries to move but he can't. I told you that this guy has got a far-away sorta dreamy look in his eyes. Also he looks as if he ain't quite certain which way he is pointin'.

I yank him off the table an' walk him around for a bit. Then I stick him in a big brocade chair an' go over to the little table. I pull the cork outa one of the bottles an' try it on my tongue. It is Scotch all right.

I pour out a coupla stiff shots an' give him one. He drinks it off like he needs it. So I give him another. I also have one myself just to be friendly.

" Well, Whitaker," I tell him. " So here we are.
All nice an' friendly. Now let's do some talkin'."

He sits there gaspin'. He looks as if he has got the
pants scared off him. He says :

" Let's get out of here. This place gives me the
creeps." He puts his hands in front of his face. " My
God," he groans. " They've given me a hell of a
time."

" You don't say ? " I tell him. " I suppose you
wouldn't have any ideas about what they've done with
your girl friend—the one you walked out on, I mean
—Geralda—the good-lookin' baby."

" How do I know ? " he says. " I don't know anything. I think I'm lucky to be alive. And Geralda
ought to have minded her own business. She ought
to have stayed out of this thing. Panzetti's a devil.
God knows what they'll do to her."

I give myself a cigarette.

" Well . . ." I say. " Believe it or not I have got
an idea at the back of my head that I'm gonna find
this dame some time somewhere. Maybe I'll take a
look when I ain't too busy."

He says : " Why don't you look now . . . ? You're
Caution—the Special Agent—aren't you ? "

" That's right, pal," I tell him. " An' you knew I
would be comin' along ? They told you to expect
me, hey ? "

" One of Panzetti's gorillas said you'd be along,"
he says. " He told me that if you came alone it would
be all right, but that if you brought anybody with
you they'd cut my throat before you could do anything
about it. I've been worrying myself sick. I thought
you might try something tough."

" Well, I didn't," I say. " I just come along all on
my own nice an' quiet."

He don't say anything for a minute. Then he goes
over to the table an' pours himself another drink. He

gulps the drink down like it was the last one he was ever goin' to have. Then he says :

" If you think Geralda's somewhere about why don't you look for her ? Why don't you . . ."

" Pipe down," I tell him. " Or else you'll get yourself heart disease. I told you I wasn't worryin' about her. We'll get around to Geralda in a minute. First of all I want to talk to *you*. You sorta interest me."

He looks at me as if I was nuts.

" I don't understand you," he says. " Why the hell don't you get a move on and do something ? You don't even seem to be worrying yourself about Geralda or anything. Do you realise what is at stake . . . ? "

" You mean the dive-bomber ? " I say. " Yeah, I realise about that, but I am a guy who never gives up hope. An' right now you can compose yourself an' take it easy an' tell me what I want to know."

I wander over to the whisky an' give myself a stiff one. After I have drunk it I say to him :

" Me . . . I am a guy with a great sense of humour. I reckon you gotta hand it to this Panzetti mug. That boy's got brains all right. He's been makin' rings around us ever since he started in on this racket. First of all he gets a bundle of jack off the German guys to get next to you an' get the blue-prints off you, an' when he's done this he then starts considerin' a little idea to double-cross the Jerries an' start doin' some more business with the U.S. an' English Governments. The boy's clever. The only thing is he might try an' be a little bit too clever an' that is where we'll get him where it hurts most."

He shrugs his shoulders.

" You'll have to be damned clever to get the better of Panzetti," he says. " The best thing for all of us is to play it his way. We've got to get those blue-prints back—no matter what it costs."

"You don't say," I tell him. "An' supposin' the big boy decides to double-cross us. Supposin' he's had a photostatic copy made of 'em an' after we've done business with him he sells *that* to the Germans. What about that angle?"

"It's not possible," he says. "I'm not such a fool as you think. The blue-prints aren't quite finished. I've left out the most important angle on the whole thing. Panzetti knows this. He knows I know it and that you'll know it. That's our guarantee."

"Swell," I tell him. "The idea of gettin' guarantees from Panzetti makes me swoon with joy. I know what I would like to do to that yellow-nosed bastard."

"Possibly," he says. "You know what you *think* you'd like to do to him. But the fact remains that at the moment he's master of the situation. He's got the blue-prints and he's got Geralda."

"That's worryin' you a helluva lot, isn't it?" I ask him. "Why should you worry about Geralda? A guy like you who would walk out on a swell package like Geralda for a cheap mobster's pet like Carlette Francini ought to have his brains attended to."

He don't say anything. He just gives a big sigh. I light another cigarette.

"O.K., Whitaker," I say. "Well, let's get down to cases. I reckon that when Mister Panzetti's boyos spreadeagled you across that table they gave you some messages for me . . . didn't they? They knew I'd be comin' down here. They knew Montana Kells would do her stuff an' pull that phoney act on me to get me down here. Well . . . where do we go from there?"

He says: "This is what they told me to tell you. Panzetti's got the Germans' money. He doesn't give a damn about them. He reckons they can't do anything to him over here. All right . . . well, he's prepared to do a deal with the Government here. He

111

wants two hundred and fifty thousand dollars. When he's got the money and a guarantee that he's going to be left alone afterwards he'll hand over the blue-prints. If he doesn't get the money within two or three days he's going to make it his business to see that Hitler gets the blue-prints and we'll never see Geralda again.

"They told me what they'd do to Geralda. . . . They said . . ." He puts his hands over his face again like he can't bear to think of it.

"Keep your mind on the ball, fella," I tell him. "This is not the time to worry about the Varney dame."

"My God!" he says. "Haven't you got any heart at all? Do you know what Panzetti's like? Can't you use your imagination and think of that poor girl in the hands of that sadistic swine. Can't you . . . ?"

"You're breakin' my heart," I tell him. "But right now we'll keep down to cases. Never mind about Geralda. We'll leave her strugglin' in the hands of Panzetti just for a minute an' concentrate on Carlo Panzetti. When did you see that guy last?"

"I've never seen him," he says. "He keeps in the background. I don't know the names of the people I've seen. But you can take it from me he's here. He's in some place in England—some safe place—and he'll stop at nothing. He's absolutely reckless and he's as clever as the devil."

I shrug my shoulders.

"It certainly looks as if that guy has got somethin' on us," I tell him. "An' I have also got an idea in my head that if we want those blue-prints we shall have to buy 'em like he says. Did these guys tell you where an' how the money was to be paid?"

He nods his head.

"The money was to be paid to me," he says. "When

I've got it I've got to ring a telephone number. Then they'll tell me where I am to go to hand over the money. When I get there they'll give me the blueprints and they'll free Geralda. They'll let her go free with me."

" Nice goin'," I say. " An' how do we know they won't knock you off again an' keep her. What guarantee have we got about that ? "

He spreads his hands.

" There's no guarantee," he says. " We've just got to trust Panzetti. But I don't see how he can cross us. After all it would be pretty difficult for him to get out of England, wouldn't it ? Supposing he *did* want to try a cross."

" He got over here, didn't he ? " I say. " If he can get in he can get out. Still it looks as if we gotta play it his way."

I throw my cigarette stub away. Right then, somewhere in the house a telephone starts ringin'. I stand up an' listen. The bell is soundin' somewhere from downstairs.

" Stick around, pal," I tell him. " I'm goin' to take that call. Maybe this is Santa Claus ringin' up just to ask how the old folks are."

I ease outa the room an' along the corridor. I run down the stairs. The telephone is ringin' in one of the rooms off the front hallway. I push the door open an' go in. By the light of my flash I can see the telephone on a table in the corner. It is ringin' its head off. All around it the furniture is as dusty as hell, but the telephone is nice an' clean, so it looks like somebody musta known I was goin' to use it an' that I like clean telephones.

I grab it. I say :

" Hello . . . this is Mr. Lemuel H. Caution of the F.B.I. speakin', an' what can I do for you ? "

There is a pause an' then a voice comes over the

113

wire. I'm tellin' you guys that this voice is not a nice voice. It is soft an' as cold as a snowball. It sounds such a goddam cruel voice that it makes my spine feel like somebody was ticklin' it with an icicle.

"My name is Panzetti," says the voice. "Carlo Panzetti. I have a little friend here who would like to speak to you, Mr. Caution. Perhaps you would not mind holding the line . . . thank you."

There is another pause. Then I hear a rough voice say :

"Get over to the phone you . . . an' talk."

I wait a minute an' then she comes on the line. Me . . . I would know that voice anywhere. Even in this goddam cold and lonely house the sound of that dame speakin' makes me go all goofy.

It is Geralda all right.

I say : "Well, Geralda, how's it comin' ? An' I hope those guys are treatin' you right."

She says : "Mr. Caution. I can't say much to you. But I have been told to tell you that unless you agree to the terms which have, by now, been discussed with you, and unless you make the necessary arrangements for the money to be handed over at the time and place of which you will be informed ; first of all the blueprints will be delivered to the Germans, and secondly I shall be killed. I am to tell you that I shall die very slowly, and that in order that you shall know that I *am* dead and how I died my body will be sent to your Jermyn Street address within one week from today unless you do what you have been told to do."

She stops speakin'. There is a click an' the phone goes dead.

I give a big sigh. I hang up the receiver an' stand there for a minute—thinkin'. I feel plenty sorry for that dame Geralda.

Then I give myself a fresh cigarette an' I go upstairs. Whitaker is standin' where I left him.

114

" That was Panzetti—that was," I tell him. " Also I had a word or two with Geralda. She told me that what you had said was O.K., that if Panzetti don't get the dough he is handin' over the stuff to the Jerries an' is goin' to give her the works. He is also goin' to push that poor kid around a bit before he bumps her."

He says : " Well . . . we've got to act and we've got to act quickly. Otherwise . . ."

" Just a minute, pal," I tell him. " Just take your coat off an' show me your arms, willya ? "

He looks at me like I was nuts, but he starts takin' his coat off. I push up his shirt sleeves an' look at his arms.

" O.K.," I tell him. " Put your coat on an' listen to me. Just sit down an' take it easy because I want you to sorta concentrate on the words of wisdom that I am now gonna tell you."

He looks good an' surprised. But he sits down.

" First of all," I tell him. " That hot momma Montana Kells told me that Panzetti had been slippin' you a lot of dope so's even if we got our hooks on you you couldn't finish off them blue-prints. Secondly she told me first of all that the blue-prints wasn't completed, an' afterwards when she'd had a few more Scotches she said they was finished."

I look at him. He don't say anything.

" You told me just now that the blue-prints wasn't finished. That they wouldn't be any good until you'd put the final touch on 'em. But just now, Geralda, doin' her stuff like Panzetti tells her, says that unless we ante up with the cash he is goin' to hand the blue-prints over to the Germans. Well, if they ain't finished an' if the bit you haven't done to 'em is the whole works, then what goddam good are they to the Jerries —even if they do get 'em ?

" Secondly, I cannot see any injection marks on your arms. If Panzetti had been druggin' you I reckon

115

he'd had given you the stuff in your arms. Maybe he
didn't do it that way. Maybe your backside is covered
with punctures, but I am not goin' to ask you to take
your pants off."

I get up.

" I am wise to you . . . you yellow-bellied love-
child," I tell him. " This whole goddam business has
stunk in my nostrils from the start. Ever since Montana
started to pull that act on me I have been stickin'
around lookin' for a fresh set-up. *An' you are it. . . .*"

He runs his tongue over his lips.

" What the hell do you mean, Caution ? " he says.

" *I mean you are not Whitaker,*" I tell him. " You
are just one more of the Panzetti beauty chorus tryin'
to make me into the world's biggest sucker. Do you
think I ain't wise to you, baby ? This set-up has smelt
from the start. Montana tells me a fairy story an' gets
me down here. I meet you an' believe you are
Whitaker. I get the dough an' hand it over to you.
You go off an' turn it in to Panzetti. Maybe you let
Geralda Varney go an' maybe you don't. *But you still
got Whitaker—the real Whitaker.*

" An' Panzetti makes that boyo finish off the blue-
prints an' then he can start off all over again an' do
a fresh deal. He can start the whole goddam market
off once more. Maybe he thinks the German U.A.-1
boys will pay some more jack. An' even if they won't
pay any more jack for the set of blue-prints they have
already paid for, maybe they will pay some more to
have Whitaker bumped off so's he can't invent any
more dive-bombers for anybody else."

He stands there lookin' at me. He is sweatin'. He
says in a hoarse sorta voice :

" Listen, Caution. I . . ."

I put up my hand.

" Save it, sweetheart," I tell him. " Because I do
not wish to listen to you any more. I would not

116

believe anything you said even if it was vouched for by a coupla angels with twenty-two carat gold wings an' all the proper fittin's. I would not believe you because it looks to me like all you guys are more scared of buckin' against Panzetti than you are of anythin' else. An' that bein' so there is only one thing for me to do."

"What are you going to do?" he says. He is sweatin' like it was midsummer.

"This is what I am goin' to do," I tell him.

I give him one sweet haymaker that sends him careerin' across the room. Then I get to work on him. I put some overtime in on this lousy bum that didn't even give me any joy. All the time I was sockin' him around the place I am thinkin' of Geralda an' wonderin' what sorta deal she is gettin'.

I leave him lyin' in the corner. He looks like somethin' that has been put through the mangle. I reckon this boyo will not be in circulation again for two or three days an' even then he won't be certain whether it is *his* jaw or one that he has hired out.

I go downstairs an' out onto the path. I ease around by the lake an' back to the car. But all the while I am wonderin' about one or two things that I cannot make out.

I am wonderin' what that guy Zokka was doin' kickin' around, watchin' my car. I am wonderin' about Geralda. I am wonderin' about a helluva lot of things.

I get back to the car an' get in. I light a cigarette an' sit there in the darkness thinkin'. Then I let in the clutch an' get out on to the road. I roll off towards Newbury.

I reckon there is only one way I can play this thing.

2

I get on the main road an' just meander along nice an' quiet. I am tryin' to get some sorta idea about what is in the back of Panzetti's mind an' how he will play this thing from now on. Because I can see how that boyo has worked it up to now.

Here is the set-up from the start. The German guys —the U.A.-1 boys in America—get at Panzetti in the first place because they probably know his record an' they think he is the boy for them. Panzetti has been outa business for some time. First of all the rackets ain't like they usta be before J. Edgar Hoover got busy. There ain't the money in the snatch game an' booze that there usta be. Now all the big-time mobsters are just fiddlin' around tryin' to angle themselves in on protection rackets and the dope an' vice businesses. The real big days for the number one mobster went out three-four years ago.

So I reckon that Panzetti is glad to get some business comin' his way at last. He tells the German guys that he will look after this business for 'em an' he puts a tail on Whitaker an' finds out just what sorta cuss he is. He finds out that Whitaker is goin' to marry Geralda Varney an' he also discovers that the boy is a bit haywire where the dames are concerned. So he tries the doll angle. He puts in Carlette Francini who contacts Whitaker an' pulls her old act on him. Whitaker falls like a sack of coke an' Panzetti, knowin' that Whitaker is a guy who will scare easy, gets some threatenin' letters written to him tellin' him what will happen if he don't come across with the dive-bomber plans.

Panzetti knows that Whitaker bein' the big mug he is will show the letters to Carlette an' discuss the business with her. Whitaker does this. Carlette then says that the only thing for him to do is to clear out an' come to England where he will be safe.

Now it is plenty easy for anybody to understand why Whitaker falls for this. First of all the goddam Germans have been makin' plenty of trouble for one an' all in the States. They know goddam well that America is practically producin' fifty per cent for Britain an' they reckon that if they can throw a spanner in the works they are as good as half winnin' the war. So they get good an' busy. Also you gotta realise these boys are well organised an' with plenty of jack to spend an' they stick at nothin' at all. They will just as soon cut your throat for Führer an' Fatherland as they will buy you a shot of rye whisky if *that* suits 'em better at the moment.

So Whitaker scrams. He probably gets himself a passport under a phoney name an' he comes over to England. This is where I reckon that little so-an'-so Carlette pulls another fast one. She probably tells him that she has got friends over here an' that he can stay with 'em an' that she will come over as soon as she can an' join up with him an' so everything will be jake. She then sends the big mug off an' he comes over an' delivers himself into the hands of Willie Kritsch or Zokka or some other of Panzetti's guys who are already fixed over here an' waitin' for him. That disposes of Whitaker.

Carlette then comes over after stickin' around to find out just what action, if any, the Federal authorities are goin' to take when they find that Whitaker has skipped. She also sticks around to find out just what the Jerries who paid Panzetti to get the plans are thinkin', an' probably stalls 'em off with some story.

All the while Panzetti will be sittin' in the background. That boyo is a leery sorta cuss an' never shows himself unless he's got to.

119

Maybe Carlette tells 'em that it wasn't safe to pinch the stuff in America. That the Feds. would kick up too much of a stink, but that the thing to do is to get Whitaker over to England an' let him finish the plans there an' then they can be delivered over to the German guys somewhere in occupied territory in France, which, if you guys like to think it out, would not be a too difficult job when you got the right boyos to work it.

Everything goes like jake until Carlette finds out that I am comin' over here. So she guesses that the Federal Government have got wise to the fact that Whitaker has skipped for England. The next thing to do is to get me well outa the way before I can start anything.

But she slips up on this, so they have to try somethin' else. They get a fresh idea. This one is that Montana Kells, who is a clever dame an' is workin' over here for Panzetti on this racket, with that chauffeur boy friend of hers, is put in to tell me some phoney story about how she wants to get away from the Panzetti bunch and will spill the beans if I will look after her. Her job is to get me to go down to this Casino Lodge dump and meet up with a guy that I am goin' to think is Whitaker. I am then supposed to hand over two hundred and fifty grand to this mug, an' he is goin' off, after which I reckon Panzetti will get to work on the real Whitaker, make him finish off the plans an' then start the market off again. He will probably hand over one set of blue-prints to us, skip back to U.S. on the safe conduct that is part of the bargain, an' I will take six to four that the dirty so-an'-so will take back photostatic copies of the blue-prints an' stick the German U.A.-1 boys for some more jack when he gets back.

All of which looks like the Panzetti technique all right, because that guy has got medals for sellin' a

120

thing about forty times to seventy different people an' then double-crossin' the lot of 'em.

He also knows that he is on a good market because both the American an' British Governments want this business about the Whitaker dive-bomber kept plenty quiet. He knows that nobody will want to make a big noise about it an' that is all to the good for him.

I would like to get my hooks on that mug. I got one or two little things I would like to try on him.

The road is as dark as hell. By now I am through Newbury an' on my way to Reading. I reckon with a bit of luck I can make Maidenhead in an hour an' I reckon that this visit to Maidenhead is goin' to be goddam important to somebody.

I start thinkin' of Geralda Varney. I hope that dame is all right, but I reckon she is—just for the moment anyhow. Panzetti will not start anything with Geralda until he finds out that I am wise to his phoney Whitaker act, after which he is liable to get very nasty with one an' all.

But there is one thing that I cannot quite get. I cannot see how this guy expects to get away with it if he has to bump anybody at all. I reckon that even Panzetti has gotta know that it's goddam difficult to get away with a killin' in England, an' at a time like this, with a war on how the hell does that guy think he is goin' to make a getaway?

But maybe there is an answer to that. England is not so very far from France an' occupied France is in the hands of the Jerries. Maybe Panzetti thought he could get over there. Maybe he's got it all fixed up.

It is ten-thirty when I get into Maidenhead. The moon has come up a bit an' an air-raid siren is soundin' somewhere across country. Maidenhead looks sorta pretty in the moonlight an' I start thinkin' of the time when I was around here last in 1936 when everything was hunky dory an' there was lights reflectin' on the water.

I park the car in some back street an' I meander along to a hotel an' ask if they know where the Melander Club is. They tell me that they heard of some such place but they don't know where it is, so I reckon the Melander Club is just another one of them funny night places that you get around this part, where they sorta keep themselves nice an' quiet without a lot of publicity.

I am just goin' in to some other dump to ask when I get an idea. It is an off-shoot of an old idea I had on this job, but the way things are I think that maybe it is worth tryin'. I ask some guy where the police station is an' ease along there. I see a police sergeant an' show him the police pass I got from Herrick an' ask him if he will do somethin' for me. I tell him that this is a very important bit of business an' that it has to be played the way I want it.

Then I tell him what I want. This shakes him a bit an' he scratches his head an' says it seems a bit irregular but that he supposes my havin' the police pass lets him out so he will play ball.

I say thanks a lot. He then gets through to the local exchange an' asks 'em for the number of the Melander Club. He gets it an' calls through. When somebody comes on the line he says :

" This is the Maidenhead police speaking. Can I talk to Miss Carlette Lariat, please ? "

I watch him holdin' on. I am wonderin' whether Carlette will be there an' if she will fall for this line. But after a minute it looks as if it's come off. He says :

" Hello . . . Miss Lariat ? This is the Maidenhead police. There is a gentleman here by the name of Fratti—Mr. Giacomo Fratti—an American. Mr. Fratti was hurt in a bomb explosion in London yesterday, and he was on his way to the Melander Club to see you but his car has broken down and he can't walk very well. He wanted to know if somebody could come along here and pick him up. You can? Very well. Thank you."

He hangs up an' says that Miss Lariat is comin' along to pick me up.

So it looks as if it's come off!

I say thanks a lot an' that I won't have to trouble him any more. Then I ease outside the police station an' stand just around the corner in the shadow. I take my Luger outa my shoulder holster an' stick it in my side pocket. Then I stick around, light a cigarette an' wait.

I am wonderin' whether Carlette has really fallen for the story. But why shouldn't she? Fratti's dead, an' I'll bet all the tea in China to a coupla last year's eggs that he was in such little pieces that they never could put him together well enough to be able to recognise him.

But Willie Kritsch an' Carlette don't know that he's dead. He was supposed to have got away from that dump at Hampstead before the time bomb went off an' unless Montana Kells has contacted those two an' wised 'em up that I have told her that Fratti is dead then maybe I can get away with this business. But I am takin' a chance. Because if they *do* know about Fratti I reckon they will scram good an' quick without doin' any investigatin'.

I stamp my feet on the ground to keep the circulation goin'. It is darned cold. I get around to thinkin' that this business of bein' a " G " man is not a very warm trade to be in. The climate is never right. Either you got cold feet standin' about in the middle of the night or else things are so goddam hot that you wish you had a job peelin' snowballs in Iceland.

Somewhere along the street I can hear a car comin'.

It slows down when it gets near me an' pulls in an' stops just four or five feet from where I am standin'. The door opens an' Carlette gets out.

The baby is lookin' swell. She is wearin' a big mink coat an' a cute hat. She slams the door an' takes a coupla steps towards the entrance of the Police Station. I ease out nice an' quiet an' just tickle her under the arm with the barrel of the Luger.

"Take it easy, baby," I tell her. "This is Mister Caution of the old firm of Faith Hope an' Charity Unlimited so don't start anything around here, otherwise the cannon is liable to go off, after which I should be able to look right inside you an' see your dear little heart beatin'."

She stops like she has been poleaxed. She says:
"Christ . . . ain't that a break or is it!"

"You said it, my lambie-pie," I tell her, "an' I also wish to tell you that if you got any of your friends inside that car an' they start anything then I shall start a shootin' match so quick that you would think I was the Italian Navy steamin' back to port after a coupla fish had looked at 'em with an angry expression."

She says a very rude word. Then she says there is not anybody in the car; that she is on her own.

"O.K., sweetheart," I tell her. "Let you an' me get inside an' do a little talkin'."

We get inta the car. She gets in the drivin' seat an' I slip in behind. I close the doors an' put the gun back in my pocket. I light myself a Lucky Strike an' wait for her to start talkin'.

"Jeez . . ." she says. "You sonofabitch. I fell for that stuff. I thought Fratti had got hurt an' just made it down here. I wondered why the hell that mug hadn't turned up. I s'pose you pinched the guy."

"Nope," I tell her. "The lamented Fratti is no

more. The guy got himself blown up instead of me.
I got his passport in my pocket."

" Well," she says. " An' what's the next move.
Where do we go from here ? "

" How's Montana Kells ? " I ask her. " I am very
interested in the health of that cutie. Is she around ? "

She shakes her head.

" I ain't seen her," she says. " An' I don't know
a thing about anything."

" That's O.K. by me," I tell her. " So all I got to
do is to take you in an' hand you over. I'm sorta
sorry because I don't like the idea of these English
guys stringin' you up. An' they do it over here, you
know. They're tough. This ain't like America. You
can't pull anything on these guys. Once they got you
you're for it."

" What the hell do you mean ? " she says. But I
can hear she is scared. " They can't do nothin' to me.
I ain't bumped anybody."

" No ? " I tell her. " Well, Fratti's dead, ain't
he ? "

She screws around in the car. I can see her eyes
gleamin'.

" So what ! " she says. " I suppose you're gonna
tell me I croaked Fratti. Why, the goddam fool musta
croaked himself. *He* was carryin' the bomb, wasn't
he ? "

" Sure," I tell her. " But you don't understand the
law over here, Carlette. It's a scream, I'm tellin' you.
The law here says that if a bunch of crooks are banded
together to do a criminal act an' one of 'em gets killed
in doin' it then all the rest of 'em are chargeable with
murder. An' that's what they'll do to you, my sweet,
an' they'll string you up by the neck an' you'll kick
like you was a fan-dancer with hysterics."

" My God ! " she says. " This don't sound so good
to me. You ain't stringin' me along, are you ? "

125

" Why should I string *you* along, Carlette ? " I tell
her. " What the heck does it matter to me ? *You're*
the one they're gonna hang."

She don't say anything. She opens up her handbag
an' gives herself a cigarette. I snap my lighter an'
light it for her. After a bit she says :

" Can't I do a deal over this ? Supposin' I do a
big squeal. Are you goin' to look after me ? "

" Hear me laugh," I tell her. " All you dames are
the same. You get caught up with an' then you wanta
do a deal. Montana wanted to do a deal too. She
put on an act when it suited her an' then tried to
throw a fast one into me. Now you're tryin' the same
stunt."

" Not me," she says. " I'm scared. This bein'
hanged by the neck until you are dead stuff is no good
to me."

I shrug my shoulders.

" You won't do yourself any harm by doin' a little
talkin'," I say. " Where is that guy Willie Kritsch ?
The guy who is totin' my identification papers about.
An' why did he have to have 'em anyway ? "

" He had to have 'em to kid Geralda Varney along,"
she says. " An' don't ask me why because I don't
know. Panzetti knows. You'll haveta ask him. An'
I don't know where Willie Kritsch is right now. He
was along at the Melander this afternoon an' then a
call came through this evenin' an' he scrammed. He
said he'd be back tomorrow."

I nod my head. I reckon I know where that call
came from.

That would be Zokka telephonin' through to tell
Kritsch that I'd arrived at Casino Lodge an' that I'd
been plenty tough with him."

" Where's Panzetti ? " I ask her.

" Search me," she says. " I haven't seen Carlo
since I left New York. But then you know how shy

that guy is. Nobody ever sees him . . . well not so you'd notice it."

" Where is Geralda Varney ? " I ask her.

" I wouldn't know," she says. " Willie knows. He's lookin' after her."

" That bein' so who is at this Melander Club dump right now ? " I ask her.

" Nobody," she says. " I was holdin' the fort. An' the goddam place gives me the creeps anyhow."

" Let's go," I tell her. " I reckon I'd like to take a look at this Melander Club, so you switch on an' get goin'. Only I would like to point out to you, Carlette, that if I find that there is somebody waitin' for me with a rod I'm goin' to give it to you so quick that you won't even know what's hit you."

She says : " I'm tellin' you the truth. There ain't anybody there except me." She looks round at me an' I get a look at her face. " I'm tellin' you the truth," she says. " I'm tellin' you I don't feel so good about this business. Maybe I got an idea . . ."

She lets in the clutch an' starts to turn the car around.

" The idea bein' . . . ? " I say.

She don't say anything. She straightens up the car an' puts her foot down. We roll down the road. By the way she is drivin' I reckon she knows the neighbourhood.

" Just let me collect my thoughts," she says. " I'm a girl who don't like bein' rushed. Maybe I'll do a little talkin' later on."

" That suits me," I tell her.

I relax back in the car, an' smoke. I keep the Luger nice an' handy.

Lookin' at the back of her head I get to thinkin' that these dames who get around with the mobs are just big female mugs. They don't know a thing. Some of 'em are just cheap chisellers an' some of 'em

127

think that stickin' around with some thug is the right royal road to bein' in the diamond market an' gettin' themselves a mink coat.

Even then they don't wear it for long. Somebody rubs 'em out, or they get pinched, or something. . . .

Because a dame in a mob—no matter how much brains she has got—is always dependent on her sex-appeal. It don't matter a cuss whether a guy has got a pan like the map of the world if he can keep his trap shut, squeeze the trigger at the right moment, an' generally do his stuff, he's O.K. an' maybe he'll live until somebody bumps him in the normal sequence of events.

But it's different with a dame. She gets inta a mob because some big shot likes her shape or the way her ankles look, or the way her eyes shine when she's had a glass of champagne. So he cuts her in an' she thinks that life is just one big lump of sugar.

An' then the big boy begins to get tired of her. Maybe he got his eye on some other frail. So he has to get rid of her. An' he knows goddam well that if he turns her off she's gonna shoot her mouth just outa jealousy.

So he don't take a chance. He fixes things so that it looks as if she ain't on the up an' up with the mob. He sorta suggests that she's talkin' outa turn or makin' things a little difficult an' sure as shootin' one of the boys will take her for a car ride an' dump the remains in the local ditch.

Sometimes they leave 'em with the mink coat. An' sometimes they even take that off for the next doll.

I grin to myself. Maybe somethin' like that is happenin' to Carlette. Maybe she ain't so stuck on Willie Kritsch as she was. Maybe he ain't so stuck on her an' she thinks she might as well get out while the goin's good.

I have got a hunch that I am right about this. Anyhow I'm goin' to play it that way.

I say sorta casual : " The trouble with you mobsters' dolls is you always mix your men an' it don't pay. You oughta look out, baby. There's somebody who don't like you . . . well . . . not very much."

She is lookin' straight ahead at the road.

" Meanin' who ? " she says.

" Meanin' Montana," I tell her, makin' the lie roll off my tongue nice an' easy. " She told me she was stuck on Willie Kritsch," I go on. " An' she sorta suggested that he was goin' for her. You better look out or that boyo is gonna ditch you."

She says : " I see . . . so it's like that, is it ? O.K. Well stick around. I'll show you somethin'. I'm gonna sell that heel out, hook line an' sinker. I'm gonna do somethin' I never thought I'd do. I'm gonna squeal."

I grin to myself.

Maybe now we're goin' to get some place.

129

CHAPTER FIVE

RUB OUT

I

AFTER a few minutes' drivin' she swings the car on to a side road an' puts her foot down. The road is good an' straight an' I am not so displeased with this because I can see by the way this doll is handlin' the heap that she is not concentratin' too much on drivin'. I reckon that maybe she has something else on her mind.

After a bit we swing left an' then right. She slows down an' rolls the car through two big iron gates that stand back off the roadway. We go along a circular drive that leads up to a house between two rows of drippin' laurel bushes. It has started to rain good an' plenty an' the general atmosphere around here is so goddam cheerful that it woulda been a pleasure to sit at somebody's death-bed for a nice change.

Carlette gets outa the car an' I go after her. She takes a key out an' opens the door of this place. It looks like an old-time villa that has seen better days. There are weeds growin' between the stones in the porch steps an' there is a smell of damp that could give you rheumatics.

" Are you gonna leave the car there ? " I ask her. " Supposin' Willie Kritsch or some of his pals blow along. They're likely to get curious about where you been, hey ? "

She says that Willie Kritsch won't be back tonight

an' that if anybody else comes around and sees the car, so what?

I step into the hallway after her an' shut the door. The place looks better inside. When she puts the light on I can see that it is a well-furnished an' comfortable sorta dump that looks as if it has been lived in.

She goes straight ahead down the passage on the other side of the hallway. Half-way down she opens a door on the right an' goes in. She switches on the light.

I stand in the doorway lookin' around. The room is swell. There are big arm-chairs an' soft carpets an' a first-class radio an' all the trimmin's. Over in the corner is a drink wagon with all the bottles on it an' most of 'em full.

She starts takin' off her coat. I light a cigarette an' throw my own coat an' hat in the corner. Then I go an' plant myself in one of the big chairs in front of the fire.

She comes over an' stands lookin' down inta the flames. She don't look so happy. I reckon she is poisonin' herself with some not so sweet thoughts about Kritsch an' Montana.

I sit there, drawin' on the cigarette, lookin' at her an' thinkin' that all dames are the same when they are stuck on some guy. It don't matter how tough an' clever a jane is in the ordinary course of events, directly she gets herself tied up to some big noise in pants she starts to go haywire. An' a mobster's doll like Carlette is just as bad as any other dame. She just forgets to use any brains she has got an' realise that a guy whose business is double-crossin' other guys is just as likely to use the same technique on *her*.

Inside I am doin' a big grin. Because if what Montana said about bein' Panzetti's frail is true then this idea of Willie tryin' to muscle in on the dame is

131

sheer hooey. But it's a useful one so I reckon I will play it along a bit.

" Why don't you relax, Carlette ? " I tell her. " It ain't no good to worry about a guy like Willie Kritsch if he's gone bad on you. Besides history always repeats itself an' I reckon that he will hand a sour deal to Montana one of these fine days the same way as he's doin' to you now."

" Yeah," she says. " O.K. But if anybody's handin' out a sour deal it's gonna be me. I reckon that when I've said my piece that black-haired momma can have what's left."

" I got it," I tell her. " So that is just the big straight squeal that is gonna put Willie in the can an' Montana in the ice-box. This is one more example of hell hath no fury like a dame who's boy friend has taken a run-out powder with the opposition show ? Am I right ? "

" You're goddam right," she says.

She goes over to the drink-wagon an' pours out some drinks. She squirts in some soda, comes back an' hands one to me. It is a half glass full of Canadian Bourbon with a spot of soda an' it tastes swell. She flops down in the chair on the other side of the fire.

" I'm sick of the whole goddam works," she says. " Another thing, I'm gettin' scared. An' I don't scare easily. An' if I want something else to bite on there's that hell-cat Montana. . . ."

I take a bite at the bourbon an' start blowin' smoke-rings. I am beginnin' to feel that maybe I'm goin' to get some place with this dame. I sorta feel that, as far as is possible with a momma like her, Carlette is on the up-an'-up.

" Montana is a cute package," I tell her. " She's got somethin'. First of all she's nearly as good-lookin' as you are, an' she has also got a way with her.

That dame is so damned allurin' that she even falls for herself, an' she is so goddam crooked that she would make a corkscrew look straight by comparison. At the same time she is a bit of a mug over *some* things.

" Such as what ? " she says.

" Such as doin' a double on Panzetti," I tell her. " By what she said it looks like she is Panzetti's girl an' if she's a member of the Panzetti harem it ain't goin' to do her any good to start slingin' the eye on Willie Kritsch. If Panzetti was to find out, what do you think would happen to the pair of 'em ? "

She looks at me. She looks surprised.

" Don't be a sap," she says. " Don't you know that . . ." She stops talkin' suddenly an' looks at the fire.

" Montana is cute all right," I go on. " She goes tailin' me around an' then tells me a funny story about this Whitaker guy bein' up at some dump at Burghclere. She tells me that the Varney dame is probably there also. When I get up there I find some guy tied to a table. This bozo proceeds to unwind a long spiel on me about his bein' Whitaker. The idea bein' that I am to arrange to get this guy a quarter of a million bucks, after which he is goin' to contact Panzetti an' get the blue-prints back, an' Geralda Varney, an' everything is goin' to be sweet an' happy for everybody ever afterwards."

Carlette looks up. She is lookin' as if she is feelin' a little bit more happy. She crosses her legs an' leans back so's I can see she is wearin' real silk tops an' black suspenders. She says :

" Would you like to give me a cigarette ? "

I give her one. She draws a deep breath of smoke right down inside her an' then lets it trickle out of her nostrils.

" So you went down to this Burghclere dump," she

133

says, " an' found this guy who said he was Whitaker tied to a table. An' what did you do with him ? "

I grin at her.

" I told him he ought not to tell me fairy tales like that," I say. " An' I smacked him around a bit an' left him there. I don't reckon he'll annoy anybody for quite a bit."

She nods her head. She is lookin' into the fire like she was tryin' to read her fortune there.

" Zokka was around there too," I tell her. " Hangin' around. I was a bit tough with that guy as well. I been doin' quite a bit of man-handlin' tonight."

She still don't say anything.

" While I was talkin' to this guy on the table—the phoney Whitaker guy," I go on, " a telephone rings some place in the house. So I go down an' take the call. An' who do you think it was on the line ? "

Carlette looks at me. She says :

" I wouldn't know. You tell *me* who it was."

" It was nobody else but Panzetti," I tell her. " He introduces himself an' then sticks Geralda Varney on the line. She tells me that unless I do what I have been told an' arrange to pay this jack over to this phoney Whitaker then they are goin' to bump Geralda nice an' slow an' send her around to me in a packin'-case, which I do not consider is a nice thing to do."

" So that was what Panzetti said ? " says Carlette. She nods her head like a wise woman. " An' he spoke to you on the telephone an' then put the Varney piece on to speak to you." She starts laughin'. " May I be sugared an' iced," she says. " Ain't life a scream ? "

" It is one long howl of merriment," I tell her. " But why does it sorta strike you like that right now ? What's on your mind ? "

" You'd be surprised," she says. " If you knew what was on my mind you'd die with laughin'." She stops talkin' an' looks at the fire again. After a bit she says :

" What sort of a deal can I make with you ? "

" That depends," I tell her. " Just how far are you in this ? "

" Not too far to get out," she says. " Panzetti put me in originally to get next to Whitaker. Some German mob in the States was payin' Carlo plenty. He told me there'd be a lot of heavy sugar in this for me. Well . . . it wasn't difficult. Whitaker was easy. Then Panzetti had him pushed around a bit an' a coupla threatenin' notes sent, the idea bein' that I was to scare Whitaker into cashin' in with the blue-prints. But Whitaker don't go for that. He goes off for a day or so to think things over an' then comes back an' says that he is gonna clear out an' come over here.

" I got through to Panzetti an' told him an' he said that was O.K., that he'd like Whitaker to come over here, an' that I was to come on after him after I'd stuck around for a bit to see if there was any big noise about his disappearance. Panzetti reckoned they'd keep it quiet because of the bomber plans. He was right. They did.

" I hung around an' heard that you were up in Kansas tryin' to find Whitaker. So I stuck on your tail an' came over on the same boat. Manders—the wireless guy—was workin' for the German mob an' you know how we framed you.

" When I got here Willie Kritsch met me. He'd got me fixed up in that apartment in St. John's Wood. Directly you showed up we got out an' came down here. Kritsch has had this place for some time."

I light a fresh cigarette.

" Well, you ain't in so deep that you couldn't be got out," I tell her. " If I thought you was bein' straight for once, Carlette, I'd get you out of this if you'd blow the entire works on the Panzetti set-up. But before I do anything like that you gotta show me that you're on the level. Because I do not like bein' taken for a sucker by good-lookin' dames like you an' Montana."

" The hell with Montana," she says. " I'm through with that dirty so-an'-so an' the whole goddam lot of 'em. All I want is a nice slice of peace an' quiet an' to get outa this business before somebody starts some sweet slaughter—which is what I think is goin' to happen in a minute."

" Nice work," I tell her. " But you better be quick, baby, otherwise somebody might wanta slaughter *you.*"

" You're tellin' me," she says. " O.K. Well, you want to know that I'm on the up-an'-up. I'm gonna prove that to you here an' now an' I'm gonna prove it so good that even *you*'ll believe it."

" Nice goin'," I tell her. " An' just how're you goin' to do that ? "

She gets up.

She goes across the room to where she has left her handbag. She opens it an' fiddles about for a bit an' then comes back with a key. She throws the key over to me.

" If you like to go around the back of the house," she says, "—you can get to it through the passage here—you'll find a lawn. You go across the lawn an' through the bushes on the other side. You'll find a one-storey stone garage just behind the thicket there. Open it up an' take a look in the back room. When you come back I'll talk turkey to you—*an'* I'll guarantee to make your ears flap ! "

" O.K., baby," I tell her. " But don't try an' take any powders on me while I am away. Anyhow you *can't* escape anywhere in this country. It ain't big enough ; they'll have you in no time."

"Don't be a fool, Lemmy," she says. "I'm playin'
this straight. When you've had a look in the garage
you'll know that."
I get up. I go over to the doorway an' I turn
around an' take a look at her.
"All right," I say. "I am the sorta guy who
will try anything once but only once. I'll be seein'
you."
I turn down the passage and walk along, through
the kitchen an' out through the back door. I am
wonderin' what is on the ice now? The rain is comin'
down like hell an' I start cursin' myself for not havin'
put my topcoat on.
I cross the lawn an' go into the shrubbery on the
other side. I stand there for a minute an' loosen up
the Luger in my shoulder holster because I have made
up my mind that I am not havin' any further funny
business with any more of these guys an' that if anybody is goin' to start somethin' it is goin' to be *me*.
On the other side of the shrubbery there is a little
clearin' with a path through it. The path runs through
a thicket on the other side of the clearin'. I pull the
Luger outa the holster an' go right ahead. When I
get through the thicket, facin' me—a few yards away
—is the stone garage.
I open the door an' go in. There is a light switch
by the door an' I snap it on. It is a fair-sized dump
with two big cars parked on the floor. On the other
side of the garage floor is another door. I go over
an' try it. It is locked but the same key fits both doors.
I open it an' go in.
The light is on. Lyin' on a work bench on the
other side of the room is Geralda. She is tied up with
bits of rope, wire an' anything else they could find
handy. An' her mouth is tied up with a red silk
bandanna handkerchief.
I give a big grin. I reckon that Carlette was on the

137

up-an'-up all right. This proves it. It looks as if that baby has made up her mind to squeal and squeal so loud that everybody is goin' to hear her.

I go over an' stand there lookin' down at Geralda. Then I take out my pocket-knife an' start doin' a big uncuttin' act. After I have got the rope an' stuff off her I take the handkerchief off her mouth.

" Goodnight, or good-mornin' to you, Geralda," I say. " I am very glad to meet you some more an' I sincerely hope that by this time you have got it into your dear little red head that I am the real, honest-to-god, dyed-in-the-wool Lemmy Caution, an' I hope you haven't been here too long."

She swings her legs down off the bench an' sits there, stretchin' an' looking at me. This baby does not look too pleased with life, but all the same I cannot take my eyes off her.

Maybe I told you mugs about Geralda before. O.K. Well, I'm goin' to do it again. Even the fact that she has been trussed up like a spring chicken does not make this honeypot anything else but one hundred per cent. She is wearin' a grey wool frock with scarlet collar an' cuffs, tan silk stockin's an' tan shoes   She is the last word, the ultimate yelp. I'm tellin' you that this dame has got so much that I can't take my eyes off her.

Then, all of a sudden, she smiles at me. It was just like the sun comin' out on a winter's day.

" You've got your nerve," she said.   " I never thought I was going to forgive you for being so im-pertinent on our last meeting—even after I knew that you were Mr. Caution.   But I can't be angry with you now. How *did* you know I was here ? "

" I didn't," I tell her.   " Carlette Francini, who has decided to swing a fast one across her pals, wised me up.   And now, if you do not mind, you an' me are goin' to do a little fast work."

I take out my cigarette pack an' give her one. I help myself and light both cigarettes. She says :

" I would like to arrange my hair—and I want to wash and get tidy. It's not been nice being in this place."

I nod my head.

" The washin' will have to wait," I tell her. " You an' me have got to have a little talk an' we've got to have it now. Before I go back an' talk to Carlette. I'm sorry but that's how it's got to be."

She tosses her head.

" I don't know that I agree," she says. She looks like the Queen of Sheba in a temper.

" Look, lady," I tell her. " What you agree with an' what you don't agree with does not matter to me at this minute. What does matter is this. Ever since this job started you have been musclin' in an' mixin' things up. You are now goin' to finish doin' things like that. What you are goin' to do is to tell me what I wanta know, after which I am goin' to get you away to London where the police can look after you till we got this mob pulled in."

Her eyes flash. I reckon that Geralda is not used to bein' talked to like that.

She says :

" Do I have to answer your questions ? I must say that for a Federal officer you do not seem to have handled this case too intelligently from the start. First of all . . ."

I put up my hand.

" Just save it, sweetheart," I tell her, " otherwise I am goin' to smack you harder than I did when we met before. I have not got any time to waste because things are poppin'."

" I have no time to waste either," she cracks back at me. I can see her eyes are blazin'. I'm tellin' you mugs that she looks marvellous. " And there's

139

something else you might care to know, Mr. Caution. If you hadn't been so unintelligent on the *Florida* the mix-up would not have happened. If you hadn't fallen so easily for that Carlette Francini woman I should have known who you were in the first place."

" O.K.," I tell her. " So they told you about that . . . did they ? "

She smiles—sorta sarcastic.

" Kritsch—the man who, at first, pretended to be you—told me," she says. She smiles some more. " The story lost nothing by the telling," she says. " Apparently you fell very easily for the charms of Carlette Francini. They seem to have made a fool of you, Mr. Caution."

" Not such a fool as that boy friend of yours made outa you," I tell her. I am feelin' as bad-tempered as an old goat. " Right from the start," I go on, " you have done everything the wrong way. Ever since this job started you played right into the hands of this goddam bunch of thugs just because you gotta stick your nose inta something that don't concern you. Besides which," I say with a grin as sarcastic as hers, " you have the goddam nerve to complain about me fallin' for Carlette. Well, what about you ? You wasn't good enough to keep your boy friend Whitaker, who you was supposed to be goin' to marry, from bein' pinched from right under your nose by Carlette. But maybe you haven't got as much allure as that dame ? "

" I do not wish to discuss allure with you," she says.

" O.K.," I tell her. " Well, we will not discuss it. Because although you are one of the swellest lookin' dames I have ever met there are moments when I could smack the pants off you an' like doin' it."

She says in an icy voice : " I am not interested in

individuals who go about smacking the pants off people."

I grin at her.

" No ? " I tell her. " But you would be if it happened to you. All right . . . well, now just relax an' try an' forget that Whitaker took a run-out powder on you—which has made you feel sore about things —an' that you made a mug outa yourself by lettin' Kritsch kid you he was me. Another thing," I go on, " I think you are also forgettin' that if I hadn't turned up at that dump in Hampstead an' stuck you in that garage—even if I did smack your tail while I was doin' it—you would be in such little pieces by now that nobody would know how pretty you are."

" I'm most obliged to you," she says with her nose up in the air. " But while I must thank you for having saved my life on that occasion I would like to point out that if *you* hadn't allowed your identity papers to be stolen I should never have believed that Kritsch was you and I should never have gone to that house."

" All right, delicious," I tell her. " Well, now if you will stop behavin' like the first woman dictator for a few minutes maybe we can get down to brass tacks. I wanta know some things. . . ."

" What things ? " she says. She goes over an' leans against the wall of the garage. She has got her hands behind her an' she looks so goddam beautiful an' provocative that I could eat her all in one piece.

" First of all," I tell her, " I wanta check on what Carlette Francini has told me. When Whitaker took a run-out powder on you, where did you scram ? When I was up in Kansas City lookin' for him I was also lookin' for you. After that guy had gone why didn't you stick around an' help the authorities to find the guy ? "

141

" Because I knew that he would come over here,"
she says. "And I intended to come here after him.
He needs me. Elmer Whitaker is a genius. He must
not be judged by the standards which might apply
to other men. He is foolish about women and is
inclined to be weak about them, but at heart he is
perfectly sound."

" Hear me laugh," I tell her. " The idea of a guy
takin' a run-out powder with Carlette Francini an'
bein' perfectly sound at heart gives me the willies. He
was so goddam sound at heart that he was scared stiff
after he got a threatenin' letter from the Panzetti
bunch. And, although he is a swell inventor of air-
planes, outside that he is just a pint size punk with
as much brains as you could stick in your eye without
noticin' the fact."

She falls for this one. She says :
" Why do you say he has no brains outside his
inventions ? "

" Honey," I tell her, " any guy who left a dame
who looks like you look for a dame like Carlette
Francini must be nutty."

She throws her cigarette stub down an' puts her
little foot on it. She don't say anything.

" All right," I tell her. " Let's go on from there.
Tell me . . . what did you think you were goin' to do
after you came over here ? An' why did you come ?
Did you know that Panzetti had got his hooks
inta Whitaker. Did you think that you could
protect Whitaker ? If you thought that Panzetti
was after him why didn't you go to the Federal
Authorities ? "

" I came over here because Elmer wrote to me
before he left America," she says. " He wrote to me
the day before he sailed. I received the letter after
he had gone. He told me that he was afraid of some
people who were trying to get his invention. He said

142

that he thought he would be safe over in England and that he would be able to complete the blue-prints in peace."

" Why hadn't he completed them before ? " I ask her. " I can answer that one. Because he was too busy runnin' around with Carlette. That's the sort of mug little Elmer is."

She shrugs her shoulders.

" Why should I try to prove anything to you," she says. " You are *so* stupid. I can tell you why Elmer did not complete the blue-prints. He explained the reason in his letter. Whilst the blue-prints were in-complete the main secret of the dive-bomber was safe. Elmer had no intention of completing the plans while there was the slightest chance of their falling into the hands of the people who wanted them."

" Maybe," I tell her. " But what about Kritsch and his bunch ? Panzetti's over here an' he's got little Elmer an' the plans an' everything he wants. He had *you* too, until just now. An' then you say that Whitaker ain't a mug."

" Panzetti can do nothing with the plans until they are complete," she says. " And Elmer will never complete them—he'll die first."

" Hooey," I tell her. " A guy who was as weak-kneed as Elmer was over this job, a guy who was afraid of a coupla threatening letters an' who had not got enough sense to stay put, tell the mob to go to hell, finish off the blue-prints an' turn 'em over to the U.S. Government like he said he was goin' to do, is not good enough to stand up to Panzetti if that boy gets tough."

Her lip curls up. She looks marvellous. She says :
" Why should I argue with you ? Apparently you know everything. I can't even understand why you should want to ask questions."

" I've got some reasons, honeypot," I tell her.

143

" An' you are one of 'em. I do not wish to have to spend my time rushin' around after you because you are always gettin' yourself snatched by some bunch of yeggs so that they can hold you as an extra induce-ment to get a quarter of a million dollars. That is one of my reasons. Another thing," I go on, " when you spoke to me on the telephone this evening, just after Panzetti had spoken to me, were you in the same room ? Did you hear anything else that was said ? "

She shakes her head.

" I wasn't in the room when Panzetti spoke to you," she says. " I was brought in afterwards by a man they called ' Frisco.' Kritsch handed the telephone to me and told me to say what I did."

" I see . . ." I say. " So you was just brought in an' told to tell me that unless I carried out the instructions I'd received you were goin' to be bumped nice an' slow an' then sent to me in a packin'-case. You didn't know who was with me when you were talkin' to me ? "

" No," she says. She looks at me with her eyes wide open.

I give a big laugh.

" This is funny," I tell her. " They put a dame in to get me down to some house—Casino Lodge—at a place called Burghclere. When I get there I find a guy who says he is Whitaker, who says that the only way to settle this business is for me to get the 250,000 dollars an' hand it over to him. That he will then get the blue-prints back an' be set free an' you will be allowed to go too. You are put on the telephone probably from this dump to tell me that is right an' that if I don't agree they are goin' to bump you an' sell to the Germans. So you see these guys are clever. The boyo who was supposed to be Whitaker was a fake. He was just another of the mob. They got the

144

real Whitaker salted away somewhere. Maybe they're cuttin' his nose off or somethin' right now. . . ."

She says : " This man . . . the man who said he was Whitaker . . . what was he like ? "

" He was an ordinary lookin' cuss," I tell her. " About one hundred an' sixty pounds, about five feet nine or ten, with black hair an' a thin face with big mournful eyes. He looked the usual sorta punk to me. . . ."

She says : " My God . . . are you a fool or are you ! " She looks at me like I was nuts.

" Listen, Geralda," I tell her, " you cannot . . ."

Right then I hear a peculiar sorta bump. It comes from somewhere outside. I pull the Luger out an' give it to her.

" Look, baby," I tell her, " I gotta go. There is something screwy goin' on around here. Stick around an' if anybody starts anything let 'em have it. But don't go outa this place. Here's the key. Lock the door from the inside."

I scram across the garage through the thicket, across the lawn an' back into the house. When I get into the kitchen I stand there listenin' but I cannot hear a thing.

I gumshoe down the passage to the room where I left Carlette. I push open the door an' I go in.

I cannot see Carlette. All I can see is that the table with the drinks on it has been turned over. I walk over there an' take a look. Then I see her.

She has got it right through the pump. The whole front of her frock is stained dark with blood. I reckon somebody has put half a dozen bullets inta her. Her eyes are wide open, starin' at the ceilin'. One of her hands is clenched but the other one is open an' in the palm of it somebody has put a penny—the old mob sign for a squealer's pay-off.

I put the drinks table back on its legs an' bend down

145

over Carlette. Round the edges of the bloodstains I can see that the front of her dress has been burned a bit. I reckon whoever it was gave it to her was shootin' at pretty close range. That means that she let 'em get up close ; that she recognised 'em. Maybe the guy had the gun behind his back an' she didn't know he was goin' to crease her.

I reckon this is a bit tough for Carlette. Here is one time she has got herself bumped for squealin' an' she ain't even had time to squeal !

I pick up one of the bottles of bourbon that has got the cork in it an' a glass. I pour myself a stiff one an' take it in front of the fire an' drink it. It looks maybe as if somethin' is goin' to happen around here. Back of my head I have got an idea as to how I am goin' to play this.

I go back to the table an' get another shot of bourbon. I am just turnin' around to walk back to the fire when somebody says :

" I hope you like your drink, pal."

I take a look at the guy. He is a tall, thin guy. He has got a thin face with high cheek-bones an' long eyes with flashy eyelids. His overcoat is well-cut an' he is wearin' a black fedora at a slant over his left eye. He looks a very smart guy an' a trifle tough.

Hangin' down by his right side, held sorta loosely in his fingers, is a three millimetre Mauser automatic. He don't look as if he is worryin' about anything very much.

He says—nice an' easy : " You wouldn't try an' start anything, would you, Caution ? If you do I'll give it to you."

He goes over to the drinks wagon an' pours himself out one. He keeps lookin' at me along his eyes.

" I bet you would, fella," I tell him. " Just like somebody gave it to her." I grin at him. " Just another of these brave guys who bump frails like that one. If it wasn't payin' you a compliment I'd tell you what a lousy yellow bastard you are."

" Don't let me stop you," he says. " The name's Kritsch—Willie Kritsch—maybe you heard it some time. Maybe you heard it from that." He points at Carlette with the barrel of the gun.

" I heard plenty," I tell him. " But nothin' I've heard is goin' to give me so much joy as the pig's squeal you'll put up when they're draggin' you along to the hot seat. An' I hope they turn the current on slow so's you get the pants burnt off you first an' die nice an' easy, you cheap lug."

" Yeah . . ." he says. " You don't say."

He comes over to me an' hits me across the face with the gun. Then he throws the bourbon inta my face. I'm tellin' you it don't feel so good either.

He goes back to the drink wagon an' pours another drink. I can feel the blood runnin' down my face but I don't do anything about it. I am not inclined to give this punk any satisfaction.

He sinks the drink an' then goes over to the chair that is in front of Carlette. He flops down into it. All the time he keeps watchin' me. After a bit he says :

" This is not quite so good. A lousy set-up an' somebody is gonna pay for it." He throws me a grin. " I reckon that somebody is gonna be you," he says.

He gets up an' goes back to the wagon for another drink. He gives himself a long slug of bourbon outa the bottle an' then meanders over to the door. This guy is one of them quiet guys who do not get very excited over anythin'.

When he gets to the door he puts his head around the corner an' calls out " Frisco." Then he goes back to the chair.

There are some steps along the passage an' then

147

another guy comes in. This guy is short an' square. His eyes are slit like he had a Chinese pa an' his nose is sorta turned up so's you can see the insides of his nostrils if you feel inclined to look that way. His arms are long an' bent—like a gorilla's.

He says :

" Hello there, boss." He takes a look at me an' grins. When he opens his mouth you can see a lotta black teeth like rocks standin' in dirty water. This bozo makes me feel sick to look at.

Kritsch looks at the guy. He has gotta sorta sarcastic look on his pan as if this guy Frisco was somethin' washed up by the tide. Lookin' at Kritsch I get the idea that he is a tough an' clever an' cruel guy.

He sits there with one leg, in nicely pressed pants, crooked over the arm of the chair, an' the gun hangin' down in one hand an' the bourbon bottle in the other. He points with the bottle behind him to what is left of Carlette.

He says : " How come ? "

The other guy looks uncomfortable. He looks as if he's goin' to cry. He shuffles his feet about for a bit an' then he says :

" I didn't stick around all the time like you said. I wanted to take a walk. It's goddam close around here. So I went out. I reckoned everything was O.K. She was here sittin' by the fire, smokin'. I stuck around the Maidenhead dump for a bit. When I started to come back she passed me in the car. This guy was inside it talkin' to her from the back seat. I reckoned this was Caution all right an' that dirty little so-an'-so was gonna sell us out. When I got back here she was in here. I asked her what the hell an' where he was. She said he was in the lavatory an' that if I'd got any sense I'd get outa this while the goin' was good. She tried to get over to her handbag

—where her gun was—while she was talkin', but I was too smart for her. I let her have it."

Kritsch says : " So you let her have it, you goddam lug. You haveta start somethin' that maybe nobody can finish off properly. There ain't been a killin' in this goddam job yet that could be traced to this mob an' you have to pull one, you bughouse bastard. Why the hell don't you do what I tell you an' leave the thinkin' to me ? "

The other guy looks at the floor. He says :

" I'm sorry, Willie. . . . I sorta thought she ought to have it . . . so I creased her . . . the lousy squealer."

Kritsch shrugs his shoulders.

He says :

" Frisco . . . meet Mister Caution, the big ' G ' man. He gotta bit fresh so I smashed his pan a bit with the rod. Maybe I put his jaw on the slant. Go an' put it right, pal, will you ? "

" Sure," says Frisco. He comes over an' stands in front of me. He says : " Boss . . . it would give me a big thrill to kick this smart guy in the guts. How about it ? Maybe he wouldn't even squirm."

" No," says Willie. " You might croak him an' I wouldn't have that . . . not yet awhile. Mister Caution an' me have gotta do a little talkin' before he leaves us. So just attend to that jaw, Frisco, an' leave it at that."

Frisco steps back an' swings one. He is not worryin' very much about me because Kritsch, lollin' back in the chair, is holdin' the Mauser on me, smilin' nice an' pleasant

I am gettin' to be very angry with these two guys. An' I time Frisco's swing very nicely. As his arm starts comin' back I do a quick side-step that brings him between Kritsch an' me. I drop my head just as his fist misses, an' bring my knee up with a sweet jerk right into his guts nice an' low down. He gives

149

a funny sort of yelp, then he drops an' starts rollin' about on the carpet. He makes animal noises for a minute an' then passes out.

Kritsch starts laughin'. He gets up an' gives himself another drink. But he never takes his eyes off me.

" That was a neat one," he says. " Sweet work." He laughs some more. " I only hope I'll be around when Frisco goes inta action on you. I reckon he will think up some sweet ones for you, pal. I reckon it's gonna be goddam funny watchin' just what that mug does to you."

" That's O.K. by me," I tell him. " Anyhow, whatever he's goin' to do to me it won't alter what I done to him. He don't look so good, does he ? "

" Not very," he says. " Maybe you croaked him." He yawns. " I've known a guy to be croaked by a kick like that before now," he says. He gives a big grin an' shows a set of very nice white teeth. " It would be goddam funny if Frisco was to get himself croaked by a short kick in the guts handed out to him by a guy who was stood up at the time . . . hey, Frisco ? "

Frisco don't say anything. He is still lyin' doubled up. His face is a sorta yellow colour. He is breathin' so hard that you would think he might burst.

Kritsch brings out a gold cigarette case. He takes out a cigarette an' lights it. I notice it is a slim, brown weed just like the ones I saw in Montana's case . . . an' the case is the same shape an' hers was gold too. I reckon both Willie an' Montana smoke *marihuana*. So maybe there was something in what Carlette thought. Maybe he *is* stuck on Montana.

He draws the smoke down inta his lungs. When he blows it out I can smell the acrid stink of a reefer.

He says : " So Carlette talked. . . . I always thought that goddam little tramp's mouth was too big. An' she scared easy. How much did she talk, pal ? "

150

" Plenty," I tell him. " She gave me the works.
She blew the whole goddam bezusus. She put the
whole thing in the bag."

" You're a liar," he says. His voice is nice an'
pleasant. " You wasn't here with her long enough. I
don't believe she gave you a goddam thing. Maybe
she hadn't even time to give you a drink."

" I ain't arguin' with you, you cheap love-child,"
I tell him. " I know what she blew an' what she didn't.
I'm wise to you an' Panzetti, an' whichever way you
play it you're gonna get it. An' you can laugh that
one off."

He says : " Maybe . . . but I ain't decided which
way I'm gonna play it except I know one thing. Whatever I do I'm goin' to see that you get yours . . . an'
just the way I want you to have it."

I shrug my shoulders.

" So what ? " I tell him. " What you do to me don't
make any difference to what is gonna happen to you.
So you get ahead, punk. Another thing," I tell him,
" you make me laugh. Besides which you want
disinfectin'."

He grins. The guy on the floor begins to stir. He
makes a moanin' noise. Kritsch gets up an' takes the
Bourbon bottle over to him. He slops some of the
spirit over his face an' then sticks the bottle neck in
his mouth an' tips it up.

Frisco starts to cough an' gag. He writhes about
for a bit an' then he opens his eyes.

" O.K., pal," Kritsch says to him. " Take it nice
an' easy. You got a lot of time. An' try not to be
sick on the carpet. It ain't polite."

He leaves the bottle on the carpet by the side of
Frisco an' goes back to the chair.

He says :

" It ain't quite so good about Carlette. I reckon
that mug Frisco is nutty to do a thing like that. It

151

sorta messes things up a bit. Still I'll think up somethin'." He shrugs his shoulders an' grins at me.
" Anyhow, it was about time Carlette got hers," he
says. " I was gettin' tired of that baby." He grins
some more. " If you'd like to walk over to the wagon
an' clean your face off with some cold water, get
ahead," he says. " Only we got a swell dame comin'
here in a minute an' I wouldn't like her to meet up
with a Federal officer with a mussed up face. An'
have a drink while you're there."

I walk over to the wagon an' soak my handkerchief
in the cold water. I clean off my face. While I am
doin' it I take a look at him but I can see that there
is no chance of startin' anything.

I walk back to the fireplace. Frisco is beginnin' to
pull himself together. He is lyin' on his side an' he
takes a long look at me. I reckon he is thinkin' just
what he is gonna do to me.

Kritsch says : " Frisco, you're gettin' soft. Any
time somebody gives you a kick in the guts these days
you wanna take a lot of time out to think about
it. An' there's quite a lot to be fixed in the next
half-hour. So just get on your hind legs an' go
get that dame. Bring her in here. I wanna talk to
her."

" What dame is this ? " I ask him.

" The one you was lookin' for," he says. " Varney
is the name." He gives a very long, slow grin. I
reckon the devil musta looked like that some time. He
says : " This dame is a very good-lookin' dame an' I
was thinkin' that we might sorta use her to make you
talk. I got an idea I wanna find out just what Carlette
did put you on to."

" Don't make me laugh," I tell him. " Do you
think that you can make me talk if I don't wanta
talk."

" Yeah," he says. " When you see what I'm gonna

let Frisco do to that dame if you *don't* talk you'll change your mind, pal, see ? "

Frisco has got up to his feet. He stands there swayin' about for a minute an' then he starts in my direction. He is not lookin' very kind.

" Nothin' doin', pal," Kritsch says to him. " You can leave him till later. I'll let you have a turn soon. But right now you can take it out of the dame. Go an' get her."

Frisco turns around an' ambles outa the room. Kritsch is sittin' in the chair spinnin' the gun on his finger. After a bit he says :

" It's maybe tough for you that Frisco bumped that doll." He throws a look over his shoulder. " If he had laid off her until I come back maybe we could all have done a little talkin'. As it is it don't look so good for you." He yawns. " When I get through with you I reckon I'm gonna have to fog you."

He stops talkin' for a minute an' sorta considers this for a bit. Then he goes on :

" I didn't want any killin' over here . . . at least not anythin' that *looked* like a killin', but I'm beginnin' to alter my opinion. Now that this silly jane has got herself creased maybe it's gonna be better if you get fogged too. I got a big idea about that. It's the sorta idea I get sometimes. It's swell." He gives a big yawn. " I'm gonna get Frisco to croak you," he says. " It's gonna work better that way. I reckon I don't want you stickin' around. I can't afford to have you around because maybe that doll Carlette squealed big enough for you to do some thinkin' on. But *I* ain't gonna do it." He gives me another sweet grin. " I'm gonna get Frisco to do it . . . like I said."

" So they can hang the rap on him," I say. " You're a sweet mobster, ain't you, Kritsch. You'd double-cross your own sister."

153

" Why not ? " he says. " Ain't it a sweet idea ?
Nobody knows me around here. When I've been here
I've stuck inside this dump. But they know Frisco
an' they know Carlette. They been in the bars an'
places around Maidenhead."

He puts the bottle neck in his mouth an' takes another
slug.

" When I bump a guy," he goes on, " I do it so's
I get away with it. I don't leave no strings untied.
Well . . . this job's easy. Carlette is creased by Frisco
an' when they do a post-mortem on her they're gonna
find the bullets came outa his gun." He gives another
big grin. " An' when they do a post-mortem on you
they're gonna find that the bullets in you come outa
Frisco's gun too. Then when the medical examiner
gets around to Frisco he finds that the bullets in *him*
come outa Carlette's gun. It's in her handbag over
there. An' so the cops are gonna reckon that Frisco
opened fire on you an' Carlette pulled a gun on him
an' shot him an' he shot her before he croaked. I just
take a quiet run-out powder an' nobody even knows
I was here tonight."

" You're a nice guy, Kritsch," I tell him. " So
you're gonna bump Frisco when the time comes.
Ain't you the pretty little mobster . . . ? "

" I'm not so bad," he says. " The scream is that
Frisco is sorta fond of me. Is that a yell or is it ? "

I don't say anythin'. Any time I take a look at this
guy I want to be sick.

An' I am not feelin' so good about Geralda. All
I hope is that when that Frisco bird starts tryin' to
bust into the garage she lets him have it where it'll hurt
plenty.

I take a sideways look at Kritsch. He is lyin' back
with his eyes half-closed but he is watchin' me underneath the lids. I reckon I can't pull anything with
this bird an' yet I've got to do something. Right

154

now I am the popular candidate for the local graveyard.

I stand there listenin'. I hope that dame gets away,
because you guys will have realised by now that this
Kritsch-Frisco combination is no sorta Friendly
Society. But at the same time there is a funny sort of
idea persistin' in the back of my head.

I reckon it is damn funny that Kritsch should be
so het up because Frisco has croaked Carlette. Why
should he care ? Well, there is only one reason an'
that is that Kritsch thought that he was goin' to carry
out his schemes over here—whatever they were—an'
get away with it an' keep his nose clean.

Work it out for yourself. They didn't mind puttin'
in Fratti to send me an' Geralda sky-high in the
Laurel Lawn dump at Hampstead because that
woulda looked like it was done by a German bomb,
but Kritsch didn't want any obvious bumpin' off
done, an' that is why he is aimin' to give it to Frisco.
He has the right idea about that. If the cops find
Carlette's body an' my body full of lead outa Frisco's
gun an' Frisco gets the heat from Carlette's rod, then
they're goin' to conclude that there's been a shootin'
match between those two with me as a stand-in an'
they ain't goin' to look for any other killer. This
leaves Willie Kritsch in the clear.

I am right in the middle of these deep thoughts
when the door busts open an' Frisco flops in. He
stands there in the doorway lookin' like somebody had
just told him that his pet canary was dead. There is
a sort of whinin' expression on his pan that makes him
look more like a dead fish than ever.

Kritsch looks at him sort of ominously. He says
nice an' quiet :

" So what ? Where's the doll, Frisco ? "

Frisco says : " She's beat it. That goddam frail
has got outa here. She's taken one of the cars. That

155

big heap of yours is gone. This goddam lug musta got the key offa Carlette. He musta . . ."

Kritsch says : " I thought I told you to stick to that key ? I thought I told you I was gonna hold you responsible for the Varney dame. What the hell's the matter with you, Bughouse ? "

Frisco don't say anything. I think this is where I get into this conversation.

" Listen, Frisco," I tell him. " You get an earful of this, you unconscious cow-head, because I reckon that this is one of the last things you are goin' to hear."

I take a quick look at Willie. He is lyin' back, lookin' at me with a half grin on his thin lips. This guy has certainly got his nerve. He don't even try to interrupt.

" While you was lookin' for the Varney piece," I go on, " I been talkin' to Willie here. He didn't want any shootin'. He didn't want Carlette creased the way you done it. This is what he is goin' to do. The bullets in that doll came outa your gun. So they'll know you killed her. Well, that cheap yellow bastard has just told me that after you've ironed me out he's goin' to crease you with her gun. See ? That plants all the evidence on you. You're goin' to stand for a double murder rap—after you're dead—while this moron gets away with a clean record. What's the matter with you ? Can't you even look after yourself, you cheap herrin' ? "

Frisco looks at Willie. Willie just smiles back nice an' easy. Frisco says to me :

" I reckon you're just a cheap lousy liar an' I'm gonna mash your face in."

Kritsch says : " Don't get steamed up, Frisco. The guy is just makin' things up, tryin' to find an out. It's understandable, ain't it ? "

Frisco grins.

"Sure," he says. "You oughta have let me mash him a little before. What do I do with him?"

Kritsch reaches for the bottle. He takes another short swig.

"Give it to him," he says. "An' let him have it in the belly. I wanta see that guy wriggle. He's been annoyin' me." He looks over at me an' he gives a dreamy sorta smile. "The last time Frisco an' me croaked a guy like that it was goddam funny," he says. He looks at Frisco. "Maybe you remember, pal?"

Frisco grins. He says yeah he remembers. He starts smilin' too. I look at 'em both. I reckon that here is the best two lousy murder guys that I have ever met up with. When these bozos decide to bump somebody they take a joy in their work. They get one helluva kick outa it.

Kritsch goes on: "We had some trouble with a palooka up in Oklahoma City," he says. "An' Frisco an' me decided that it was time somebody gave this mug the heat. So we made a date to meet up with him some place an' he comes along thinkin' that we're gonna buy him dinner. Then we tell him."

Frisco says: "Yeah . . . wasn't that a scream. You never saw a guy so surprised in your life. The guy was scared . . . he was . . ."

Kritsch busts in: "Close your trap, Frisco . . . I'm tellin' this story. Well . . . this guy gets scared an' so Frisco starts playin' games with him. He gives himself a good time. He tells this mug that if he likes to cash in he'll make it a quick job an' that if he don't he's gonna get it where it'll hurt a lot. So the guy starts offerin' Frisco all sorta goddam things. He tells him where he's got some dough hidden away an' one or two good bits of ice. So Frisco gets sorta avaricious. He thinks he can make this guy talk some more so he shoots him through the knee-cap. Then he tells the

157

sap that if he don't come across with some more
information about where he has got stuff he's gonna
shoot the other knee-cap off. Was that a scream or
was it, Frisco?"

"Yeah," says Frisco. "I nearly killed myself
laughin'."

"So at the end of all this," says Willie, stretchin'
himself, "this guy reckons that he is gonna be ironed
out quick, but he's wrong because Frisco gives it to
him in the belly, just an inch or two underneath the
navel where it hurts plenty an' we stuck around an'
drank Scotch an' watched this mug pass out. I'm
tellin' you it was goddam funny . . . hey, Frisco?"

Frisco says: "Yeah . . . it was a yell."

Me . . . I don't say anythin'. You guys can guess
that I am just dyin' with laughin' at this humour that
is goin' on around here.

"So you're gonna get it in the same way," says
Kritsch. "An' I hope you like it. Get busy, Frisco
. . . just hand it out to our pal here . . . nice an' easy.
Just one slug in the right spot."

He sprawls back in his chair.

"O.K.," says Frisco.

He is grinnin' like a Chinese idol. He puts his
hand in his coat for the rod.

The telephone bell starts janglin'.

Kritsch puts up his hand.

"Hold it, Frisco," he says. "Answer the phone."

I let my breath go. I am tellin' you guys that I
am not feelin' so good at this moment. There is too
much death an' kisses hangin' around this dump for
my likin'.

Frisco grabs the telephone. He listens. Then he
screws around at Willie like he had been poleaxed.

"Yeah," he says. "I got it. The police. O.K.
I'll tell Mr. Kritsch. Yeah . . . I'll tell him right now.
Just hold on, willya."

Kritsch don't bat an eyelid. He just says sorta soft :

" What the hell ? "

Frisco puts his hand over the transmitter.

" It's the cops," he says. " Maidenhead Police. They wanta speak to you personal. They know you're here. They wanta talk to you—somethin' to do with *him*." He stabs a dirty thumb in my direction. " What the . . ."

" Pipe down," says Kritsch. " Tell 'em I'm comin'."

He lounges over to the telephone. All the while he is lookin' at me over his shoulder, holdin' the gun on me. His hand is as steady as a rock.

" Yeah . . ." he says into the telephone. " Oh certainly. . . . Yeah, sure he's here. We was just talkin' a little business. Yeah . . . I'll tell him right now. He's just washin' his hands. Yeah, he'll be right over. . . ."

He hangs up. When he looks around he looks like about fourteen different devils all rolled into one. He stands there, with one shoulder droopin' an' the gun hangin' down by his side. He says to Frisco :

" You nuthouse carrion . . . I'd like to watch you roastin' ! Ain't you the clever bastard ? So you let that dame take a powder. So the clever red-headed bitch pinches my best car an' drives around to the cops. She tells 'em that Caution is here. She tells 'em that *I'm* here, you cheap goddam lug outa hell, an' she tells 'em that *you're* here. She asks 'em to ring through an' tell Caution that they've moved his car outa the road an' put it in the police park back of the station. They wanted to know if that was O.K. by him or if he wanted somebody to bring it around."

Frisco just looks at him. After a bit he mutters : " Jeez ! . . ."

" Yeah . . ." says Willie. " You just made a sweet

159

mess of the works this evenin', pal. You been really brilliant." His eyes start glitterin'. "You get outa here," he says. "Scram an' get the other car outa the garage an' bring it round front. When you've done that take Carlette's car an' get outa here. You know where to go to. An' don't make any mistakes this time or I'm gonna do somethin' to you. . . . Now get!"

Frisco don't say anything. He just gives me a long sorta disappointed look an' scrams. Willie lounges back to where he has left the bottle. He takes a drink an' throws it in the corner. It smashes up against the wall. He lights a cigarette. Then he turns around an' looks at me. He is still smilin'. He says:

"I reckon this is your night out. Through that goddam dame you get a break. One of these days maybe I'm gonna catch up with that baby when there ain't anybody around an' she's gonna pay plenty."

I grin at him.

"I bet you're feelin' sour, fella," I tell him. "She just bust up your little idea, didn't she? If you iron me out now you're plantin' your finger-marks on everything. If I don't show up to take my car away they'll come around here an' find Carlette. There'll be a wireless call out after you in no time. They'll knock you off before you've got ten yards."

He grins.

"They won't," he says. "Because you won't let 'em." He flops down in the chair. "You got some brains I've heard, Caution," he says, "an' so have I. I'm gonna get out of this nice an' easy. I'm gonna play it my way . . . see? An' you're gonna help me because you wanta play things your way. What didya come over here for? You came over here to get them blue-prints of the Whitaker bomber. You didn't come over here to pinch Frisco for foggin' that fool dame Carlette. But you ain't got anything on me. So far as

160

you're concerned I've kept my nose clean. . . ." He grins. " Officially, I mean . . . if you get me."

" Meanin' what ? " I ask him.

" Meanin' this," he says. " I'm gonna blow. But you ain't gonna put any cops on to me. Because if you do you won't ever see Elmer Whitaker alive an' you won't ever see them goddam plans. *I'm tellin' you.*"

" O.K.," I tell him. " So what . . . what about that ? " I point over to where Carlette is lyin'. He looks over an' shrugs his shoulders.

" I'll give the cops somethin' for that," he says. He starts smilin' again.

Frisco comes in.

" I took the heap around to the front," he says. " She's O.K. for gas an' water."

Willie says : " That's fine. Now you take Carlette's car an' get outa here. You know where to go. An' keep on the main London road. Don't try any clever stuff. An' get there as soon as you can. Scram, lug ! "

Frisco says : " Sure . . . so long, Willie."

He goes out.

Willie pulls a pair of drivin'-gloves out of his pocket. He puts the gun down in front of him an' starts pullin' the gloves on. He don't take his eyes off me. Outside I can hear the noise as Frisco starts up Carlette's car in the front of the house an' drives off.

Kritsch says : " Look, Caution. . . . You got a break tonight an' maybe it was lucky. Maybe I like it this way better too. You gotta deal with me an' you know it. You're the guy who always brings back what he went out for, ain't ya ? Well, you went out for them blue-prints, didn'tya ? I think you're a goddam sap. You won't get Whitaker an' you won't get the prints unless you cash in. Whitaker told you the way we want it played—the way it's gonna be

161

played. We want the cash on the line before you get
a smell of anything . . . see?

" Well . . . you'll get another chance. You're
gettin' it because I ain't ever had a killin' hung on to
me although I've croaked a few guys. I don't like
bein' mixed in killin's officially—if you get me. So
you get a break. You get a break just because that
goddam Varney doll had enough sense to play this so's
I showed in it." He grins. He looks like Satan in a
bad temper.

I stretch myself.

" Look, you lousy yellow heel," I tell him. " You
think you're doin' fine, don't you? You reckon you're
right on top of this job, but I ain't even worryin' about
you. You are such a small-time punk an' you are so
goddam crooked that any time you tried to think
straight you'd have a coupla fits. You're a swell guy
when you gotta gun or when you got that nuthouse
guy Frisco stringin' along with you to crease 'em while
you stick around an' watch. But you'll get yours all
right," I tell him. " An' I hope I'm around when the
big moment arrives."

" Hooey, Caution," he says. " You're dreamin'.
Besides which you oughta be very grateful to me for
not lettin' Frisco iron you out. Some of you guys are
never satisfied."

He gives a big laugh.

" I'm on my way," he says. " But before I scram
I wanta show you that I am a guy who is on the side
of law an' order." He twists up his mouth like the
joke was killin' him. " Get an earful of this. . . ."

He goes to the telephone. He says into it . . . nice
an' quiet :

" Operator, give me Police quick . . . Maidenhead
Police."

He twists around an' gives me a big smile. Then
he starts in again :

" Maidenhead Police. . . . This is Mr. Kritsch speaking from the Melander Club. I had an appointment
here tonight with Mr. Lemmy Caution of the F.B.I.
. . . you heard about him ? O.K. Well, Mr. Caution
has asked me to ring through to you an' tell you that
there's been a killin' around here. Yeah . . . some
dame called Carlette Lariat . . . Mr. Caution knows
her too. Well, the guy who done this has taken a
run-out on us. His name is Charles Paolo—he's
usually known as Frisco—yeah. . . . Well, this guy
can be picked up. He's drivin' a blue Ford sedan
CXT 3465. He's on the way to London now. . . .
You can get him easy. . . . Yeah . . . that's all. Mr.
Caution says he'll be glad if you'll get around here
in about fifteen minutes. He says he'll wait for
you."

He hangs up.

" I reckon I'm gettin' tired of that goddam Frisco,"
he says. " He always was a bum. They'll swing him
off for this ! Jeez . . . Will he be surprised when them
cops catch up with him. . . ."

He lights a cigarette.

" I'm on my way," he says. " Any time—providin'
it's soon—that you wanta get them blue-prints an'
collect Whitaker, you let me know. I'll sorta keep in
touch with you. An' don't try any funny ideas out.
I can get outa this goddam country any time I wanta
. . . see ? "

I don't say anything. I am thinking what I would
like to do to this guy.

He comes over an' stands in front of me. He says :
" Well . . . goodnight, pal. . . . I'll be seein' you."

He strolls over to Carlette's handbag an' puts it
under his arm.

" I noticed you eyein' this bag," he says. " Ever
since you knew she had a rod in it. I reckon you'da
given somethin' to be able to get your hooks on a gun

163

tonight. But this is one time when you've hadta take it an' like it.

"I'm goin' now," he says. "An' I'm gonna lock the door. If you wanta get out you can try, but by the time you make it I shall be well on my way. An' when them coppers get here you can give 'em my best wishes."

He steps backwards to the door, keepin' the gun on me. He fumbles for the handle, finds it, opens the door behind him an' eases out. I hear the key turn in the lock.

I take out my pack of Lucky Strikes an' light one. Then I go over to the drink wagon an' find a half bottle of gin. I take a long drink. I reckon I need one.

2

It is still rainin' when the Divisional Detective-Inspector—the guy who has come over from Slough to take a look at the Carlette killin'—an' me scram out of the Melander Club an' go back to the police headquarters at Maidenhead.

I have not told this guy too much. I have kept the Willie Kritsch angles under my hat because, anyhow, Frisco has been picked up an' charged with the killin', an' I reckon I do not want to get any wires mixed. The D.D.I. has been through to Scotland Yard an' they have given him the O.K. on me an' so everything is under control.

Walkin' through the rain I grin to myself when I think of the police car slidin' up against Frisco's car as he was rollin' along to London an' pinchin' him on a murder rap. Well . . . that is one rat outa the way.

When we get to police headquarters the D.D.I. asks me if there is anything he can do for me. I tell

164

him yes there is two things. First of all I want a word on the telephone with Herrick an' secondly I would like to know how long he reckons it would take a dame to drive from Maidenhead to Burghclere. He has a look at the map an' he says that allowin' for the fact that the night is a dark one without any moon an' that there is no road lightin' an' no headlamps, he reckons that it is goin' to take anybody a good two hours to do it—especially if they don't know the road.

I do a little calculation. I reckon that it was about an hour ago that Geralda bust outa the Melander Club an' scrammed. Allowin' for the time that she spent in the police station tellin' 'em to get through to Kritsch about the car—which was a sweet piece of work—I don't reckon that she has got to Reading yet.

" O.K., chief," I tell him. " Well, here is what I would like done. I reckon that the dame who came into the police station here an' got the sergeant to call through to the Melander Club, headed for Burghclere directly she went. I want that baby picked up. I reckon that if you could get through to the Reading police an' ask them to put a car out an' pick her up I would be glad. I don't want her arrested or anything but I want 'em to keep her there until I get along an' have a little talk with her."

I give him a description of Geralda an' I also tell him what the car was like. He says that this will be O.K. an' that if she's got through Reading they can get on the line to the Newbury police an' have her picked up there. He says it will be easy about stoppin' her without makin' an arrest an' that they can hold her to be questioned by me under the Defence of the Realm Act an' that when I am through with her I can either let her go or ask the police to return her to London.

165

I say thanks a lot but I would like to make up my mind about that after I have talked to her. He goes off to fix all this an' I wait for the call to Herrick to come through.

Sittin' there, in the Station Inspector's room, drinkin' a cup of tea an' smokin' a cigarette, I do some heavy thinkin' about the guy Kritsch.

You gotta hand it to that guy. He has got a sweet nerve. Beyond that he is just a cheap, yellow sonofabitch that is out for what he wants an' don't give two shakes in hell how he gets it.

But I sorta feel that the boyo has got something up his sleeve. He ain't worryin' very much. An' he ought to be worryin'. Even though he reckons that this Whitaker blue-print business is so important that a murder or two—especially when it is a mobster's doll that gets fogged—don't matter so much, he still oughta be worryin'. An' the only reason that he don't give a cuss is that he has got an idea at the back of his head that he is goin' to get away with this business and this can only mean one thing.

It means that Willie has got somethin' hot up his sleeve an' I reckon I got an idea what it is. He figures things out like this. He reckons that nobody is goin' to worry about pinchin' him as an accessory to the Carlette killin' because he is too big a bird. He knows that both the U.S. an' the British Governments have got to have the Whitaker Dive-Bomber an' they are not goin' to let anything stand in the way of their gettin' it. He knows that if the worst comes to the worst they will pay the 250,000 dollars for the plans.

But even then they ain't goin' to be so pleased with Willie. When they have got the plans they're goin' to try an' wipe up just as many of the Panzetti mob as they can get their fingers on. Even if they have promised 'em a safe conduct outa the country.

166

But Willie is still not worryin' because he *knows* he is goin' to be able to make a getaway. The whole job has been so well fixed that he thinks nobody can upset it an' that is why he is not worryin'.

That is one thing I am thinkin' about an' the other thing is Geralda.

This babe is cute all right. When they was handin' out brains that doll was standin' right in the front row. Look at the way she has handled this business tonight. First of all, just when I heard that noise that made me scram outa the garage an' go back into the house an' run into Willie Kritsch, she was gettin' good an' annoyed with me. She sorta indicated that I was a fool. Why? Well, I know why if you don't. She thinks I am a mug because the guy I was talkin' to at Burghclere, the guy I found spreadeagled on the table *was* Whitaker! She knew that directly I described the bozo.

So right away she starts plannin' a big rescue act. All she wants to do is to get along up to Burghclere and rescue Whitaker, because—an' it is as plain as your ugly Aunt Lizzie—she is still stuck on that mug even if he does get around with other janes an' go rushin' about the place just because he gets scared. She is still for Whitaker hook, line an' sinker an' nothin' is goin' to stop her tryin' to get him away from the Panzetti bunch.

I reckon that directly I left her to go an' see what was goin' on in the house, she opened up the garage doors an' ran one of the cars out the back way. Then maybe she gumshoes back again, an' while Frisco is lookin' all over for her she comes back inta the house an' hears Willie Kritsch, who has by now got me on ice, givin' me the works an' tellin' me just what he is goin' to do to me. She don't like this at all so she aims to kill two birds with one stone. She scrams but stops off at the police station an' gets the station

167

sergeant to ring through about my car, knowin' that this will make Willie think plenty before him an' Frisco start any more killin'. After which she steps on it an' goes off to do the big rescue act with my gun in her mitt.

All of which will show you guys that this Geralda is a jane with character an' she has also got plenty of guts—especially where her boy friend Whitaker is concerned.

I reckon that Geralda is a dame with a will of her own. An' when a doll is like that you got to play her along easy, otherwise she goes off pop an' does something that is liable to upset the whole shootin' gallery.

I remember some frail I met up with in Witchita. She was a helluva jane. She had black hair an' black eyes an' a figure that looked like a serpent with nerve troubles. Except for the fact that she hadn't had her face lifted she mighta been your favourite film star. That baby was the berries.

She usta get around with a mobster an' when this mug got pinched an' thrown in the can for stickin' up a bank she crashes around to police headquarters an' tells one an' all that it was impossible for this bozo to have done the job because all the while he was with her in her apartment.

The police chief who is handlin' the case tells her that she is talkin' seven different kinds of hooey an' that everybody knows that it was her boy friend who heisted the bank. But she sticks to her story an' the District Attorney is gettin' worried because he reckons that if she gets up on the witness stand an' shows them legs of hers an' swings it a bit then the jury might not concentrate on the business in hand an' believe her an' acquit the mug.

So the D.A. asks me to take a hand in this business. So I stick my hat over one eye an' ease around to her

168

apartment. When I get in she is lyin' back on a couch in a black lace negligée lookin' like Desdemona three minutes before Othello put the half nelson on her. She has got about thirty-six inches of silk stockin' showin' just to cheer up the troops an' every time she looks at me she droops her eyelids an' looks at you like she was a cobra workin' out how to get a quick stranglehold on a rabbit.

I tell her that I don't want to waste a lot of her time but that the D.A. has told me that she is a witness for the defence because she says that the accused mug was with her at the time of the job. I tell her that she needn't worry because she won't have to appear in court because I know the guy never did the job at all, an' that I know it because when the bank was stuck up he was around at the Yelt Hotel with a blonde that I know very well personally, an' that this baby who is a very truthful jane has said with her hand on her heart that at the time of the stick-up this palooka was readin' a book called *True Tales of Passion* to her because she always had difficulty in gettin' off to sleep. So that everything is O.K. an' she needn't worry about anything at all.

After which she takes a jump in the air, uses some language that woulda made an old soldier look like Aunt Sissy an' says that she is goddamed if she is goin' to stand for havin' some other dame go into court an' make out that she is losin' her boy friends. She says that the blonde is a so-an'-so liar an' that she is puttin' up a fake alibi an' that it was impossible for the mug to be with *her* because at the time stated he was stickin' up the bank.

All of which will show you that the course of true love never did run smooth an' that you have only got to make a dame jealous an' she will take a bite at any-body—even her own boy friend—just as soon as sneeze.

169

But believe it or not this Geralda is goin' to be a very difficult proposition. First of all she is so stuck on this Whitaker guy that nothin' else matters, an' secondly she is not so pleased with me. Thirdly, she is liable to go off the handle at any minute in order to try an' rescue this mug Whitaker, which is a business that is liable to interfere with my own ideas.

I am just strugglin' with all these big thoughts when an officer comes in an' tells me that Herrick is on the telephone. When I get on the line I tell him that I am very sorry about havin' stood him up so much over this job but that things have been poppin' around here an' that I think I am not doin' so bad about it, an' that beyond nearly gettin' myself creased by the Frisco guy I am very well, an' full of bright ideas.

He says that this is O.K. by him, but that it looks as if I am usin' my old technique quite a lot an' that he hopes that I am not goin' to pull somethin' that is goin' to start a real *blitzkrieg* at Scotland Yard, an' that he will be very obliged to me if I will try an' be as orthodox in my methods as I can, an' what do I propose to do now because he would like to know. He says the only information he has got up to the moment is that Carlette Francini has got herself killed an' that Frisco has been pulled in for it.

I tell him that he should not worry a lot. I also tell him that it is very difficult for me to be orthodox when some guy is tryin' to shoot me in the belly an' that just as soon as I can get through with one or two angles that I am on I will have a long conference with him an' get things straightened out.

I then ask him if he has had any reply to the Trans-atlantic call I asked him to put through to Head-quarters in Washington askin' them for the last known whereabouts of Carlo Panzetti. He says yes, the reply is through an' that they say that Panzetti is in Chicago an' has been there for the last four months without movin' outa the city.

This gives me a big grin because I had an idea that this is the way it was.

" O.K., Herrick," I tell him. " Now there is just one little thing that you can do for me. Can you rush a wireless or a telephone call across to Washington good an' quick ? "

He says he will do his best an' what is the message.

I tell him to get himself a piece of paper an' write it down. I give it to him. Here it is :

" *To Director Federal Bureau of Investigation, Department of Justice, Washington, U.S.A. Urgent.*

" *Request immediate arrest of Carlo Panzetti stop Arrest on charge of attempted sale of U.S. Navy Department Whitaker Dive-Bomber plans. Suggest that Carlette Francini has squealed complete story. Threaten life sentence unless Panzetti produces and hands over uncompleted blue-prints of Dive-Bomber in his possession. Please inform me results immediately.*

" *Caution.*"

Herrick says he will get this off over the U.S. Embassy wire just as soon as he can make it. He wants to know when he is goin' to see me for a conference an' I tell him that I reckon I will be around my dump some time midday tomorrow an' that I will telephone him.

I then hang up. I reckon this guy Herrick is a good guy an' that it is very tough on him that I have not been able to work in with him more than I have. But life is like that.

I go back to the Inspector's room an' the D.D.I. is waitin' for me. A message has just come through from the Reading police. They have picked up Geralda on

171

the Reading-Newbury road an' she is at the Police Station at Reading. They say they will keep her there until I show up. They also say that she is not very pleased.

I go off with the D.D.I. to his dump an' have one little shot of whisky an' a cigarette with him. I also borrow a fur coat from his wife, after which I grab my car outa the police car-park an' roll off.

Maybe I am beginnin' to see a little daylight.

CHAPTER SIX

I

BY THE TIME I get to Reading I have mapped out a sorta plan of campaign. This campaign is just monkey business but it looks to me like it might come off given a fair chance an' no interference.

It is nearly half-past three when I pull in an' it is doin' everything it can. It is rainin', tryin' to snow, an' it is so goddam cold that it would freeze the ears off a brass monkey. Just to make things a bit more comfortable there is a nice mist comin' up.

I do not know if you guys realise what is back of my mind, but if you do you will also see that from now on the main job looks like handling three people—Geralda, that lousy bastard Willie Kritsch an' Montana. I am not particularly worryin' about anybody else at the moment because I reckon that right now they don't matter.

Some guy tells me where the police station is an' I pull in there an' show my pass. The sergeant on duty takes me inta a back room an' there, sittin' over the fire, with a policeman's overcoat around her shoulders, is Geralda.

I give her a big grin. The sergeant guy scrams an' I go over to her an' stand lookin' down at her with the fur coat over my arm.

" Me . . . I am the thoughtful little fella," I tell her. " I reckoned that you'd be good an' cold after your drive here without any coat so I borrowed this for you."

173

She looks up at me like I was a piece of cheese. I'm tellin' you mugs that Geralda is not so pleased with me or anythin' else.

She says : " I suppose you're pleased with yourself. I suppose you think you've done something clever . . . you . . . you . . . moron. . . ."

" So I'm a moron, am I ? " I say. " An' if I am a moron what do you think you are ? Anyhow my intentions was good."

" The road to Hell is paved with good intentions," she says. " But I want to know why I am being kept here ? What law have I broken ? Or is this just another brilliant idea of Mr. Lemmy Caution, the famous ' G ' man ? "

I take out my cigarettes an' light one. All the while she is watchin' me under her long lashes.

Sittin' there, lookin' sideways at me, she is a picture. I'm tellin' you bozos that if this baby had lived in the time of Charles the Second, Sweet Nell of Old Drury would still be in the orange business an' there would be millions of dames named Geralda kickin' around. She is one hundred per cent plus an' when she is in a bad temper like she is now she looks better than ever. Me. . . . I think I am goin' to enjoy myself.

" Sure it was," I tell her. " But I am very grateful to you, Geralda, because I reckon that if you had not thought of that idea of gettin' the Maidenhead cops to call through to Kritsch just at the right minute, by now I would be nice an' dead, which is a thing I do not like. So I want to put it on record," I go on, " that with me you are the berries. Also you look so marvellous I could eat you."

She tosses her head.

" Think nothing of it," she says. " It evens things up. I was grateful to you for saving my life at the Hampstead place—even if you did rather spoil the gesture by . . ."

" Givin' you a smack on the tail-piece ? " I say.
" Well . . . I reckon that any dame is all the better
for a smack now an' again. But that was only a little
smack. Maybe one of these days I'll have to get
around to smackin' you properly."

" I dislike you," she says. " I think you are rather
cheap and fresh and coarse. . . ."

" Which makes me like a nice cod steak," I crack
back at her. " What I wanta say is . . ."

" I'm not interested in what you want to say," she
says. She is so goddam angry she can hardly speak.
" I want to know by what authority you have me
chased about the place by police cars and brought
here ? I suppose you guessed I was going to Burghclere."

I grin at her.

" Why don't you stop bein' a silly coot, Geralda ? "
I ask her. " Why don't you be your age an' get wise
to yourself ? Did you think I was such a mug as to
let you go playin' around at Burghclere ? What the
hell good did you think you was goin' to do around
there ? An' you wasn't such a silly little beanhead as
to think that you'd find Whitaker still there. Just go
on lookin' sweet, honey, and leave the thinkin' to
Lemmy."

" I can look after myself," she says. " Besides I had
a gun . . . *your* gun."

" Much good that woulda done you with that mob,"
I tell her. " They got one or two boys workin' for 'em
over here—Zokka, an' such like guys—who would
love to take you apart just to see what makes you tick.
All you gotta do is to go back to London an' be a
nice sensible jane an' not interfere."

" An' what about Elmer ? " she asks in a cold sorta
voice. " What about him ? Does nobody care ? "

" Why get excited about that angle ? " I ask her.
" They ain't goin' to do anything to Elmer—well, not

175

yet. That mug is their best bet. While they got him they're safe. They know durned well that we're not goin' to get too tough while they got Whitaker. Believe me, honey, you don't haveta get worried about that poor fish."

" He is not a poor fish," she says. " And why should you talk of him like that ? He's got more brains in his little finger than you have in your whole carcase. Elmer is a genius."

" A genius for gettin' himself in a tough spot maybe," I say. " But *I* think he is a mug."

" And I think *you* are a mug," she says. " Just imagine . . . you were down there with him—armed. You could have got him away. You didn't do it. Why ? "

" Because I didn't believe he was Whitaker," I tell her. " Work it out for yourself. I go down to that dump because of a story that is told me by Montana Kells, who is Panzetti's number one girl friend. Well, that story smelt from the moment she started to tell it to me. So naturally I think it is a frame. When I get down there an' meet this guy an' he says that the only thing to do is to cash in the dough, it looks like it's a clever little idea to get the dough an' then keep the real Whitaker."

" Well . . . you were wrong," she says. " Directly you described him I knew at once that it *was* Elmer. And you manhandled him, you knocked him about. You . . . you gorilla. . . ."

Her eyes fill up with tears. She looks so good I cannot take my eyes off her. I am beginnin' to wish that I was Elmer myself.

" If you'd done what he wanted you to do this business could all have been settled. *He* is the most important thing. And both of us want the Whitaker Dive-Bomber to go to Britain. But it seems to me that there is only one way to get it. You've got to

pay the money. They'll hold him to ransom until
you do, and if you try to arrest them they'll kill him
and then there will be nothing for any one."

"Don't you believe it, honey," I tell her. "We're
goin' to get the Dive-Bomber plans an' we're goin' to
get Elmer back safe an' then you can ask me to the
weddin' . . . that is if you've forgiven Elmer by that
time. . . ."

"What have I to forgive him for?" she says.

I raise my eyebrows.

"What about the late Carlette Francini?" I ask
her.

She looks at me. She says :

"Is she dead?"

"Yeah," I tell her. "One of Willie Kritsch's pals
fogged that dame just as she was about to spill everything. But you haven't answered my question. Haven't
you got to forgive Elmer for takin' a run-out powder
with that baby? Or do you like him gettin' around
with mobsters' frails?"

She shrugs her shoulders.

"How could *you* understand?" she says. "I'm
certain that there was *really* nothing between Elmer
and that woman. He's impulsive, that's all. He's
always been like that."

"That musta been nice for his ma," I tell her.
"But I still think Elmer is a punk. Just fancy, here is
a big inventor gets the pants scared off him because
a mob write him a threatenin' letter. So he takes a
run-out with a dame that they put in to take him for
a walk up the garden. O.K. An' then before he
scrams he writes you an' tells you that he is scrammin'.
What does he do that for? The answer is because he
is a punk."

Her eyes flash.

"You fool," she says. "How could *you* understand
a man like Elmer Whitaker? *I* know why he wrote.

177

He wrote me because he realised that he had made a fool of himself over this Francini woman. He hoped that I would forgive him. He hoped that I would come over here too. I am certain that he had already made up his mind to get away from her. He wanted me to be here but he was too proud to ask me to come. He just hoped I *would* come."

I give a big sigh.

" They christened that guy wrong," I tell her. " They oughta have called him ' Little Lord Fauntleroy.' . . ."

She interrupts.

" Why should I discuss it with you ? " she says. " What I should like to know is what you intend to do. *Something* must be done at once. I insist that every possible step is taken to rescue Elmer *and* the airplane plans—and quickly."

" Maybe," I tell her, " but it ain't goin' to be done by you rushin' down to the Burghclere dump in a car pinched from Willie Kritsch, wavin' my Luger about. That ain't goin' to get anybody any place. An', by the way, I'd like the Luger back. I'm sorta fond of that gun."

She brings it out from under the coat she has got around her an' I slip it back into my shoulder holster.

She says : " Well . . . what *are* you going to do ? Can't you think of *anything* ? I thought Special Agents were brilliant men."

I grin at her.

" They are," I tell her. " You'd be surprised if you knew how brilliant some of those guys are."

She throws me a quick look.

" It would be strange if *you* were," she says. " But perhaps it's not quite impossible. Half the time while you are talking to me I get a definite idea that you are thinking about something else. . . ."

" You're telling me," I say. " You don't know how

right you are, Geralda. All the time I am talkin' to you I am thinkin' that you are just the sort of dame that I have always been wantin' to meet up with. You got the whole issue beat. Me . . . I think that your hair sorta looks like it oughta look an' you walk the right way an' has anybody ever told you about the shape of your mouth ? "

I give a big sigh.

" One of these days," I go on, " when I got time you might remind me to tell you what I really think about you."

She don't say anything for a minute or two. Then she says :

" If you think so much of what I look like you might spend a little more time in thinking about getting Elmer back."

" An' what good is that goin' to do *me* ? " I ask her. " Elmer gets rescued an' I get a kick in the pants. Lady, you are too fond of that palooka."

" I admire his brain," she says.

" That's O.K. by me," I say. " An' I am very glad to hear that it is his brain you admire because that bozo has got a pan like a wet fish."

She don't say anything. She just sits there lookin' at the fire. She is leanin' forward a little an' I get to thinkin' that the guy who designed this baby's curves certainly knew his oats.

Suddenly she turns around and looks at me. There is a little smile playin' about her mouth. She says :

" Really you and I are somewhat alike, Mr. Caution. We are both people who know our minds and just what we want. We are both people who go out to get it. But surely you can understand my interest in Elmer Whitaker. Perhaps there *is* something maternal in it. Supposing he is weak and supposing he has been influenced by women ? He's just a child with a great brain."

179

"An' a big konk," I tell her. "I've never seen so much nose on any one guy's pan before . . . but maybe that's a sign of brains."

She don't take any notice of that one. She says :
"I want him to get the recognition he deserves. I want him to get the reward he has earned. Instead of which his life is in danger."

I don't say a word. Maybe this dame expects me to burst into tears because Elmer's life is in danger. Personally speakin' I would like to give Elmer a good kick in the pants.

She puts her hand on my arm. She says sorta soft :
"Mr. Caution. . . . I want you to know that in spite of the fact that I'm annoyed with your attitude about Elmer, I trust you. I believe that if you wanted to you could get him out of this mess and put him back where he belongs."

She gives a big sigh.

"If you could do that," she says, "I should be very grateful. . . ." She slings me a long sideways look that registers on me plenty."

I think for a minute. Then I say :
"Well . . . there might be a bargain in that. Supposin' I clear up this business about Elmer. Supposin' I bring you two together again. Supposin' I get those goddam blue-prints back. In other words supposin' I clean up all this business an' straighten everything out to your satisfaction. So what ? "

She smiles at me.

"I think there is nothing that I wouldn't do," she says. "But I don't believe you will ever get Elmer away from those people *alive*, unless they get the money. They are quite ruthless. They will stick at nothing. I think that unless you can persuade the Government here to give them the money they want quickly they will kill Elmer. And what then . . .?

Even supposing you catch them eventually, what good will it do ? "

I throw my cigarette stub in the fire an' light another one. While I am drawin' the smoke down into my lungs I am doin' some quick thinkin'. After a bit I say :

" Look, Geralda, between you an' me an' the gate-post I think you are right. I reckon that the only way we are goin' to get Elmer outa this mess an' get the blue-prints back is by cashin' in an' givin' these thugs what they want. But even if we do that there is one thing that frightens me."

She leans forward. Her eyes are bright. I can see I have got this baby really interested.

" What is it ? " she asks. " What are you afraid of ? "

" When I was talkin' to Whitaker down at the Burghclere dump," I tell her, " he told me one or two things. I didn't believe 'em then because I didn't believe he was Whitaker. But I do now. An' here is what I am scared of :

" Whitaker hasn't finished the blue-prints yet—not quite. He's left a bit undone—an important bit. The main parts of the blue-prints—the parts they have got —are no good without this last bit. You got that ? "

She nods her head. She is hangin' on every word I say.

" O.K.," I go on. " Well, supposin' we give 'em the dough right away. Supposin' we give it to Whitaker to take to them—which is what they told him we got to do. Well, they hand over the blue-prints—the parts that *are* completed—but we haven't got any guarantee that they're goin' to let Whitaker complete the un-finished part, an' we haven't got any guarantee that they're goin' to let him go, have we ? "

" No," she says. " I'm beginning to see what you mean."

" Supposin'," I go on, " havin' got the two hundred an' fifty thousand dollars, they decide that they are *not* goin' to play ball with us. Well, it's easy for 'em, ain't it ? They make Whitaker complete the blue-prints—an' don't tell me that they couldn't make him do it because, believe me, those guys have got ways of makin' people do anything—then when the whole thing is complete they bump little Elmer an' scram."

" Why should they do that ? " she asks. " What good would the blue-prints—even if they were completed—be to them ? "

" None at all, honey," I tell her. " But they'd be a helluva lot of good to the Germans."

" My God," she says. " I never thought of that. Of course. If they could get out of England they could sell the invention a second time—to the Germans."

" Right, baby," I say, " an' so we got to find a way of doin' this job that is goin' to show us a good chance of gettin' Whitaker an' the *complete* blue-prints when we pay over the dough."

She puts her hand on my arm.

" Perhaps I've misjudged you, Mr. Caution," she says. " Perhaps you aren't so unintelligent after all—in spite of the fact that you can be extremely annoying at times. . . ."

" Don't apologise, honey," I tell her. " You don't have to. I could annoy you all day an' not even notice it. An' don't call me Mr. Caution, because you are one of those dames that I always like to call me by my first name—that is when they ain't callin' me something worse."

" Very well," she says. " Well . . . Lemmy . . . Do you think the British Government will put up so much money ? Two hundred and fifty thousand dollars is a lot."

" Not in this war," I tell her. " Two hundred an'

fifty thousand dollars is under sixty thousand pounds. What the hell's that to a country that is spendin' nine or ten millions a day? I think that end of the job will be all right. I think if we can show the Government here that we are goin' to get the Whitaker Dive-Bomber they'll put up the dough fast enough."

"Very well then," she says. "Then we've got to find some way of making certain that when the money *is* paid we get the completed plans *and* Elmer. But is it possible to find a way? These gangsters have the whiphand. We've got to do what they want. We can't even argue with them."

I grin at her.

"Can't we?" I say. "Maybe we can't argue, but we don't wanta argue. What we want is an idea. An' I think I've got it."

"I see," she says. She throws me a quick smile. "And that's why you stopped me from going to Burghclere. You already had the idea, and I might have spoiled everything." She draws her chair closer to mine. "So you've a scheme," she says. "Wonderful. What is it?"

"Just a minute, honeybelle," I tell her. "Maybe you won't like the idea when you've heard it. Maybe it won't sound so good to you."

"Tell me what it is," she says.

"It's this," I tell her. "Up to tonight Panzetti an' Kritsch an' the rest of 'em had three things to bargain with. They had the completed portion of the blue-prints, they had Whitaker an' they had you. Now they've only got two things—the blue-prints an' Whitaker. *We've* got you."

"Yes . . ." she says. She looks puzzled.

"I'm goin' to propose to give you back to 'em," I tell her. "I'm goin' to suggest that the deal is done this way : I'll make contact with these mugs an' tell

183

'em that you're crazy about Whitaker an' that you want to know that the deal is goin' through straight —for his sake. So what we want is this : First of all Whitaker is to finish off the part of the blue-prints that he hasn't done yet. Directly he's done that they're to hand that part over to us. So they will be keepin' three-quarters of the prints an' we shall have the last bit.

"In return for this bit we give 'em *you* as security that we will see the rest of the deal through. See ? "

She lets her breath go.

"I see . . ." she says.

"All right," I go on. "Well, then the position is this. They've got three-quarters of the blue prints— which are no good to 'em, an' we've got one quarter which is no good to us. But now neither side can twist the other. We can't double-cross them because they are holdin' you an' Whitaker as hostages an' they can't double-cross us because we shall have the last quarter of the blue-prints and the rest of the plans are no good without that quarter.

"All right. Well, then we pay over the money. When we pay it over they return Whitaker an' you an' the blue-prints they've got, an' we give 'em the two hundred an' fifty thousand bucks an' let 'em go. An' if it works that way it'll be worth the money."

She nods her head.

"There's only one thing," she says. "Supposing they pretended to agree. How do we know when Elmer finishes off the blue-prints that they wouldn't photograph them or copy them before they were handed over to us ? "

"That's easy," I tell her. "The bargain would start with you goin' down an' meetin' Elmer at some place agreed an' taking him away until he had done the completion of the prints which you would bring straight back to us without them ever seein' it."

" But would they agree to that ? " she says. " They might say that when I returned to you with the print I might not go back to them."

" They needn't worry," I tell her. " They would still have Whitaker."

" Marvellous," she says. " The scheme is absolutely watertight. I think it's swell."

" All right," I tell her. " An' would you be prepared to go through with it ? "

She smiles at me.

" Try me," she says.

" O.K., I will," I say. I put my arm around her an' give her one helluva kiss. Does that baby struggle ? Does she try to get away ? She does not. No, Sir. She just *gives*. Oh boy . . . !

After a bit she says : " I didn't mean *that*. And you ought not to have done it. Elmer wouldn't like it ! "

I take a quick look at her. Her face is serious, but her eyes are laughin' like hell.

" Me . . . I do not get this Elmer business," I tell her. " I thought you was so stuck on that guy ? "

" I told you I admired his *brain*," she says. " And after all I think you're entitled to a little encouragement. You *are* trying to save Elmer." She throws me another of them sideways looks. " Of course, when I'm married to him, I probably shan't kiss anyone else."

I don't say anything. I think " probably " is a helluva good word.

" I get up. I reckon we got to get a move on.

" Come on, Geralda," I tell her. " We've got a job to do. Get inta this coat an' lets scram."

I put her into the fur coat that I borrowed off the D.D.I.'s wife at Reading. While I am helpin' her on with it I get a breath of the perfume she is wearin'. Well . . . I have met some scents and some scents but this scent is definitely *scent* if you get me. It sorta knocks you sideways without bein' obvious.

185

We say goodnight to the cops an' scram. I start up the car an' we roll off towards the London road.

After we have been drivin' for half an hour I take a look in the drivin' mirror an' behind me I see a black police car pacin' us about fifty yards in our rear.

I grin. I reckon that Herrick has told the cops that he don't want to lose me again.

An' believe it or not I don't blame him.

2

It is six o'clock when we get back to London. It is as black as a nigger but the rain has stopped an' the all-clear syrens are goin'. Me . . . I am so goddam tired that I can hardly see. Geralda is smokin' cigarettes one after the other to stop herself goin' to sleep, an' the petrol tank is nearly empty. We just made it.

I drive down to Geralda's hotel in the Strand an' park that baby. I tell her to stick around until she hears from me an' not try any more funny business. She says she won't.

" I'm leaving this to you from now on, Lemmy," she says. " And I hope you're going to pull it off."

I tell her not to worry, that I shall be seein' her, an' that my advice to her is to go to bed an' get rested up because I reckon she is goin' to have some work to do pretty soon.

Then I drive around to my apartment in Jermyn Street an' take a shower. I dress an' make myself a cup of coffee an' do some thinkin'.

Me . . . I am not feelin' too bad about this business right now. I have got a whole lot of ideas about it an' even if only half of 'em are right maybe I'm goin' to get some place.

I take one little swig at the rye bottle just to keep the germs away, after which I ease downstairs, get in the car an' roll around to the garage near Montana's dump—the place I got the car from. On the way there I am wonderin' what has happened to that chauffeur guy that I left under the table with the milk bottle. Maybe Montana took a look around there an' maybe she didn't. I hope she didn't.

I leave the car away down the block an' walk to the garage. The door downstairs is locked but I open it up with a skeleton key I got on my chain. I ease up the stairs an' go into the flat upstairs. Everything is as quiet as a morgue. I switch on the light an' go into the kitchen. I give a big sigh of relief because the chauffeur guy is still there.

He is asleep where I left him an' he has drunk all the milk. I reckon that mug must be pretty stiff by now.

I bend over him an' give him a good shake. He opens his eyes an' looks up at me. He calls me a very rude name.

I take out my pocket knife an' start cuttin' him loose. When I have done this I grab a chair an' sit down. I watch him while he rubs his wrists an' ankles an' tries to limber up.

" Well, pal . . . " I say. " An' how're you feelin'. Personally, I'm a bit surprised to find you here. I thought maybe Montana woulda taken a look around here an' cut you loose."

" You're a goddam liar," he says. " Why the hell should she come around here ? She knew you'd got the car an' she told me to scram. She thought I *had* scrammed. One of these days I'm gonna even up with you, smart guy."

" Oh yeah ? " I say. " Well, I reckon that you'll be a lot older than you are now before that time comes around. Me . . . I think you are a mug an' no ordinary mug either. Just a big double-gutted, god-dam outsize in mugs who can't see when he's bein'

187

used as a stooge an' to carry the baby when the time comes for the big boys to get out."

" What the hell do you mean by that ? " he says.

I tip my chair back an' put my hands in my pockets. I look at him an' grin. He is sittin' there by the table on his haunches, lookin' like hell an' devils.

" I mean just what I say, punk," I tell him. " You are just a big bonehead. When your Ma had you she woulda done better to have got herself a cheap radio set. It looks better than you do an' if you don't like the programme you can always turn it off."

" You don't say, wise guy," he says, sorta soft.

He gathers his legs underneath him an' gives a leap at me. He shoots himself offa that floor at me like somebody fired him out of a cannon.

I go with him. I let the chair go backwards because I know that about ten inches behind me is the wall, an' I bring up my knee just as he contacts. It hits him in the belly an' knocks the wind outa him. He falls offa me sideways an' as he is goin' I clock him a sweet one on the jaw just to show him that there is no ill-feelin'.

I reckon that this guy is a mug all right. But this don't surprise me because I cannot see Montana havin' a mobster around her who was *not* a mug. I reckon that baby likes to be the only one in the vicinity with brains.

He lays where he has fell. He is breathin' in an' out like an old whale that has come up for air. I tilt the chair back, get up, an' go through the pockets of his livery coat. In the top right hand pocket I find a leather wallet. Inside it is an American passport, some English notes an' some American dollar notes.

I take a look at the passport. When I see the name on it I give a grin. The name is Guilio Paolo. So it looks to me that the boy is a first-generation wop an' I

have got myself a lot of medals for handlin' punks like
this.

I put my hand in his collar an' yank him up. Then
I trundle him into the sittin' room an' throw him in an
armchair. I sit down in the chair opposite him an'
light myself a cigarette. I give him plenty of time to
get his wind an' get settled down. Then I start in on
him.

"Look, punk," I tell him. "The time has come
when you an' me had better have a little straight talk,
an' I ain't even particularly interested if you don't
listen. If you *do* like to open them windmill-sails you
call ears an' take in the pearls of wisdom that I am
about to drop maybe you will do yourself a good turn.
But if you wanta go to sleep you go. Why should I
worry if in ten or fifteen years' time you are rottin'
around in one of these prisons they got over here—
Portland or Maidstone or wherever it is they send the
hard cases to—because that is what is goin' to happen
to you an' believe it or not they are very tough with
cons over here. You can't buy a goddam thing an'
you can't bribe anybody an' there is no parole boards
an' just sweet nothin' at all. So now you know."

He puts on a big sneer.

"Tryin' to scare me, hey?" he says. "Well, you
try some more, you lousy gumshoein' dick. You ain't
got anythin' on me an' you can go jump in the lake so
far as I am concerned. You make me sick."

"I'll make you plenty sick before I'm through with
you," I tell him. "But you just relax for a minute,
sourpuss, an' listen to me. I'm goin' to tell you a
little story. I'm goin' to tell you why you're so goddam cocksure of yourself."

"You don't say?" he says. "All right—go ahead.
Maybe this is gonna be funny."

"Look," I tell him. "Any time when I find a
crook as fresh as you are I always reckon that the mug

189

thinks he has got somethin' up his sleeve. He thinks he has got an out. Like you think you got an out.

" Boneheads like you are always easy to make suckers out of," I go on. " Just like Panzetti an' Montana an' Willie Kritsch are goin' to make a sucker outa you."

He gives another sneer. But it ain't a good sneer. It looks to me like I have started to register on this guy.

" Oh yeah ! " he says. " An' how are they gonna do that ? "

" They're goin' to drop you over when the time comes," I tell him. " They're goin' to ditch you as sure as God made little green apples. An' why the hell should they do anythin' else ? "

I lean forward an' put the fluence on him.

" Look, unconscious," I tell him. " I ain't a mind-reader but I'll bet you half a year's pay that I'm on to your end of this job. You are just a small-time mobster an' you was brought over here by Montana to act as chauffeur an' general stooge. They got you a passport. They been payin' you well. I reckon you liked the idea of comin' over an' makin' yourself a slice of dough.

" All right . . . well, you know what the game is. You know goddam well that these boyos are stickin' up the Government here for some big money for the Whitaker plans, an' you think they are goin' to get away with it. An' you think that when the deal's done you're goin' to get a nice piece of jack.

" An' you ain't even got to worry about a getaway. Because you know that is all arranged. You know just as well as they do that if the Government an' the cops here could pinch the lot of you *after* they'd bought the blue-prints offa you they would do it. But you ain't worryin' about that. Panzetti an' Montana an' Kritsch have got such a perfect getaway planned that you know everythin' is goin' to be just too perfect. So that's why you ain't worryin' about anything much.

" But you're makin' a very big mistake. An' you
ain't the first guy to make it either. Another guy in
this mob made the same error as you're makin'. . . ."
He starts gettin' interested. He says :
" What guy an' what error ? I don't know what the
hell you're talkin' about."
" You will," I tell him. " Listen, pal," I go on,
" your name's Paolo. Well, there was another guy
playin' around with this mob. His name was Paolo
too. They usta call him Frisco. Maybe that guy is
your brother, hey ? You got the same sorta konk that
looks as if it's been hit by a flatiron an' knocked up-
wards. Maybe that guy is a relation of yours. . . ."
He looks serious.
" Well, what about him ? " he says. " Supposin'
he is ? "
I shrug my shoulders.
" Listen, sourpuss," I say. " I reckon you might as
well order yourself a nice funeral casket because you're
gonna need one before you're much older. Willie
Kritsch has had Frisco knocked off. The cops have
got him on a murder rap."
His eyes pop.
" Like hell . . ." he says. " You're bluffin'. You're
workin' the old game. . . ."
" All right," I say. " If I'm bluffin' I'll take you
along to see him. Maybe you'd like to feed him buns
between the bars."
He says : " Why the hell should Kritsch want
Frisco knocked off ? What the hell is all this you are
tryin' to pull on me ? "
" I ain't pullin' a thing," I tell him. " I don't have
to. You are the guy who has got to try an' pull something if you wanta keep all in one piece. Work it out
for yourself. . . ."
I do some quick guessin'. I put two an' two together
an' let him have it.

191

"You know how it was," I tell him. "It was all fixed that Frisco should stick around at the Melander Club at Maidenhead with Carlette Francini an' this Geralda Varney dame. O.K. Well, I put through a phoney call an' got Carlette outa the place. She came to meet me. She'd made up her mind to squeal because she reckoned it was the only thing she could do.

"Well, Frisco had gone out for a walk an' I suppose Carlette thought he would be around some bar or somewhere an' wouldn't be back. She made a mistake. Frisco saw her meet up with me an' he followed the car back on foot. When he arrives I am outa the way, talkin' to the Varney dame, an' Carlette tells him that I am in the lavatory. She's stallin' for time . . . see? Frisco smells a rat an' when she goes for her handbag where he knows she has got a rod he fogs her. Later on Willie shows up. Willie don't like this set-up a bit an' he reckons that he's goin' to give me the heat too. But he can't make it because the cops get through to the house askin' after me. So he decides to call it a day.

"So what does he do? He tells Frisco to get out an' drive up to London, an' when he has scrammed, Willie gets through to the Maidenhead Police an' reports the Carlette killin'. Not only does he do that but he tells 'em that Frisco pulled it an' he also tells where they can pick him up.

"A clever mug, hey? He knows goddam well that the cops are goin' to have somebody for that killin' so he gives 'em Frisco. He thinks that leaves him in the clear to complete this deal. See?"

He don't say a word. He just sits there lookin' straight in front of him. I can see that I have definitely registered on this guy.

"Well . . . what d'ya think they're goin' to do with you, you big half-wit?" I ask him. "They handed Frisco over to the cops an' Frisco is goin' to swing for creasin' Carlette—you can take that from me. So how're they goin' to think about you ? They'll know you'll find out about it some time. They'll know you won't be so pleased ; that when you find your brother Frisco is goin' to be jumpin' around on the end of a rope maybe you'll get annoyed an' start something. Well . . . are they goin' to risk that ? An' if they ain't, what are they goin' to do ? They'll crease you like Carlette was creased. They won't take a chance on you. An' how d'ya like that ? "

He says : " Jeez . . . that lousy Kritsch. What am I gonna do to him for that ? "

" You ain't goin' to do a thing," I tell him. " The only way you're gonna play this business is the way *I* want it played. So you can make up your mind here an' now just what you're goin' to do."

" What's the choice ? " he says.

" If you don't like my proposition," I tell him, " I'm gonna hand you over to the cops now an' have you thrown in the can. They got about nine hundred charges under the Defence of the Realm Act they can hold you under. An' I'm goin' to make it my business to see that you get a sweet sentence when the time comes. But if you like to play it my way maybe I'll give you a break. Maybe I'll fix it for you."

" How do I know you'll fix it ? How do I know you won't walk out on me ? "

" You don't know," I tell him. " You got to take a chance on that."

He gets up an' he walks over to the window. He pulls the blind on one side an' looks out. It is gettin' light now an' it as cold as hell.

He turns around.

" You wasn't stringin' me along about Frisco ? " he says. " That stuff you gave me was the real works ? "

" Yeah," I tell him. " But you don't haveta believe it. If you wanta come along to Cannon Row you'll find

193

Frisco in a cell an' he can tell you himself. That guy will be swung off before three months have gone. They got a quick way with killers in this country."

He comes away from the window. He stands lookin' at me with his hands in his breeches pockets. There is a big bruise on his jaw where I clocked him.

He says : " I'm gonna take a chance on you. I'm gonna play this your way. An' you gotta give me a deal when the time comes. . . ."

" That's O.K.," I tell him. " But let me give you a tip. Don't try any double-crossin' acts. They won't get you no place."

He says : " I'm on the level. Me. . . . I was sorta fond of that mug Frisco. I'm gonna get even with that bastard Kritsch for turnin' him in."

" O.K.," I say. " I always thought that louse Willie would be too goddam clever one day. I think you're bein' a wise guy."

He says : " What d'ya want me to do ? "

" You sit yourself down in that chair," I tell him, " an' smoke a cigarette an' open up them airplane-flaps you call ears."

He sits down. I give him a cigarette. I tell him what he's got to do.

3

It is eleven o'clock an' a nice, cold, sunny mornin' when Herrick arrives around at my apartment. I have had a hot shower, a four-finger shot of rye an' a big breakfast. Beyond the fact that I am good an' tired I am feelin' swell.

Herrick plants himself down in a chair beside the fire. He says :

" I got your telephone message an' came round right away." He gives me a rueful sorta grin. " The

Assistant Commissioner says he would be glad to know *something* about what's been going on."

He pulls out a pipe an' starts fillin' it.

" You're just a cuss, Lemmy," he says. " You just have to do everything off your own bat, don't you ? "

" Look, Herrick," I tell him. " It is not that way at all. Things just broke an' had to be played along. But I don't think we've got to worry. We're goin' to be O.K. We're goin' to get those Whitaker plans all right."

He raises his eyebrows.

" That means you know where Whitaker is," he says.

I shake my head.

" I don't know where he is right now," I tell him. " But I'm goin' to know."

" How're we going to get those plans ? " he asks.

" We're goin' to buy 'em," I tell him. " I've got it all fixed. We're goin' to pay 'em a quarter of a million dollars for the complete plans. . . ." I grin at him.

He looks as if he had been hit with a poleaxe.

" Am I dreaming ? " he says.

" Look, Herrick," I tell him. " You ain't dreamin'. This thing has just got to be played out my way an' you got to play ball. I got an idea that I wanta finish off this job without somebody gettin' their throat cut. So let's get down to cases."

" All right," he says. " Start from the beginning."

I get a bottle of whisky, a syphon and some cigarettes. Then I give him the works—the whole bag of tricks—right from the start.

4

At half past twelve I doll myself up in a very nice grey pin-head suit I have got, with a pale blue silk shirt an' navy tie an' I go visitin'.

I take a taxi an' roll around to Montana Kell's apartment. On the way round I am wonderin' whether I am goin' to find that baby there, or whether she has decided to take herself off some place. But I am layin' a slight shade of odds that she will be there because I have got a very definite idea as to how she is playin' her hand.

When I go into the dump I take a look at the indicator in the hall an' it says : " Miss Montana Kells—IN." I go up in the lift an' ring the bell. After a minute some neat package in a very tight black dress that is kind to her curves an' a lace apron asks me what I want. I tell her that I wanta talk to Miss Kells. She says she is not certain as to whether Miss Kells is in but that she will go an' see.

I tell her not to worry. I give the door a push an' go in. I tell the dame in the apron to scram an' I walk across the hallway an' open the door on the far side.

Montana is in all right. I have bust right inta her bedroom. She is sittin' in front of a swell mirror, wearin' a bad tempered expression, a brassière, pink silk french pants an' biege silk stockin's.

This outfit, combined with the fact that she is sportin' a pair of black patent court shoes with four-inch heels, makes her look like the front page of *La Vie Parisienne*, in the good old days when France was France an' not pretendin' to be a hick station on the Berlin-Rome main line.

She screws around an' takes a look at me.

"Well. . . . I'll be goddamed," she says. "If it ain't Mister Caution." She puts on an expression of injured innocence. "Say, can't I get any privacy around here?" she says. "This is my bedroom an' I'm a very particular dame when it comes to guys takin' a gander at my nether limbs by daylight."

"Look, delicious," I tell her. "I have seen dames in pink silk pants before. In fact I would go so far as to say that if all the pink silk pants I have seen was added up they would stretch twice around the world an' still leave a pair over for you to keep in your handbag."

"Yeah," she says. "I've heard about you. Just another tough copper. It's always the same story. The dame always pays."

"Don't you believe it," I tell her. "At least, not when the dame is *you.*"

I take off my overcoat an' put it, with my fedora, in the corner of the room. When I come back from doin' this Montana has inserted herself inta a crepe de chine lounging gown with a fur collar. Some of you guys may think this is modesty but don't get me wrong—this dame could still manage to show all the leg she wants even if she was dressed in armour.

"Are you wantin' somethin', Lemmy?" she says sorta sweet. "Or maybe you only come around to say thank you for the big tip-off I handed out to you. Maybe you went down an' saw Whitaker an' got everything fixed. An' what about a little drink, you big hero?"

"You got something there," I say.

She goes off to a cupboard an' comes back with glasses, a bottle of Scotch an' a syphon. She mixes the drinks an' hands one across to me. Then she sits back in the corner of the settee an' relaxes.

197

"Is anything wrong, honey?" she says. "You look sorta worried."

I shrug my shoulders.

"Believe it or not, Montana," I tell her. "I am plenty worried. I made one helluva big slip up. Me. . . . I feel like the village idiot only worse."

She puts her nose in the glass an' smells the liquor. She says :

"What didya do, big boy . . . tell auntie? It ain't like you to slip."

"Well I slipped," I tell her. "Plenty. I went down to that Burghclere dump an' saw Whitaker. When I got down there he was waitin' for me—trussed up like a chicken. But I thought it was a plant. I thought it was some guy they had put in to pretend to be Whitaker so I sorta messed up the situation."

She takes a drink.

"That wasn't like you," she says. "But maybe you didn't believe what I told you. Maybe you was tryin' to be *too* clever."

"Maybe," I say. "Anyhow that's how it was. So I scrammed outa there an' got myself inta a tough spot with Willie Kritsch at a dump called the Melander Club at Maidenhead. I got outa that all right but Carlette Francini got herself ironed out an' the cops have pinched some guy called Frisco on a murder charge."

"Life can be excitin', can't it?" she says sorta casual. "Did you see anything of the Geralda dame?"

"Yeah . . ." I tell her. "I brought her back with me. She's here in town, so that's something."

She nods. She comes over an' takes my glass an' fills it up again.

She says :

"So you're pretty well where you started. It's a

bit disappointin' . . . after I tried to help you all I could."

" Yeah . . ." I tell her. " That was the trouble . . . you helpin'. Naturally I didn't believe anything you told me. I expected the whole goddam thing was a plant."

" Jeez . . . ! " she says. " Can you beat that ? I was tryin' to do every goddam thing I could to help you. Tryin' to give you a break. All I hoped was that you would pull these mugs in an' then I should feel nice an' safe. Didn't I tell you how I wanted to get away from Panzetti an' . . ."

" Hooey," I tell her. " If you wanted to make a break, why didn't you ? What about that note I gave you to Herrick at Scotland Yard askin' him to get you outa the country ? Well . . . you ain't even tried to go. You're still stickin' around here powderin' your nose an' waitin' for . . . what ? "

" Well, I like that," she says. " There's gratitude for you. Never again will I do anything for a goddam copper so long as I live. I tried to help you because you know goddam well that I'm crazy about you. An' this is all the thanks I get.

" Another thing," she goes on, " I *was* goin' to get outa here. I was goin' today. I told the maid to get my things packed this afternoon an' then I was goin' down to Scotland Yard to see your pal Herrick an' arrange about gettin' back quick to the States before Panzetti. . . ."

" Bunk, Montana," I tell her. " You're talkin' hooey. I woulda paid some sweet dough to see you meanderin' down to Scotland Yard on them four-inch heels an' gettin' yourself chucked in the can."

" What the hell are you talkin' about ? " she says. " Why should they wanta throw me in the can ? "

" Because I called through to Herrick an' told him

199

to chuck you in the can any time you called around with that note," I tell her.

" Whoever told you that you could pull somethin' over me musta been nuts," I go on. " You are the original brown snake. You are so goddam cunnin' that one of these days you are goin' to double-cross yourself by mistake. All you got is a swell pair of legs, a figure that waves in the breeze, a pair of come-on eyes an' a look-me-over-kid-I'm-hard-to-get look. To me you are the most unconscious dame that ever tried to wriggle a pair of thirtyfour hips inta a size thirty wrap around. You are so goddam obvious that it positively hurts.

" Anytime I fall for a dame like you I hope that somebody will take me outside an' cut my head off quick because I would rather be tied up to a coupla wild alligators than get myself hitched on to you. So now you know . . . you female whip-snake, an' if you don't like it you can go fry an egg."

" You lousy gumshoein' dick ! " she hollers. " You right royal bastard. You heel. After I done what I've done for you an' told you. I was nutty about you— even if I did know you got yourself a crick in the neck through lookin' around at every dame you ever met up with . . . . An' this is the deal I get from you. Me, I would rather die four hundred an' fifty times than get within a mile of you. If I had you stickin' around me I'd take poison."

" If I was stickin' around with you I'd *give* you poison," I tell her. " Only it probably wouldn't act. You drunk so much hard liquor in your life that your stomach is probably armour plated. If I had my way I'd give you a Mills bomb for breakfast . . . after I'd pulled the pin out."

" Jeez . . ." she hisses. " Listen to that ! Me ! . . . I don't reckon I have ever been so insulted by a goddam copper in my life."

She comes over to me an' stands there lookin' down at me.

She is almost black in the face with rage.

" You half-witted love-child," she says. " What the hell do you think you're talkin' about? You are the sorta low-down cuss that plays around with a delicate an' sensitive dame like me, gets her to give a lotta information about her pals an' then under pretence of protectin' her has her thrown in the can. An' to think that I was stuck on you . . ." she raises her eyes up-wards. . . . " For chrissake," she says, " I was stuck on you. I coulda given you everything. There was nothin' I woulda kept back from you. . . ."

" Well, you ain't keepin' much back now," I tell her. " Because your dressin' gown is undone an' sittin' here is like bein' in the front row of the stalls at the strip tease festival."

I finish my drink.

" Take it easy, babe," I tell her. " I am wise to you. So let's start from the beginnin' an' try an' straighten things out."

" An' what the hell does that mean? " she howls. " What the . . ."

I get up. I pick her up an' carry her over to the settee. I drop her down on it an' I give her a good smack on the spot intended for same. She tries to give me a back-handed kick in the eye but it don't come off. I go back to my chair.

" Look, Desdemona," I tell her, " I am now goin' to give you some free advice an' if you got anything besides sponge cake in that head of yours you're goin' to listen."

She turns over an' sits up. She looks at me like a snake. Her eyes are gleamin' an' I reckon that if she coulda got her fingers on a rod she woulda fogged me as soon as look.

" All right," I go on. " First of all I would like to

201

inform you that for a clever dame you can be so goddam silly that you would make a lunatic look like an outsize brain guy. . . ."

" Yeah . . ." she says. " You're talkin' plenty, but you ain't sayin' much. I reckon this is just another of them bluffs of yours. I know you. You're tryin' to swing one on me but it ain't gonna come off. You . . ."

" Can it, sister," I tell her. " I am tryin' to swing nothin'. An' when I've said my piece you're gonna admit that I know what I'm talkin' about."

" First of all," I tell her, " you are such a goddam liar that you would make Ananias look like the winner of the Veracity Stakes. When you was pullin' that act on me just before I went rushin' off to Burghclere you told me you wanted to get away from Panzetti ; that you was frightened sick of that guy. An' the idea was that I was to wipe these boyos up an' get you back to America. Well, if you wanted to get away from Panzetti why go back to where he is ? You knew goddam well that Panzetti had never left the States. You knew goddam well that that mug has been sittin' on his backside in Chicago ; that he has never been near this country."

She opens her mouth to say something.

" Pipe down," I tell her, " an' don't make things worse than they are. All that stuff you told me about wantin' to get away from Panzetti was just so much apple sauce. What you wanted to do was to get back to that guy. So's you could go on workin' for him over there like you been workin' for him over here."

I light myself a cigarette an' take a look at her. She don't say anything. She is lying back on the settee, with her hand behind her head, lookin' at me sideways. I got the idea that she is thinkin' pretty hard too.

202

"Panzetti had Willie Kritsch an' some other guys planted over here," I go on. "They was planted here before Whitaker ever got near this place. Kritsch an' Frisco, Zokka an' probably one or two more. *You* was here too. Just to see that the mugs did their stuff an' didn't try any funny business. Am I right, baby?"

She throws me a big laugh.

"Go on," she says, puttin' on an act. "You interest me. I wouldn't stop you for worlds."

"Carlette Francini is left over there to find out what goes on after Whitaker has come over here," I say. "She finds out that I am gumshoein' around up in Kansas City tryin' to find this mug Whitaker. She also finds out that Whitaker has written a letter to Geralda Varney tellin' her that he is comin' over here. So she reckons that Geralda will come over an' she probably cables you to keep an eye open for her. She then sticks around an' tails me when I come over here. She fixes with Manders, the wireless officer on the *Florida,* who is workin' for the Germans, to pinch my papers so that Willie Kritsch can have 'em an' put an act on to Geralda that he is me.

"When I get here another of the boys is put in to stall me from goin' to Scotland Yard an' I am told a phoney story to get me up to that dump Laurel Lawn in Hampstead, the idea bein' that Geralda will also be sent along there an' that sap Fratti will come around an' blow the two of us an' the dump to hell.

"So it looks like Panzetti wants to get rid of me an' he wants to get rid of Geralda. As usual he is sittin' very nicely in the background, keepin' his nose clean an' with a cast-iron alibi. While all this is goin' on he is in Chicago an' so nobody can accuse him of anythin' that happens over here."

"You astound me," she says. "Ain't you the brainy guy!"

203

"I'm not so bad when I start tickin' over," I tell her. "Well . . . it don't come off. The Fratti business flops an' the next thing to do is to try somethin' else. But Kritsch thinks that he don't wanta have to iron me out. He don't wanta start any obvious killin' around here until he has got the big business settled. So I reckon that you an' him have a meetin' an' you decide that the thing to do is to play me for a sucker. You are to contact me an' tell me that you are sick of the whole business an' that you wanta get out. You are to tell me where Whitaker is—the idea bein' that when I get there that poor mug has been told just what to say if he wantsta save his own life an Geralda's as well. But I make a sap outa myself. I don't believe it is Whitaker so I miss a chance of doin' somethin'."

"Yeah?" she says. "An' if—mind you I said *if*—all this was true, what was you supposed to do?"

"I was supposed to cash in with the dough that Panzetti wants," I tell her. "An' when it had been paid over I reckon that you baskets woulda stuck on to Whitaker. You woulda kept him an' made him do another set of prints all over again. You'da sold 'em to the Jerries. In other words youda sold the whole issue *twice* an' we shoulda been left lookin' like somethin' that the cat has brought in."

"Nuts," she says. "Are you expectin' me to fall for this stuff? D'you mean to tell me that you an' the Government an' all the cops over here woulda been prepared to pay plenty for plans that had been got off a guy who'd been kidnapped? D'you expect me to believe that?"

I shrug my shoulders.

"What the hell is a quarter of a million dollars in a war like this?" I tell her. "Another thing is we can't afford to have anything happen to Whitaker. If Whitaker got bumped off one of the greatest air inventions is lost for ever. That's where Panzetti was clever. He knew we'd *got* to do business an' on his terms ; an' this is one of the reasons that I've kept the cops here outa this. I knew that if they started cavortin' around, Kritsch would probably make Whitaker finish off the prints, cut his throat, scram back to U.S. an' sell the stuff to the Jerries. That's why I been playin' this thing on my own like I have."

She says : " Well, you heel . . . if that's all that's worryin' you . . . it can still be played that way, can't it ? Except for one thing maybe."

" What thing ? " I ask her.

" Francini," she says. " Didn't you say that she'd been creased. What're the cops here goin' to do about that ? They ain't gonna let that go . . . are they ? "

I grin at her.

" That is where I got to hand one to Willie Kritsch," I tell her. " I don't like that guy but I got to admit that he's got brains. He handed 'em Frisco on a plate for that killin'. He rung the police up an' told 'em it was Frisco. They picked the mug up an' he'll swing for it an' so that's that."

She nods her head.

" You brown-eyed hell-cat," I say. " You wouldn't know anything about *that*, would you ? You wouldn't know a thing. Willie Kritsch hasn't been through an' told you all about it, has he ? "

I give her a big horse-laugh.

She says : " I don't know a goddam thing except what I wanta know. Believe it or not I'm stuck on you, Lemmy, an' all I wanta do is to help you."

" Honest ? " I say.

" Honest," she says.

" Boloney," I tell her. " Anytime I want to get some help from you I'll go throw myself down a pit filled with crocodiles instead."

"All right," she says. "Well, if you feel like that, what the hell are you doin' round here? You ain't got anything on me. You got a lotta theories but I don't care for theories, an' you can't do much with 'em. What's the big idea?"

"Listen, gorgeous," I tell her. "Even if you are so crooked that you would make a corkscrew look like the shortest distance between two points, there are moments when you got your uses. This is one of 'em."

"Strange," she says. "So you're actually gonna use me. How thrillin' . . ." she wriggles around an' looks at me. "What have I gotta do now," she says. "An' I hope it's somethin' I wouldn't mind bein' photographed."

"Well . . . here it is," I tell her. "Me . . . I know when I got to do a deal. Let's start off fresh. Let's see if we can't put this business through so that everybody is happy an' nobody else creased. Carlette's dead . . . but then Carlette was just another mobster's dame without too much brains.

"All right. . . . Panzetti wants a quarter of a million dollars. An' I don't mind payin' that providin' I'm goin' to get a square deal. But I got to know that I'm goin' to get a square deal an' I gotta know that Whitaker is goin' to be released an' not hurt or croaked or anythin' like that. In other words I've got to have some sorta guarantee."

"Yeah . . ." she says. "An' how're you goin' to get that?"

I take a look at her. This baby is lookin' pretty pleased with herself. An' maybe she's got a reason. She's a helluva looker an' she has got more brains than a snake. Montana is tough medicine, I'm tellin' you.

"I got an idea," I tell her. "I got an idea by which I know that I'm goin' to get a square deal

206

when the dough is paid over, an' you an' Kritsch an'
Panzetti know that you're goin' to get a square deal
an' get the money paid."

" I wish you wouldn't associate me with these
guys," she says. But she is grinnin' when she says it.
Flashin' her little white teeth an' generally enjoyin'
herself. This dame has got a sweet nerve, I'm tellin'
you.

" We don't wanta argue about that," I say. " I've
made arrangements to get that dough quick. All I
want is action. I want to get outa this country. I
wanta get back to the States with those plans in my
pocket an' Whitaker on the end of a string."

" So you got the dough," she says. " Well . . .
maybe you're wise to play it that way. Maybe those
mugs *are* clever too."

" Not forgettin' yourself," I crack at her.

" I never forget myself," she says. " O.K. Well,
what is the next move ? What do I have to do ? "

" I got to have a talk with Kritsch," I tell her. " I
got to get this thing straightened out. An' I got an
idea as to the way we can do it so that everybody's
pleased."

She looks at me for a long time ; then she says :

" Willie might think you're gonna make some funny
business with him. He might think you're goin' to
try a pinch or somethin'."

I shrug my shoulders.

" If he wants to think that I can't stop him," I say.
" But what's he worryin' about. How can I pinch
him. He's got Whitaker, ain't he ? "

She smiles at me. She looks like the cat that has
swallowed the canary.

" That's right, honey," she says. " So he has. An'
even if you did pinch Willie I reckon he would still
have somebody left to cut Whitaker's throat."

" Even if you had to do it yourself," I say.

She gives me a languid smile. Then she gets up an' stretches.

" So you want . . . what ? " she says.

" I want to meet Kritsch," I tell her. " I want to meet him an' get this thing fixed. An' so does he . . . an' so does Panzetti an' so do *you*."

" Yeah ? " she says. " Well . . . I'll see what I can do. You got a telephone number ? "

I write down my number on a piece of paper.

" I'm a generous sorta dame," she says. " I always do my best to help any guy who needs it. That's always been my trouble," she says. " I'm too generous . . . too yieldin'."

She picks up the piece of paper.

" I'll call through to you, Lemmy," she says. " Maybe I can do what you want. Maybe I'll be able to give you a ring tonight.

She comes over close to me. I can smell the scent she is wearin'.

" But you wouldn't try anythin' funny, would you ? " she says, sorta soft. " No monkey business ? "

" Do I look that sorta guy . . . ? " I say.

" Yeah . . ." she says, " you do . . . an' then some." She smiles at me. " But this time I don't think you can make any monkey business. It looks like for once somebody has got you where they want you . . . just for once. . . ."

She stands there lookin' at me. Her eyes are shinin'.

" Well," she says, " an' that's that. What're you goin' to do now, Lemmy ? "

" I'm goin' to scram," I tell her. " I owe myself some sleep."

She looks over at the bed. She locks her hands behind her neck an' takes a quick look at me.

" That's a swell bed," she says. " It's O.K. by me if you like to take a rest here."

208

"That's nice of you, pal," I tell her. "You're sweet, ain't you?"

"It's just the mother in me," she says. "Are you gonna stay?"

I pick up my coat.

"No thanks, honey," I tell her. "I am an old-fashioned guy. I'd just hate to wake up an' find somebody had cut my throat by mistake."

I ease over to the door.

"So long, lambie-pie," I tell her. "Don't do anything your mother wouldn't like an' don't get your feet wet."

"Nuts!" she says, but she is smilin' when she says it.

I scram.

I walk up into Regent Street an' chase around for ten minutes or so. I keep an eye open in case somebody is tailin' me. After a bit I take a cab down to Piccadilly. I pay off the cab an' go down into the subway. I find a telephone box an' call through to Herrick.

When he comes on the line he says: "Well . . . Lemmy . . . did she fall?"

"Did she?" I tell him. "She fell for it hook, line an' sinker. So all you got to do is to get that dough."

"Right," he says. "Is it to be English or American money?"

"Make it English," I tell him. "Maybe they'd like that better."

I hang up. I walk along to my dump in Jermyn Street an' go to bed. Lyin' there, lookin' at the ceilin' I get to thinkin' about some of the dames I have met on this job.

Carlette . . . who is no more . . . was just another little mug. Montana is pure poison . . . that dame is dangerous. And Geralda . . . there is a doll!

209

I roll over. There is one thing about a bed. It don't matter what trouble you get inta with dames you can always go to bed . . . by yourself I mean.

An' a bed will never let you down.

Not unless some baby has been tamperin' with the springs.

CHAPTER SEVEN

THE DAME ALWAYS PAYS

I

THERE ARE guys who do not like the business of sittin' around an' waitin' for something to happen. But I don't mind it. It sorta gives you time to think about things . . . an' dames. Thinkin' about dames has always been a hobby of mine an' it is an easy sorta thing to do an' not so risky as gettin' around with 'em.

There is a big fire in my apartment an' it is seven o'clock an' the rye tastes as good as rye always does. I sit back in my armchair an' do a little ponderin' about the dolls that have showed up in this business.

I reckon Carlette was a mug. She was the sorta mug that a big mobster like Panzetti always has hangin' around. She is a good-looker with a swell figure an' beyond that she ain't got anything. She is just one of them frails that get pushed around an' told what to do an' she does it. She spends most of her time wonderin' what is goin' to happen next an' tryin' to keep her nose clean. When something busts she is the sorta dame that the cops go for because her type is the type that always does a big squawk when it gets scared, after which somebody takes her for a ride for squealin' an' nobody gives a cuss.

The frail was just unlucky. But she was goin' to be unlucky anyhow. I don't reckon that Panzetti woulda let that baby go on livin' anyway. Maybe he woulda waited until she got back to the States an' then fanned her. She mighta guessed too much. In any event

I reckon that Carlette had it comin' an' if she got it a little time before it was due that was just too bad.

I get around to thinkin' about Montana. Here is a jane that has got somethin'. She has looks. She is tough an' she has got brains. She is the sorta dame that can string along with a guy like Panzetti without gettin' her throat cut. She is the sorta baby who carries a seven-inch knife stuck in her stockin' top just so's she can open anybody up who don't agree with her at any given moment.

She is the brain baby. I reckon Panzetti put her over here to keep an eye on things generally, but not to mix in enough to make anybody take a lot of notice of her. Willie Kritsch was the executive guy. He was the bozo who has to get things done while she sticks around as a sorta sleepin' partner—with one eye open.

Zokka, Frisco an' his brother Guilio Paolo an' Fratti—the guy who tried to blow the dump up at Hampstead—are all small-timers. Short-weight mobsters who think they are on the way to bein' big-shots, but who never get further than fetchin' an' carryin' with an occasional bump-off thrown in just to keep 'em from gettin' stale.

But the interestin' thing is that Panzetti musta done some very nice organisation. He musta known what he was about. Gettin' this bunch over here an' organisin' 'em was nice work especially, when you got a bunch of first generation wops to handle, because all this bunch are half Italian—even if they are graded as American citizens.

Then there is Geralda. I start smilin' to myself when I think of this dame. I think Geralda is cute. Maybe she's a bit nutty to be stuck on this Whitaker guy, but then all the best dames are a bit nutty about somethin' . . . or they *say* they are.

I remember a bozo I knew up in Laminton, Pa. This guy was about seventy years of age an' had got himself married about eight times to different dames. The older he got the younger they got. The last time he got married he hitched himself up to some swell baby of twenty-five who had already divorced four husbands an' was still lookin' around an' sighin' for love.

He says that this is his most successful marriage an' that the dame is nutty about him an' when I ask him what it is he's got that keeps 'em so sweet he says that he always let's 'em have a hobby to keep 'em occupied an' that if their minds are sorta busy they don't get time to get bored with life.

I say that this is a swell idea an' I ask him what his present wife's hobby is an' he says good works. He says that every afternoon she gets around an' takes cripples for a walk in bath-chairs an' he reckons that it is a very good thing for her. I think so too.

An' about three afternoons afterwards I am walkin' through the woods around there an' when I get to some little clearin' I take a look through the bushes an' there I see this dame pushin' an invalid chair along a path with a guy in it who ain't got any legs an' who has got one arm in a sling.

When they come to the clearin' she pushes the chair off the path an' he gets out. He draws his legs from under him—because he has been sittin' on 'em, throws the sling away, produces a bottle of Scotch from under the seat, an' proceeds to start neckin' the dame like it was his last day on earth.

All of which will show you guys that the old bozo was right an' that there is nothin' like a good hobby to keep a dame outa mischief.

Me . . . I reckon that Geralda has been goin' in for a bit of hero-worship. I reckon she thinks that this Whitaker hound is the berries. Even if he ain't a lot

to look at an' even if he does get frightened when
mobsters write him letters, she reckons that he is a
genius an' that it is better to get hitched up with a
genius with no looks than a guy who looks like Clark
Gable but hasn't got anything to think with.

Even so I bet she thinks in her heart that Elmer
is a bit of a mug an' that maybe when we get him
outa this jam she will tell him off just a little
bit so's he won't get around to doin' anything silly
again.

Some dames are like that. But what Geralda don't
realise is that if she had to live with this mug Whitaker
maybe she wouldn't be so stuck on him. Right now
he is a sorta little hero to her, but the bein' a hero
stuff wears off pretty soon an' a guy has gotta have
somethin' else besides Einstein's theory to keep a dame
stringin' along an' likin' it.

Inventors maybe are O.K. When it comes to
workin' out the specific gravity of somethin' or the
stresses an' strains of this an' that these guys are the
berries. But specific gravity is no good when it comes
to givin' a dame a tumble an' the stresses an' strains
that really matter to a swell baby are not those that
you find on bridges. I'm tellin' you!

I reach for the rye bottle an' right at that moment
the telephone decides to start janglin'. I go over an'
grab the receiver.

It is Montana.

She comes through like butter wouldn't melt in her
mouth. She says in a soft little voice that sounds like
a coupla doves cooin' :

" Hey, Lemmy, is that you ? "

" Nobody else but," I tell her. " An' what can I
do for you, sweetheart ? "

She says : " Well . . . it's about that little thing we
was talkin' about earlier. You wanted to meet a friend
of mine. Well I been able to fix it."

" Fine," I tell her. " Where do I go ? "

I hear her laugh.

" You don't," she says. " This boy friend of mine is a careful sorta guy. He ain't keen on havin' his address flung around. See . . . ? What he says is that if you like to come around here an' pick me up we could go on an' meet him . . . that is providin' nobody was tailin' us to see where we was goin'."

" That's O.K. by me," I tell her. " I'll come around. When ? "

" About nine," she says. " Come around an' have a little drink, Lemmy. I'd be tickled to death to see you. You're such a nice guy to have around the place. You're always so goddam polite." She gives another laugh.

" All right, Montana," I tell her. " I'll be there. So long an' don't do nothin' that you wouldn't like your ma to hear about."

" I ain't likely to," she says. " Not with you around . . . you human ice-box. Well . . . Oh, I forgot," she goes on. " My friend says that he wants this business settled good an' quick. He says he's plenty busy. I thought I'd pass that along."

" I'll remember that," I tell her. " Well . . . so long. . . ."

" I'll be seein' you," she says.

She hangs up.

I wait a minute an' then I call through to the Yard. Herrick comes right on the line.

" Look, pal," I tell him. " The baby has just been through. I reckon they wanta get the business done good an' quick. Are you ready your end ? "

" Absolutely, Lemmy," he says. " And here's some information for you. We've got a reply to that telephone message we sent to Washington." He reads it out. It says :

215

" *To L. H. Caution,*
Care Commissioner of Police London,
Scotland Yard, London, England.

" *Panzetti arrested as requested on Federal charge.*
Threatened with trial in camera under Federal Secrets
Act and life sentence if guilty. Has handed over incom-
plete set of Whitaker D.B. blue-prints. He is being held
incommunicado *till further report from you.*
" *Director, F.B.I.*
Department of Justice, Washington."

" Swell, Herrick," I say. " Here's how it is this
end. I'm goin' to see Montana at nine o'clock. So I
reckon I shall be seein' Kritsch somewhere around ten
at latest. Montana gives me the tip-off that Kritsch
wants this business finished off as quick as possible.
So it looks as if the big boy has got everything ready-
eyed to scram out. Have you got the dough ready ? "

He says yes.

" O.K.," I tell him. " That's fine. Stick around
an' I'll call through later. I *hope.*"

He says so does he. I hang up. Then I give myself
a big shot of rye just to keep the cold out, a cigarette
an' a big grin.

2

Montana is sittin' in front of her mirror in the bedroom when the maid shows me in. She is dressed for
a big killin'. An' believe it or not she looks the berries.
Standin' there, lookin' at her, I get to wonderin' how
it is that a dame can look so good an' be such a goddam
hell-cat.

She says : " Hello, pal. You're right on the dot.
Let's go have a little drink."

216

She gets up an' comes over to where I am. She is wearin' a black lace dinner frock, cut very plain but with a helluva nice line. It's a swell frock an' it shows off her figure like she meant it to.

She swivels herself around.

" How do I look, Lemmy ? " she says. " D'you think I'll get by ? "

" You'll manage," I tell her. " You'll scrape through somehow."

We go into the sittin'-room. She mixes me a drink an' one for herself. Then she sits down an' gives me a big smile.

" You're lookin' plenty pleased with yourself," I tell her.

" I'm always glad when I can do a pal a good turn," she says. " Like I have for you—even if you don't appreciate it."

" Look, kiddo," I say. " You ain't still stickin' to that old old story about your not bein' in on this job, are you ? Because if you are I think you ought to cut it out. It creaks."

" Maybe," she says. " But it's my story an' I'm stickin' to it an' you an' anybody else can't prove it's not true."

" You got something there—maybe," I tell her. " I suppose the only guy who could really throw you down is Panzetti . . . an' I can't see him doin' that."

I light a cigarette.

" What did you fix with Willie ? " I ask her.

She says : " We . . . it was darned funny, but believe it or not he called through five minutes after you'd gone. So I told him what you wanted an' he said that it was O.K. by him. He said that he could fix to see you tonight. So I'm gonna take you along."

" Swell," I say. " That's fine."

" Yeah . . ." she says. " I'm glad you like it. There's just one little thing. . . ."

217

"Such as?" I ask her.

"Such as—don't try any funny business, Lemmy," she says. "You are a copper an' I don't like coppers. I hate 'em like hell. But I got a sorta soft spot for you. I wouldn't like to see you make a goddam mug of yourself. So take a tip from me an' don't try anythin', because there ain't anythin' to be tried . . . that's what Willie says."

"That was nice of Willie," I tell her. "An' what else did that big galoot haveta say for himself?"

"He wantsta get this deal done quick. He's gonna be very busy," she says, "an' he wants it fixed as quick as he can get it. I thought you'd like to know."

"Swell," I tell her. "He can fix it as soon as he likes. I've got the dough waitin'. All I want is to know that I'm goin' to get a square deal an' then I'm ready to settle everything."

"O.K.," she says. "An' thank you for returnin' my car, Lemmy. The chauffeur come through this afternoon an' said you'd brought it back."

She gets up an' stretches. Then she walks over to the drinks wagon an' pours out half a glass of neat Scotch. She sinks it like it was water.

"Come on, big boy," she says. "Let's scram outa here."

"Are we goin' to use your car?" I ask her.

"No," she says. "I'm not goin' to use it now." She smiles at me. "I reckon we'll be usin' it later," she says. "So I'm givin' the chauffeur a rest. We'll take a taxi."

"All right," I say. "Let's go."

She slips inta a fur coat an' we go downstairs. It is pitch black outside but there is a cab trundlin' past an' I grab it. She tells the driver where to go an' we get in.

The cab jolts off. It is so dark that I can't see where we are goin'. Montana wriggles up a big closer.

She says : " Have you gotta gun on you, Lemmy ? "
" I have not," I tell her. " Because this is one of
them occasions when I don't think a rod is necessary.
This is big business—not a free-for-all. I hope that
Willie is lookin' at it from the same point of view."

" He sure is," she says. " Willie reckons that he
wantsta get this business settled an' done in a nice
friendly spirit. He don't want no bad feelin' or
creasin' people about it."

" That's darned nice of him," I say. " It's a helluva
pity that Frisco didn't think that way about Carlette."

She shrugs her shoulders.

" Carlette was a mug," she says. " I never did like
that jane and anyhow . . ."

I finish the sentence for her : " An' anyhow she
was goin' to get it sooner or later, hey ? " I tell her.
" I bet she was. That baby mighta guessed too much
an' so I reckon she woulda been ironed out anyway."

" I wouldn't know about that," she says. " Me
. . . I do not like people bein' ironed out when I'm
around."

" Sure," I tell her. " You only like it when you've
scrammed an' somebody else can do it. You're just
a little saint on wheels, ain't you, Montana ? "

She says : " I'm not so bad, big boy, an' I'm *still*
stuck on you. An' I ain't gonna lose my temper with
you anyhow . . . not tonight. An' have you gotta
cigarette ? "

I give her a cigarette. She sits back in the corner
of the cab an' I bend over an' light it for her. In the
flame of the lighter I can see her face, an' her eyes an'
her hair. She is as pretty as paint an' as lousy as a
bad apple.

I light myself a weed an' sit back in the other corner.
She don't say another word. I reckon I like it better
that way.

After about twenty minutes' drivin' we pull up at

219

some dump. I pay off the cab an' take a look around. It is so goddam dark that I cannot even see where we are.

Montana says : " This way, handsome. . . ."

She takes my arm an' we step across on to the pavement an' then into a sorta covered passageway. We walk for about fifty yards an' then she stops in front of a door. Somewhere around I can hear music. Some band or something is playin' swing.

Montana rings a bell. After a minute or two a guy opens the door a bit. He is wearin' a tuxedo an' has got a pan that looks as if he has been indulgin' in the seven deadly sins since before he was born. He gives her a grin an' opens the door. We go in.

We are in a well-furnished passageway. We go along an' inta a lift. We go up to the second floor. Away along at the end of the passage I can see a big curtan over double doors an' the music is comin' from inside. So I reckon this is some sorta club.

The ugly guy leads the way along the passage an' turns off at the end. He opens a door an' we go in.

The room is swell. It is all grey an' black. There is a grey ceilin' with some black stars on it, a grey carpet that is so soft that it is like walkin' through snow, with black stars on it, an' the furniture is all grey as well. The room is definitely class of a certain sort, if you get me, an' I reckon it is the office-room of some sorta night club.

In the corner is a table. On it are some plates with sandwiches an' stuff an' a coupla bottles of champagne.

Montana slips off her coat. She throws it on a chair. She goes over to the table an' knocks off the neck of one of the bottles. She pours out a couple of glasses an' hands one to me.

" Here's to you, handsome," she says. " An' may crime flourish."

I grin at her.

"It looks like it's flourishin' all right to-night," I tell her. "I reckon it is doin' good business."

The door opens an' Willie Kritsch comes in.

The boy is well dressed. He looks good. If you did not know that this heel was a cheap mobster with a definite likin' for usin' a rod on guys you might even think he was good-lookin'. He is wearin' a tuxedo with nice linen an' some good studs. He has also got a nice soft smile plastered on his face. I reckon he's pleased with himself.

He comes over. He opens another bottle an' pours himself a drink.

"Here's to us," he says. "I'm glad you got along O.K., Caution. An' here's to you, Montana." He sinks the drink.

I put down my glass.

"Look, Caution," he says. "Don't let's waste any time about this job. Let's get down to cases. I wanta get it settled an' done with an' so do you."

"That's O.K. by me," I tell him. "An' just how soon do you want to get it settled ? "

"Tonight," he says. "We gotta get it through tonight."

I shake my head.

"That ain't possible," I tell him. "I don't see how it can be done."

He pours himself out another glass of champagne. He looks at me an' hands out one of them smiles of his. I am thinkin' that I would like to knock his teeth down his throat.

"Why not ? " he says. "Sit down. I don't think there's any difficulty we can't get over," he says.

I take a chair. I am thinkin' what I would like to do to this guy.

I say : "The thing is this : Before I'm goin' to pay over this dough I've got to know that I'm goin' to get a square deal. All right . . . well, I've got a

221

little scheme that ought to appeal to all parties but I'm afraid it can't be done too quick. It's goin' to take a few days."

" Yeah ? " he says. " What's the scheme ? "

" Here it is," I say. I am just about to go on talkin' about this business when there is a knock on the door an' the guy with the ugly pan puts his head in.

" There's a call for Miss Kells," he says. " It's a lady speakin'. She wouldn't leave her name. She said Miss Kells would guess who it was."

Montana gets up.

" I reckon I know who that is," she says. " I'll be back in a minute. You two guys carry on with the good work."

She goes out.

Kritsch looks after her. " There's a dame," he says. " She's got everything. Looks an' beauty an' everything. *An'* class. That dame is the tops."

" Yeah ? " I say. " Well if she is the tops I would like to see somebody who was right down low down. It'd be a nice change."

He says : " O.K. You don't like Montana. Well . . . that's all right with me. You don't haveta like her. So let's have the scheme you got."

" The idea is this," I tell him. " We don't want any slip-ups over this. You don't like me an' I certainly don't like you. But we got to do this business. O.K. At the present moment you have got about three-quarters of the Whitaker blue-prints. The other quarter is the bit he hasn't yet done. That quarter is no good without the rest an' the rest is no good without that.

" So the idea is," I go on, " that you telephone through to Geralda Varney—this dame who is so stuck on Whitaker—an' nominate a time an' place when an' where she can meet up with him an' stick around while he does the last bit of those blue-prints.

When he's done it she brings it straight back to us. You got the idea?"

"I got it," he says. "That means that you got one bit—which is no good to you—an' we got the rest which is no good to us. O.K. I got that."

"Now," I go on, "we know we're protected about the blue-prints. We know you can't make any funny business. All right. Then we pay over the dough. We send Geralda Varney along with the dough. She hands it over to you an' you then allow her an' Whitaker to go with the rest of the blue-prints. Then we let you scram outa this country without takin' any steps to stop you."

He grins at me. He has got a sorta patronisin' look on his clock. Believe it or not I would give a year's pay to take one good poke at this bastard.

"Don't worry about that last thing, pal," he says. "You needn't worry about that. You *couldn't* stop us makin' a getaway. So you can leave that out."

"Well . . ." I say, "that is the scheme. Now what have you got to say about it?"

He says: "That's O.K. by me. But I can save a whole lot of time over this. About this idea of the Varney dame collectin' that last bit of the blue-prints from Whitaker. You don't have to worry about that. That last bit's done. He done it this morning. I told him to. An' I told him what for. An' here it is."

He puts his hand in the breast pocket of his tuxedo an' he brings out a big envelope. It is sealed down with a blob of wax an' a seal.

"There's your guarantee," he says. "Nobody's seen that but Whitaker. There's a note inside from him tellin' you that he sealed it up himself an' handed it to me. If you don't believe me you can call through to him on the telephone an' he'll tell you the same."

I take the envelope an' bust it open. Inside is a blue-print drawin' of some engine part of an airplane.

There is a note from Whitaker inside that says that he has done this print because Kritsch has told him he is goin' to hand it direct to me as a guarantee of good faith. There is also a replica of the seal on the envelope so that I shall know that the envelope hasn't been tampered with.

"Well, Kritsch . . ." I tell him, "it looks as if you've saved a lot of time. All we've got to do now is to exchange the money for the rest of the blue-prints an' Whitaker. If you'll telephone through to the Varney dame she'll take it along to wherever you say, hand it over an' come back—*with* Whitaker."

He nods his head. Then he shoots another of them slow grins at me.

"That's just the one thing that you haven't got a guarantee over," he says. He leans back an' takes out his cigarette case. He lights one an' blows out a cloud of smoke. "You got to leave it to us that Whitaker an' Varney are *allowed* to come back," he says. "But don't worry. I'm gonna play ball with you. We'll let 'em go after we got the money."

"You bet you will," I say. "An' there's a goddam good reason why you will."

"Yeah," he says, "an' what is it? It'd have to be a darned good one supposin' I did intend to try any funny business."

"Nuts," I tell him. "We got Montana. She's pinched !"

He grabs the arm of the chair.

"What the hell do you mean by that one?" he asks. His face is sorta tense.

"That phone call that come through for her was phoney," I say. "I fixed that. The cops was waitin' for her when she went downstairs to telephone."

I sit there grinnin' at him.

"I reckoned that Montana would take darned good care that when we come here nobody tailed us," I say.

" I knew she might have an idea that I might try an' pull somethin'. Anyhow, in this black-out it woulda been goddam difficult for anybody to have tailed along after us. But there was one thing she didn't think of . . . the cab-driver. . . ."

He nods his head.

" Smart stuff, hey ? " he says. " So the cab-driver was a cop ? "

" Correct," I tell him. " The cab-driver was a cop. An' we got Montana an' how do you like that ? "

" You ain't got nothin' to charge her with," he says.

" I ain't chargin' her," I tell him. " I'm holdin' her as security that the Varney dame an' Whitaker are released after we paid over the dough. When that's done Montana can scram."

He laughs.

" I reckon it's goddam funny," he says. " But it was a nice piece of work. I bet she used some language when they grabbed her."

" I bet she did," I say.

I light a cigarette. I am watchin' him through the flame of the lighter.

He says : " Well . . . let's get this job settled right away."

" That suits me," I say. " I can put my hands on the dough in half an hour."

" Two hundred an' fifty thousand dollars," he says with a grin. " How much is that English ? "

" I'm payin' over fifty-seven thousand pounds in English dough," I tell him. " In five hundred pound Bank of England notes."

" O.K.," he says. He looks at his watch. " It's ten-thirty now," he goes on. " You give me the Varney dame's telephone number. I'll call through to her at eleven-thirty. When I call through I shall tell her to go to a certain place. She'll find a car there. She gets in the car an' it takes her to where we'll do the

225

exchange. When she hands over the money we'll present the car to Whitaker an' her. They can have it to drive back home in."

"That suits me," I tell him. "An' we'll give the car to Montana. She can bring it back when we let her scram."

"All right," he says. He gets up. "It's been nice seein' you like this, Caution," he says. He grins. "Maybe we'll do another little deal sometime."

"Maybe," I tell him.

I pick up my hat an' I go. When I get to the doorway I take a look at him. He is still grinnin' as he pours himself out another glass of champagne.

I reckon he is drinkin' his own health.

It is drizzlin' with rain when I get outside. I walk for a bit an' then ask some guy where I am. He tells me that I am somewhere off Baker Street. I ease along to the Station an' go into a call-box. I get through to Herrick. When he comes on the line I say :

"Look, Herrick, I am still all in one piece. Right now I am on my way to see Geralda Varney. You send a guy down to her hotel with the dough an' tell him he is to wait for me in the lounge. You got that ? "

He says he's got it.

"The next thing is to send a guy with a car to wait for me at the corner of Cork Street," I go on. "I shall want the car later. I'll give this guy a message for you when I see him. An' that's the lot. With a bit of luck we shall be O.K. Have you got Montana there ? "

He laughs.

"We've got her," he says. "An' I've never heard such language in my life. Well . . . good luck, Lemmy."

"An' to you," I tell him.

I hang up.

I walk along until I see a cab crawlin' along an' I grab it an' drive down to Geralda's hotel. The

226

plain-clothes guy from the Yard is waitin' for me with a small suitcase. I show him my pass an' he hands it over to me an' scrams.

Then I go up an' see Geralda.

When the bell-hop opens the door she is standin' in front of the fire. She is smilin' an' she looks as pretty as anything you ever saw. I tell you this dame is marvellous.

She says : " Would you like a drink or anything . . . and is everything all right ? "

" Everything is swell, Geralda," I say. " An' I would like a lot of whisky with a very little soda in it, because with a bit of luck I shall be drinkin' yours an' Elmer's health within a few hours."

She says : " So it's like that. You've got things fixed ? "

" Practically," I tell her. " There's one or two little things have gotta be done, but I think the job is very nearly O.K."

She nods her head. She looks in the fire.

" Well . . . what the hell ? " I tell her. " You oughta be excited over this. You'll have little Elmer back in no time now. I can hear weddin' bells ringin' in my ears already."

She looks up. She throws me one of those sideways looks. She is smilin' an' showin' her little white teeth.

Lookin' at her makes me catch my breath. I'm tellin' you that this baby is about the biggest eyeful that you ever saw, an' if I've said somethin' like that before I'm sayin' it again an' you just can't do anything about it.

She is wearin' a long sapphire blue velvet house-coat with little velvet slippers to match an' she has got a velvet ribbon to match tied in that Titian red hair of hers. You tie all that up with a pair of sapphire blue eyes, a skin that looks like the cream off the top of Grade " A " milk, a figure that makes you think

227

of willows blowin' in the breeze an' you understand why a tough guy like me occasionally gets poetic.

She says : " It will be very nice when Elmer comes back. But I suppose it will have its disadvantages. I shan't see *you* again, shall I ? "

" You won't want to, honey," I tell her. " Me . . . I am just one of those guys. If I get stuck on a dame I get stuck on her an' that's the way it is. Well . . . with Elmer stickin' around it wouldn't be fun for anybody."

She laughs.

" It certainly wouldn't be fun for Elmer," she says.

I am goin' to say something about this crack of hers but I think that I had better keep my mind on the business in hand.

" Look, Geralda," I tell her. " Here is the works an' don't make any mistakes. Pretty soon Willie Kritsch is goin' to call through here. I've given him the number. He's goin' to tell you to go to a certain place somewhere around London—I don't suppose it'll be far from here—an' you'll find a car waitin' for you. He'll tell you how you can recognise the car. O.K. Well, you get in an' it goes off to some place where you'll meet Kritsch an' Whitaker. You take this suitcase with you."

I open the case an' show her the packages of notes.

" There is fifty-seven thousand pounds in here," I tell her, " so don't drop the case. When you arrive you hand over the dough an' they hand over Whitaker an' the rest of the blue-prints. I've already got the last bit—Elmer did it this mornin'—so that's O.K. Have you got all that ? "

She says yes, she's got it. She don't even turn a hair.

" An' don't start anything or do anything else but what you have been told," I tell her. " Just keep your eye on the ball an' no nonsense."

"All right," she says. "I'd better get into some street clothes." She comes over an' puts out her hand.

"You've been pretty swell," she says. "I'm sorry I interfered . . . at first."

"Hooey . . ." I tell her. "Everything's goin' to be all right."

"Is it ?" she asks.

She looks at me an' the first thing I know is that she is in my arms an' I am kissin' her like somebody was payin' me double overtime rates for doin' it. An' can that baby kiss or can she ! Me . . . I have kissed dames in practically every part of the world an' the only baby who ever come anywhere near Geralda from a technical point of view was a Polish jane who was arrested for kissin' her boy friend to death on a Christmas night in Warsaw. An' when she was tried the defence proved that the mug's last words were : "It was worth it," after which the jury acquitted her as one man an' the old judge lost seven stone during the next four weeks runnin' around to her flat every evenin' after the court was closed to reconstruct the crime.

After a bit she says : "This isn't right . . . it *isn't* right . . . ! "

"You're tellin' me," I tell her. "But whether it is right or not, it is very swell an' I like it."

She looks sorta grave. She says :

"I'm afraid I do too . . . but I was thinkin' of Elmer. . . ."

I change the subject.

"Look, honey," I tell her. "You've got to get a move on. Go get into your other things an' step on it. Kritsch ought to be comin' through any time now . . . an' good luck to you."

"And you, Lemmy," she says. "I shan't ever forget you."

"You won't get the chance," I tell her as I scram outa the door.

I ease downstairs an' grab a taxicab. I tell the guy to drive me to Piccadilly Circus an' get there as quick as he can. A moon is comin' up an' it is gettin' lighter all the time. Away, on the other side of the river, I can hear some goddam Jerry droppin' bombs an' the fire-bells ringin'.

The guy drivin' the cab makes good time. I pay him off on the west side of the circus an' walk up Regent Street. I cut through into Cork Street an' make for Montana's garage. When I get there I open the door with the skeleton key an' go inside. I shut the door behind me, an' take out a vest-pocket flash I carry. I go over to the side of the garage where Montana's car used to be parked. The car is gone. I go over to the corner of the two walls an' flash the torch on the walls. Right in the corner, just about the height of my eyes, is some writing in pencil on the whitewashed wall. I put the flash on it. It says :

"*Benden Hall, Winchelsea. Between there and Fairlight.*"

I scram. I get outa the garage as if hell was after me. I ease down to the bottom of Cork Street an' on the corner I see the car. It is a black police tourer an' there is a plain-clothes cop inside.

I show him my pass.

"O.K., pal," I tell him. "Thanks for waiting. Have you got a notebook?"

He says he has. I tell him to write down "*Benden Hall, Winchelsea. Between Winchelsea an' Fairlight*" an' to grab himself a cab an' scram back to Herrick at the Yard an' give him that address. He says O.K. He also says that there is an A.A. book in the car if I want it.

I get out the book an' look at the map under my flash. This place is about sixty-three miles but the moon is right up now an' it is easy to see.

I slip in the gear an' I go. Outside London I put my foot down an' let her roll.

An' all the time I am thinkin' of that dame Geralda, which will prove to you mugs that it don't matter how you are or what you are doing there is always some dame will make you think of her ankles or her eyes or her nose or something just at the time you oughta be concentratin' on drivin' a car.

So what . . . !

3

It is just after half-past one when I pull in behind the woods that are at the back of this Benden Hall dump. I have got the low-down on this place from a police patrol who pulled me up seven miles away, an' I am plenty glad I met up with that guy because this countryside around here is good an' deserted an' there ain't any signposts an' you could go on drivin' for ever.

I drive around the right-hand side of the woods an' get on the main path that leads to the Hall. After a bit I see the big iron gates an' the carriage drive runnin' up to the house.

I pull inta the shadows at the side of the road, light myself a cigarette an' do a little thinkin'. I reckon I have got some time in hand, because first of all I don't reckon that Geralda woulda started off from London for a good twenty minutes to half an hour after me, an' then on the road comin' down I reckon I have made another twenty minutes, so I can afford to take it easy.

I start grinnin' to myself an' wonder what Geralda

231

will be thinkin' on the way down. First of all I got an idea in the back of my head that she will be doin' a little quiet spot of rumination about Lemmy Caution, an' the second fella who comes inta the picture will be little Elmer. Maybe Geralda is not quite so stuck on that guy as she was. But dames are funny things. You remember she said somethin' about feelin' maternal about this guy. Maybe she'll sorta think she oughta go through with the business an' marry the slob.

All of which will show you bozos that dames are not always so smart as they think they are.

The moon is swell. The whole place looks like one of them fairy dumps you see on the cards at Christmas, but I reckon that it ain't quite like that. Not with some of the boys who are usin' it around the place.

I throw my cigarette stub outa the window an' roll down the road. I wonder how Frisco is feelin'. As I ease along, keepin' well in the shadow on the side of the road, I start rememberin' the sweet time I had down at the Melander Club when Frisco was gettin' ready to give me the works. I reckon Geralda picked just the right moment to get the police to put that telephone call through, otherwise I would probably at this moment be laid out in the Maidenhead morgue, an' Frisco would still be his own sweet self instead of stickin' around in a police cell wonderin' just how it will feel to be kickin' on the end of a rope.

By now I am about a hundred yards off the main gates an' I pull the car off the road an' leave it in a thicket. Then I scram across the road an' start walkin' around the high wall that leads round the park. I go on walkin' until I reckon that I have come to the far side of the Hall, the side that is facin' seawards. After which I start lookin' for a place to climb.

It takes me five minutes to find a tree that is near the wall. I scram up it, take a chance an' a long jump an' make the top of the wall. I drop down over the other side, winnin' some cuts on my hands an' a tear in my pants in the process.

Between me an' the Hall is a thick shrubbery. I start gumshoein' through. All the trees an' branches are wet an' drippin' an' by the time I get through this I am feelin' I would be glad to be hung out on the line to dry.

On the other side of the shrubbery is a big lawn, an' then some flower gardens. I ease over, keepin' in the shadows. When I have worked along through the gardens I get around the side of the Hall. In front of me is a square courtyard. There are two cars standin' in it, close to the house, an' one of 'em is Montana's Lancia.

I start gumshoein' over towards the Hall. I am goin' easy because there is a big patch of moonlight between me an' the house an' the courtyard is paved with flat stones that reflect the light. I get as close as I can in the shadows an' then take a chance. I lope across the courtyard an' fetch up by the wall of the house, standin' up in some bricked up doorway.

From there I can see the Lancia. The bonnet is up an' the front near-side wheel is off.

I stand there listenin'. Away over the sea I can hear gulls screechin' but apart from that the place is as quiet as a goddam morgue.

What the hell. I get back in the shadow of the stone doorway an' sit down. I take out a cigarette an' light it carefully, shadin' the end with my hand. I stick around an' wait.

After a while I take a look at my watch. It is two o'clock. All of a sudden I hear some guy whistlin'. He is whistlin' Annie Laurie an' he is doin' it like he was very interested. It is just a nice soft easy whistle an' it gets nearer an' nearer.

A guy comes around from the other side of the house. As he comes round the corner I can see he is

233

wearin' a dark-blue chauffeur's uniform an' cap. He is smokin' a cigarette an' when he takes it outa his mouth he starts whistlin' again.

He comes along an' stands lookin' at Montana's car. He is on the far side. After a bit he comes around an' I get a good peep at this guy.

It is Paolo—Montana's chauffeur.

After a bit he puts the bonnet of the car down an' starts trundlin' the wheel that is off over to the wall. I let him get good an' near an' then I say :

"Hey, Paolo. . . ."

He puts the wheel up against the wall. He is screwin' his head around tryin' to find out what the noise was.

I say a bit louder : "Hey, Paolo. . . . I'm here in the doorway. This is Caution. Just ease along here as if you was gettin' outa the wind to light a cigarette."

He gets it. He throws his cigarette stump away an' starts fixin' a hand-pump to the wheel valve. After a bit he takes out a packet of cigarettes an' sticks one in his mouth. Then he takes out a lighter an' comes along to the doorway.

He says : "So you got it all right ? I didn't have time to leave a note but I guessed you'd take a look on the wall near the car. I guessed you'd know I'd write it up somewhere."

"Yeah," I tell him. "What happened ? "

He says : "I was supposed to drive Montana down here but she didn't show up. That bastard Kritsch called through an' told me to bring the car down here an' stick around. When I got here I faked a puncture an' took the wheel off for an excuse to get outside. I thought maybe you'd be around."

I ask him who's in the house.

"Kritsch an' Zokka," he says. "I asked Kritsch where Frisco was an' he said he was sick in hospital." He pulls a face. "I reckon what you told me was

234

true," he goes on. " He was sorta grinnin' at Zokka when he said it. That bastard was enjoyin' the joke. Well . . . maybe he won't be so pleased. . . ."

" You're tellin' me," I say. " Listen," I tell him. " Can all that stuff for a minute an' tell me how I can get inta this dump."

" It's easy enough," he says. " Kritsch reckons that the whole thing is in the bag. An' he's got somethin' up his sleeve. I don't know what an' Zokka don't know what. But there's somethin'. If you ease along the wall there's a little doorway at the end. It leads down to the kitchens. Well, don't go down the stairs. Kritsch an' Zokka an' some other guy are in the big room on the right of the front hallway. If you go up the stairs that face you when you get inside an' turn right at the top you come to a sorta balcony place with a fanlight. It looks down on the room they are in."

" O.K.," I tell him. " An' what are you proposin' to do ? " I ask him.

" Just stick around," he says. " I suppose somethin' is gonna happen sometime."

" Look, pal," I tell him. " This is what you do. Stick the wheel on the car as quick as you can an' scram. Just get yourself back to London an' take a night's rest. Tomorrow mornin' go down to Scotland Yard an' see Chief Detective Inspector Herrick. Say your piece an' you'll get an easy break. I told him about you."

" Thanks," he says. " O.K. I'll think about it."

He throws the cigarette away an' goes. I see him disappear around the side of the house.

I wait for a few minutes an' then I start gumshoein' along the wall. After a bit I come to the little green door. I try the handle an' go in. Inside it is good an' dark but somewhere I can hear some guy laughin' an' there is a gramophone playin' a nice bit of music.

235

I stick around for a minute or two an' get used to the dark. Then I take a chance an' start goin' up the stairs one at a time. When I get up about ten stairs I switch on my little vest-pocket torch an' ease up good an' quick.

At the top there is a big passage. On the walls, shown up by the moonlight that is comin' through the windows, I can see a lot of oil-paintings an' stuff. I walk along this passage an' at the end I go through a door an' into a sorta gallery that runs round a big glass fanlight that is in the middle of the room with a balustrade around it. The balcony is fronted glass an' there is plenty of light comin' through from the room underneath.

I go in an' take a look at the fanlight. Away across on the other side one of the glass pieces is lifted up on a pulley to let air into the room underneath. I gumshoe around there an' lay down on my belly by the side of the balustrade. This way I can see down into the room.

The room is a big room. It is furnished like a library. There are bookshelves all around. There are no windows but there is a door each end—a big door at one end an' a little one at the other.

Standin' in front of the fireplace, smokin' a cigarette, is Kritsch. He has got a drink in his hand. Zokka— who has still got a bruise on his jaw from where I took a poke at him—is sprawlin' in a chair opposite Kritsch on the other side of a big table. At the far end—not lookin' so happy—is Whitaker.

A nice set-up !

This guy Kritsch looks plenty pleased with himself. Standin' down there he looks like a prosperous guy on the stock market or somethin' like that. I reckon he's thinkin' he's plenty clever. Well, maybe he is, but I still don't think he's quite good enough. But is he pleased ! He looks like the cat that has swallowed the canary.

Zokka is stickin' around an' bathin' in the reflected glory. I remember what I did to this boyo up at Casino Lodge at Burghclere when I found him kickin' around my car. The thought pleases me. I take another look at him an' see that his nose is still bulgin' from the poke I gave him. I hope it stays that way.

I get up an' lean over the balustrade. Just then the big door opens an' Paolo comes in. Kritsch starts grinnin' an' Zokka gets up. Whitaker raises his head. I reckon Geralda has arrived !

They are all standin' up now an' lookin' towards the big door that Paolo come in by. He has scrammed out somewhere.

I get out of the gallery quick an' ease down the passage. I reckon that if I turn right from the green door downstairs I shall come to where the small library door is. Anyhow I am goin' to try it.

I gumshoe down the stairs an' go down the passage. When I get to the end I see I am right. The little door into the library is right in front of me an' half open.

I flatten myself up against the wall by the side of the door an' 'ook inside.

Kritsch an' Zokka are both standin' up with their backs to me. Whitaker is still sittin' down. They're all lookin' towards the doorway at the other end of the room. Geralda is just comin' through it.

Kritsch goes over towards her. He is smilin'. He says :

" Well, Miss Varney, it's a pleasure seein' you. Have you got the dough ? "

She holds up the suitcase.

" Here it is," she says. " Here's your money."

She holds the suitcase out towards Kritsch. She holds it right away from her as if she didn't wanta get near that bozo.

He says : " Don't get that way, lady. An' it's not

237

a good thing for you to get that way. You an' me are gonna be seein' plenty of each other."

Geralda says : " I don't know what you mean." She looks over at Whitaker. " Come on, Elmer," she says. " Thank God this business is over. Let's get away from here."

Whitaker don't say anything. Peerin' at him sideways through the door, I see a funny-lookin' grin on his face. Kritsch starts laughin'. He turns around to Whitaker. He says :

" Ain't it a scream ? Don't you think we'd better tell her about it ? "

Whitaker gets up.

" Well, she's got to know sometime," he says.

He looks at Geralda. He is grinnin' like a devil. She looks at him. Her eyes go from one to the other. She says in a cold sorta voice :

" I don't understand. What is this ? "

Kritsch is still laughin' an' there is a big grin over the face of that mug Zokka. Whitaker takes out a cigarette an' lights it.

" It might interest you to know, my dear," he says, " that our friends Panzetti an' Kritsch are associates of mine. It might also interest you to know that when we leave here we shall take a short trip to occupied France. I hope you'll enjoy it."

Geralda's mouth drops open. She says :

" My God ! "

Whitaker says : " You see, my dear, the rather clever idea of selling the blue-prints first of all to the British Government, and then to the German Government originated I am afraid in my own brain. Having got £60,000 from our friends on this side we shall get very much more from the Germans on the other side."

Geralda don't say a word. She stands there as if she was paralysed. She stands lookin' from Kritsch to Zokka, from Zokka to Whitaker. She looks just like a dame who has been hit over the head with a coke hammer an' is tryin' to come back to earth.

Then she says in a sorta hoarse voice : " This isn't true. This is a joke. My God, Elmer, you can't mean . . ."

Whitaker waves his hand.

" My delightful girl," he says, " you have got a lot to learn about men and a certain amount to learn about women. I know you must have felt very disappointed when I walked out on you for the unfortunate Carlette, but if you'd taken a look at yourself in the mirror, you'd have known that at least I should have enough taste to arrange to get you later on. I've never really forgotten you, Geralda."

He stands there leerin' at her like a codfish.

Kritsch says : " Oh, come off it, Elmer. What about me ? I think she's marvellous, too." He shrugs his shoulders. " But still," he says, " you an' me are too good pals to let a dame come between us. Maybe we can arrange to share, hey ? "

He takes the suitcase with the dough in it to the table. He opens it.

I slip the Luger out of the shoulder holster an' I step inta the room.

" I wouldn't worry about countin' that dough, Willie," I tell him. " It's phoney anyway, except the few notes on the top."

The three of 'em spin around. Geralda looks up an' sees me. I see her eyes flash.

" So it come off," I tell 'em.

I walk inta the room.

" Just sit down everybody," I say. " Kritsch, Whitaker an' Zokka, just take three chairs an' stick 'em against that wall an' squat. Another thing," I go on, " if any of you mugs make a move I'm goin' to give it to you."

239

Geralda says : " Lemmy . . . ! "

I grin at her.

" Ain't you the little mug ? " I tell her. " I've been on to this thing for some time. All the way along I've been tryin' to show you what this guy Whitaker was like an' you couldn't see it."

I take out my cigarettes with my free hand an' hand her the pack with my lighter. She lights one for me an' sticks it in my mouth.

I go over to Kritsch.

" Hello, big boy," I say. " How's it comin' ? " I stand there lookin' at him. " You had a big time with me at the Melander Club," I go on, " I just took everythin' that was comin' to me because that was the way it had to be played. Now have a piece of this."

I smack him across the jaw with the barrel of the Luger, an', believe it or not, I can hear the bone crack. I turn around to Geralda.

" Didn't you get it ? " I tell her. " This job was arranged between Panzetti an' Whitaker from the start. I reckon when we get around to checkin' up on little Elmer we'll find he's a Nazi—one of those lousy guys who believe in everything else except their own country.

" From the first the Navy Department had difficulty in gettin' him to finish those plans. He stalled the whole time. Then he gets a big idea. He walks out on you an' pretends to fall for Carlette Francini. Carlette is put in by Panzetti to keep contact between him an' Whitaker, but she don't know anythin' about the big job. Then Panzetti has a threatening letter sent to Whitaker an' Whitaker decides to scram over here. Before he goes he writes you a letter an' tells you what he is goin' to do, because he knows you'll come over to England after him an' he wants you out of the way. You know too much about him. You might start puttin' two an' two together without makin' seven out of it.

"Carlette Francini is left behind after he's gone to see what the Government do. She finds out that I come gumshoein' around up in Kansas City. Then I come over to England. She comes too. They pinch my papers an' Willie Kritsch kids you he's Caution, gets you along to that dump at Hampstead, an' Fratti —frontin' as a man from Scotland Yard—gets me along there. They got a nice scheme. They blow the place to hell an' they get rid of the two people who might know somethin' about Whitaker. An' everybody woulda thought it was a German bomb."

I look at Whitaker.

"You musta thought I was a mug," I tell him. "You musta thought I was a big sap. When I came down to that dump at Burghclere an' found you tied up on the table an' pretended that I didn't think you was Whitaker, didn't you think I'd got some guys to give me a description of you over in the States? I knew you was Whitaker but I wanted to play it that way. Another thing," I go on, "Montana didn't do you any good. That cutie told me that you couldn't finish the plans because Panzetti had been injectin' morphia inta you. That's why I had a look at your arms. I was lookin' for the needle marks. Well, there wasn't any. That told me that either you wasn't Whitaker or Montana was lyin'. Well, you *had* to be Whitaker, so she was lyin'. An' the only reason why she would be lyin' about a thing like that would be that you was playin' along with Panzetta—that you was in the job. That, ladies an' gentlemen," I tell 'em, "is the little mistake that the criminal always makes."

I give Elmer a poke in the snoot with the Luger. His nose starts bleedin'. He gives a whimper like a kid.

241

He says : " Maybe you're very clever, Caution, but you've only got the last bit of the blue-prints. We've got the rest an' you'll never find 'em. We've still got somethin' to deal with."

Kritsch says : " Yeah, that's right. What're you gonna do about that ? "

" Hooey," I tell 'em. " Panzetti's been pinched by the Feds. in America. They threatened him with a life sentence. He's handed over the first part of the blue-prints that you left with him, Whitaker—the stuff that he was goin' to negotiate with the Jerries with. So we got that. An' we got the last part. An' how do you like that ? We got the lot for nothin'.

" You're a nice bunch of guys," I tell 'em. " You've had Francini croaked an' you handed Frisco over to the cops for doin' it. You know we've got Montana in the can, an' you'da walked out an' left her in there. You didn't give a hell. You got a nice getaway all planned. You thought you'd get the dough. You thought you'd got everything."

I grin at 'em.

" You were so goddam certain you were goin' to make a getaway that I guessed what it was. England's not far from occupied France. It is good an' foggy these days. I reckon there'd be a seaplane comin' over to pick you up, to take you over there so that you could meet up with your pals the Germans." I grin. " That's just another Jerry seaplane that won't get back home," I say.

Outside there is a helluva bangin' on the door.

" Geralda," I tell her, " go an' open up the front door. That would be Mr. Herrick from the Yard. He's come down to collect the pieces."

Kritsch says : " What the hell ? "

He bends down as if he was goin' to tie up his shoe-lace. Then he makes a dive for the little door. Zokka gets up too. I trip Zokka, but Kritsch makes it. He gets through the door. I hear him scrammin' down the passageway. Geralda gives a little cry.

"Don't worry, baby," I tell her. "This is a small country. They'll get him. Go open the door for Herrick."

She goes out.

I say to Whitaker : "This is where you get it, pal. Your big dream ain't comin' true. You'll spend the rest of your lifetime in Alcatraz thinkin' about it, an I hope you'll like it. You're a nice guy," I tell him. "I suppose you'da bumped Geralda when you was through with her."

Herrick comes through the doorway with half a dozen plain-clothes guys. He says :

"Well . . . well . . . Lemmy. It looks as if the old technique has worked again."

He gives me a big smile.

"Pretty well," I tell him. "I'm only sorry about one thing. Kritsch has made a break."

"No, he hasn't," he says. "Somebody was waitin' outside—a man in chauffeur's uniform. He shot Kritsch as he went out the big door."

I shrug my shoulders.

"That's the way it goes," I say. "That was Montana's chauffeur Paolo." I look at Whitaker. "That guy got sorta annoyed that Kritsch handed his brother Frisco over to the cops for bumpin' Carlette. That's what they call retribution."

Geralda comes over to me. She says :

"I don't know what to say to you."

"Don't say anything," I tell her. I throw the gun on the table because it looks to me that this is a time when a dame like Geralda is goin' to faint, an' I like to be ready for a thing like that. I put out my arm an' catch her.

When I look up they are stickin' the handcuffs on Whitaker an' Zokka.

243

After a minute Geralda opens her eyes. She looks around the room. Then she remembers. She puts her arm around my neck. I give her one big kiss. I see her eyes are laughin' like hell. She says :

" You shouldn't do that, Lemmy. Elmer wouldn't like it."

4

Some guy once told me that it is pretty swell to drive through the English countryside in the moonlight. This guy knew his onions. The road is stretchin' along in front of me lookin' like what the poets would call a white ribbon in the moonlight. I am feelin' pretty good. I roll Montana's Lancia along the road towards Rye. I don't even care where I'm goin'. Why should I ? Life can be swell sometimes.

Geralda says : " Whoever said crime doesn't pay was right."

" Yeah," I tell her. " He ain't always right—not all the time. *You* very nearly paid, baby."

She looks at me. She says :

" But I didn't. Thanks to you ! This is one time when the woman doesn't pay."

" I wouldn't bet on that," I tell her.

I ease the car inta the side of the road an' slow down. I take out my cigarette case an' we start smokin'.

" One time," I tell her, " when I was up on a case in Gettysburg, I was playin' poker with a dame. She was a honey, this dame, even if she wasn't in your class, Geralda. I thought I knew something about poker an' I was playin' all I knew because the stakes we was playin' for was very interestin' stakes, the idea bein' that the loser paid."

I draw the cigarette smoke down inta my lungs an' let it trickle out of one nostril.

" We was playin' a round of jackpot, an' I couldn't do any good. I never got a card worth playin', but every time it was her deal my cards got better. It wasn't till two three weeks afterwards that she told me that she was fixin' it that way. I forgot to tell you she was a very good card player—she had very nice fingers for cards."

Geralda says : " But I don't see that, Lemmy. If she dealt crooked and gave you the good cards, that meant you'd win."

I grin at her.

" Yeah," I tell her. " She wanted me to win."

She says : " Oh ! "

Then she looks outa the wind-shield. I take a side-ways look at her. I'm tellin' you that this dame is so lovely that it almost hurts.

I let in the gear an' we slid off again. After a bit she says :

" I'm rather fond of poker, Lemmy. You and I must have a game one day."

" You bet," I tell her.

Just a little way ahead there is a big tree an' the branches come down right over the road. There is a nice piece of shade there. I pull the car in an' stop. She turns her face towards me.

" Your deal, my lovely ! " I say.

THE END

〉〉〉 If you've enjoyed this book and would like to discover more great vintage crime and thriller titles, as well as the most exciting crime and thriller authors writing today, visit: 〉〉〉

The Murder Room
Where Criminal Minds Meet

themurderroom.com